D0867416

Devotion

A Club Destiny Novel

Nicole Edwards

Copyright © 2013 by Nicole Edwards

All rights reserved. Except as permitted under the U.S. Copyright Act of 1976, no part of this publication may be reproduced, distributed, or transmitted in any form or by any means, or stored in a database or retrieval system, without prior permission of the publisher. This book may not be resold or redistributed without the express consent of the author.

Devotion – **A Club Destiny Novel** is a work of fiction.

Names, characters, businesses, places, events and incidents are either the products of the author's imagination or used in a fictitious manner. Any resemblance to actual persons, living or dead, or actual events is purely coincidental.

ISBN: 978-1-939786-09-8

Cover Image by:
© Claudio Ventrella www.123rf.com
© ensup www.123rf.com

Because you asked for it...

Devotion (*Club Destiny, #5*)

Is a follow up on the life of Luke McCoy, Sierra Sellers, and Cole Ackerley from Temptation, Club Destiny #2. **If you have NOT read Temptation, please do so before reading this book.** This book also contains information regarding the characters from the other books within the series and may contain spoilers if you intend to read them.

With that said,

There has been an overwhelming interest in understanding how these characters moved on with a normal life and how they are living in a ménage. As much as I'd like to tell you that their lives were just rainbows and butterflies after they accepted their love for one another, I can't. Although Sierra is the lifeline for both of these men, they have a deep, desperate love for one another. For two highly complex, extremely alpha men, this isn't necessarily an easy thing for them to embrace. One thing they aren't willing to sacrifice is their devotion to one another.

Enjoy!

~Nic~

Dedication

To Denise.

I'm not sure what I would do without your daily inspiration.

Prologue

With a sigh, Luke leaned back in his chair and ran his hands through his hair. He needed a haircut. For weeks now, he felt as though he'd been running in circles with absolutely no relief projected anywhere in the near future, which meant he probably would be going another week before he could pencil in the time to do something that mundane.

At the moment, he was sitting in his newly designed office, running through his inventory list, waiting patiently for Trent Ramsey to show up and shower him with the same shit he'd been dishing out for the last couple of weeks. Seemed like that's what the man lived for these days.

Between Trent and his desire to ensure that the Walker brothers didn't show them up with their fancy new resort – his exact words – and the fact that Sierra had been having Braxton Hicks contractions for the better part of the last five weeks, Luke was damned close to losing his mind. Despite his minor blow up at the doctor, both she and Sierra had assured him that it was common. Nothing to worry about.

Right.

Every single morning, Luke woke up, practically wired for sound, unable to sit still as he waited for the other shoe to drop. Although everyone seemed to think he wanted their praise for his new outlook on life, he was getting a little irritated by everyone's concern. Shit, it would be easier if he just went back to being the ornery asshole they expected him to be.

Except he couldn't. Not anymore.

Despite his frazzled nerves, Luke woke up every morning with a smile on his face. It was hard not to when the first thing he saw most of the time was Sierra's beautiful face. The second thing he saw was Cole's sexy smirk, and he'd be damned if he didn't know which one was better. Nor was he sure why he forced himself to get out of bed when he'd much rather spend the day there with them.

But he did and here he was. Although he was quite agitated by the long days, he found it difficult to be in a bad mood. Even Trent wasn't able to leave a dark cloud in his day, although the man was trying pretty damned hard. Or so it seemed. Trent was pushing his limits and quite frankly, Luke felt as though he deserved some credit. After all, he hadn't killed him yet.

Today, they were supposed to meet to discuss the possibility of taking Club Destiny in a decidedly different direction. The thing was, Luke wasn't entirely opposed to the idea. With the club currently up in the air as far as which direction it would take, he was willing to listen to suggestions. With both Sierra and Cole backing whatever decision he made, Luke felt as though he needed to give them some sort of security when it came to the future of the club.

Only he didn't have a fucking clue what that was going to be.

The vibration of his cell phone on his desk made him growl. If Trent decided to stand him up one more time…

"What?" he barked into the phone without looking at the caller id.

"Luke?"

"Baby?" Luke panicked from the strained tone of Sierra's soft voice. He'd been preparing for this phone call and without her even saying anything, he knew. "Are you ok?"

"That depends," she said, and this time he heard the smile in her voice.

"On?"

"Whether or not you're ready to be a daddy."

"Are you fucking serious?" Luke growled the words and stormed out of his office at a flat out run.

He was halfway down the stairs to the main floor before he realized he didn't have his keys. Or his wallet. Shit. Or his phone. Wait. Phone was on his ear.

Halting mid step, and damn near face planting down the remaining steps, Luke abruptly turned, grabbing hold of the railing to keep from falling. Running back to his office, he snatched his keys and wallet off of his desk and headed the opposite direction once again.

"Where are you?"

"Cole is taking me to the hospital," she said sweetly, although he could hear the hint of discomfort she was clearly trying to hide. "You might want to hurry."

At least she didn't have to question whether he was going to be there. For the last week, he'd been going over the plan – which they both tried to tell him there wasn't one. Since he insisted on at least one of them being with her until the baby was born, Luke felt a little better. Not much, but a little.

"Baby, I'm on my way now. Don't hang up." Luke was descending the steps two at a time, sending up a quick prayer that he didn't break his neck, unable to focus on anything except the woman breathing in his ear. "How far apart are the contractions?" he asked.

Contractions. It was almost laughable that he even knew what those were, but thanks to the Lamaze classes he attended with Sierra and Cole, he was well aware. More knowledgeable than he ever imagined he would be.

"Three minutes," she replied, and Luke heard Cole's voice in the background.

"Kane!" Luke bellowed as he turned toward the back entrance. "I'm on my way to the hospital! If Trent shows up, tell him I'll call him later."

"Shit!" Kane's voice echoed through the cavernous bar behind him as he disappeared down the short hallway that would lead to the parking garage.

"Baby, are you there?" Luke asked once he was inside the truck. As he fishtailed onto the main road just a minute later, Sierra's deep breaths filled the interior of his truck through the Bluetooth speaker.

"I'm here," she whispered. "Please hurry, Luke."

"Don't worry, baby. I'll be there in five minutes."

Or two more contractions.

Holy fucking shit! Any minute now, he was going to be a dad!

No one ever bothered to clue him in to the fact that minutes rarely factored into childbirth.

Ten long hours later, Luke was standing at the hospital nursery, staring at the beautiful baby girl lying in one of the newborn bassinets on the other side of the glass partition.

"Damn, bro. It's a good thing that little girl looks like her momma." Logan's laugh echoed through the hall. His brother's firm grip on his shoulder shook him slightly, and Luke smiled at his attempt at humor.

"I was thinkin' the same thing," Tag added, standing on the other side of Cole.

Luke glanced over at Cole who was standing next to him, smiling as he did. He looked about the same as Luke felt. Bewildered. Amazed. There were a shitload of adjectives that could be used to describe it, but no matter what, Luke was happy.

"Shouldn't you be taking care of your wife?" Luke asked, his gaze once again fixated on the tiny body wrapped in a pink blanket just a few feet away on the other side of the protective glass panel.

"What do you mean by 'take care of'?" Logan smirked. "We already had to find a way to pass the time for a few hours."

"Nope. Don't want to hear it," Luke said with a growl that quickly morphed into a laugh. Shit, even Logan couldn't get under his skin today.

The warmth of Cole's shoulder against his was a lifeline that Luke found himself hanging onto. Ever since the phone call the previous day, he'd been going a little crazy. Watching Sierra in so much pain wasn't what Luke considered a good time by any stretch of the imagination. He quickly learned that the nurses weren't all that fond of him barking out orders either. Although, Sierra seemed to take it all in stride. How, he had no idea.

Between her and Cole, they'd managed to keep him from going insane, albeit barely. Since the doctor finally announced that it was time, Luke's heart hadn't stopped pounding. Even now, as he stared at the precious little dark haired girl sleeping so soundly just a few feet away, his chest continued to ache. In a good way.

"You hanging in there?" Cole's voice was lowered, although Luke knew Tag and Logan heard every word.

"Yeah. You?"

"Barely," Cole whispered. "It's still a little surreal."

Leave it to Cole to be honest with what he was feeling. That was something Luke was still working on.

"Is she as perfect as she looks?" Luke asked, not intending for the words to come out.

"She is," Cole reassured him and their hands touched, their fingers linking together between them as they both stood in awe.

"Like I said, just like her momma." Logan once again chimed in, but this time he sounded just as awed as Luke felt.

"So, what's it feel like to be an uncle?" Luke asked Tag and Logan, not directing the question at either one specifically.

"It feels like I'm gonna get to give you a hard time about a lot more now. A girl, huh? I hope she gives you two a run for your money."

Luke didn't spare Logan a glance, but he laughed anyway. Yeah, he was pretty sure they were going to have their hands full with this one. If Sierra's personality was anything to go by, then their little girl was going to be spunky and wild. And Logan was right about one thing, she certainly looked like her mother with her pretty blue eyes and dark hair.

Then again, he'd overheard Sam and Ashleigh talking, and there was a very strong possibility that she might just look like her daddy after all. According to them, dark hair and blue eyes were exceedingly common for babies.

They'd just have to wait and see.

Part One

Chapter One

Seven weeks earlier…

Reluctant wasn't a strong enough word to describe Cole's feeling about tonight.

Did he want Sierra going with them? No, not really.

Did he have much of a say in the matter? No. And there wasn't a *not really* about it either.

Sierra was adamant that Luke and Cole take her to the club. According to her, if Sam was getting to see it, she was going no matter what they said. Needless to say, he and Luke had lost that battle.

And here they were walking down the narrow corridor that would lead them to the very private, very secret fetish club. The same one that was supposed to be closed down entirely. It would be too if it weren't for the fact that Luke was trying to get a decent feel for what the Walkers intended to do with their resort. Since Travis hadn't been able to outline what he was planning to do with the two clubs that were supposed to be inside the walls of the super exclusive resort, Luke had offered to give them a tour.

Considering Cole hadn't been there since he met Sierra, he wasn't exactly sure what they'd see. With a majority of the members now relieved of their contractual obligation, he wasn't expecting much. He couldn't say he was disappointed about it either.

Worst case scenario, some of the few remaining members would be in attendance and having a grand time putting on a show for the few people that would likely be there.

At least Cole wasn't going to have to worry about anything getting too far out of hand. Although Sierra had been quite adamant that she not get left out of the tour, he could tell by looking at her that she wasn't feeling well. As the baby continued to develop, Sierra was overcome by exhaustion easily these days, which meant their evenings out usually ended early. He didn't expect tonight to be much different.

"You feeling all right?" Cole asked Sierra, his hand sliding protectively against her lower back as he walked beside her down the corridor that would lead them to the double doors into the club.

"A little tired, but yes, I'm fine." Her sweet smile told him she wasn't telling him the whole truth, but then again, Sierra did her best not to worry them. Sometimes she overdid it, just to avoid their concern. Especially Luke's.

Since they had already endured an hour and a half at dinner, Cole knew Sierra wasn't going to want to be out much longer. Not only would she be getting tired, but she had been complaining that her feet were bothering her. He could only imagine. It seemed as though in the last couple of weeks, the baby had gotten significantly bigger.

However, because Luke was required to be here, and Sierra's curiosity was going to easily trump her discomfort, Cole had resigned himself to the outing. So far it had been interesting, especially listening to Travis Walker and his recent, and not so minor, changes to the resort. Since the conversation started, Luke and Logan hadn't weighed in, but Cole knew they were probably cataloging every word. It seemed as though Travis was seeking input, but his brothers had been all the support he needed by the time dinner was over.

Having dinner with seven extremely outgoing, distinctly different brothers, was entertaining in itself and Cole found himself laughing on more than one occasion at the banter between them. Having grown up an only child until Tag's father married Cole's mother – after he had moved out on his own – he didn't have any experience with that type of sibling interaction. Again, interesting was a fairly decent description.

As they walked inside the club, most of the others stopped immediately to observe their surroundings, leaving Cole and Sierra wandering behind them. As he watched the intrigue on their faces, he couldn't help but wonder what the outcome was going to be for their club. Being that Luke abruptly closed the doors a short time ago, there'd been little discussion about reopening them. Well, at least not without some significant changes.

Without a vested interest, apart from being in a permanent relationship with Luke, Cole wasn't sure what he hoped would happen. Initially, he'd thought that Luke would have more free time, but that didn't seem to be the case. In fact, Luke was probably spending more time at Club Destiny than before he closed the doors. It was clear that the current situation was weighing heavily on Luke's mind. No matter how much he and Sierra tried to reassure Luke that they would stand beside him on any decision he made, it was clear Luke had some concerns.

They did seem to be making some progress on the inclusion factor though. Luke was insisting that both he and Sierra provide their input, and he wasn't at all tolerant of their evasiveness.

Since the three of them were lovers, partners in every sense of the word, it was a no-brainer that they'd support Luke, but other than that, they wouldn't be able to persuade him to make a decision either way. They knew it, and Luke knew it. Luke was going to do what he wanted to do. That's the way Luke was. One of the many reasons Cole loved him. Unconditionally.

As the group began to break up, Cole remained with Sierra, keeping an eye on her as she began venturing through the club slowly. She didn't try to keep up with Sam, and Cole noticed that Ashleigh had taken off in another direction with Alex, likely looking for some interesting fodder for one of her upcoming novels. If anyone would benefit from the visit, Cole had no doubt it would be her.

Cole noticed that Luke and Logan were giving a brief tour to Travis and Sawyer while several of the others went their own way. Trying not to hinder Sierra from getting what she came for – which he still had no idea what that was – he remained quietly by her side. He didn't need to follow Luke because he knew the history better than most. Having been a member since Club Destiny's inception, Cole even knew what the former club's design was, which was in no way as upscale as this one.

The Destined Hearts Club had obviously needed some radical revamping as well as a financial boost by the time Luke came along and managed to save what was left of the failing establishment. Only Luke took it one step further and developed both a nightclub and the fetish club, though most people were oblivious to the latter.

Although Luke spent the better part of the last five years growing the club into something no one had probably ever anticipated, it seemed that it had begun to deteriorate in the last few months. Blackmail and deception had clouded much of the member's judgment and once that rolled over into Luke's and Logan's lives, well, that's when Luke put an end to it all.

It hadn't been an easy road either. After some pictures of Samantha McCoy surfaced and were used to blackmail Luke and Logan, they'd made some decisions they swore they'd never make. In an attempt to salvage Samantha's reputation, as well as that of the high profile company she was working for, they'd allowed the blackmailer admission, which had come back to bite them in the ass.

The members that Luke and Logan worked so hard to protect reacted exactly how everyone should have expected. They didn't care that the reputation of many were going to be affected if the pictures got out, and they insisted that their anonymity be protected at all costs. According to them, it wasn't because they were ashamed of their lifestyles, but it was in their best interest not to attract the attention of the media. Cole called bullshit.

So far, the McCoy's had done a remarkable job at keeping things under wraps. Luke took care of the bullshit and the deception. He shut down the club and officially cancelled the membership agreements with about ninety five percent of the members. Based on what Cole saw tonight, it looked like most of the other five percent were in attendance, which wasn't all that surprising.

Cole understood both sides of the argument, however, his loyalty was to Luke and Sierra only. Which was why he supported Luke's decision, promising he'd help to rebuild in any way that Luke deemed necessary. At this point, Cole still wasn't sure whether Luke was going to move forward.

Based on the conversation they'd engaged in recently, he got the impression that his lover might just be looking to take the club in another direction. He also knew the potential changes weren't completely Luke's idea. Trent Ramsey, another silent partner, played a prominent role in swaying him. Up to this point, final decisions hadn't been made, so Cole continued to wait to see what Luke wanted to do.

Despite what people thought, the BDSM and fetish industry were growing leaps and bounds lately. The sheer volume of applications that Luke received bordered on ridiculous. Luke and Logan managed to keep their membership numbers relatively low due to the hefty price tag they placed on membership. He knew the Walkers wouldn't have to worry about that since they were keeping theirs on an invitation only basis.

And it would appear that tonight was all about proving to the Walkers that Luke didn't go into business as a nightclub owner. The few members that remained were some of the kinkier and the most discreet, and the selected few had been informed that the doors would be open for one night only.

As Cole continued to walk with Sierra around the perimeter of the room, he kept an eye on her as well as notated the few changes he noticed since the last time he was there. There weren't many. Based on the scene taking place in the large glass room on the main floor, Mistress Serena was still in charge and putting on a rather entertaining show tonight.

Mistress Serena was officially the manager of the fetish club, as well as a Domme who loved to show the patrons exactly who was in charge. There probably wasn't a night that went by in which her presence wasn't requested in at least one or more scenes. Tonight wasn't any different.

Sierra stopped in front of the glass enclosed room, watching intently as Mistress Serena directed some pretty intense interaction between two men and one woman. Based on the little bit that Cole had heard, one of the men was about to understand what it meant to submit to another man.

"Do you come here often?" Sierra asked, dividing her attention between what was taking place a few feet in front of them and him. Sliding his hand in hers, twining their fingers together, Cole grinned down at her.

"No." It was the absolute truth and based on the small smile Sierra gifted him with, she appreciated his response.

Cole rarely had the urge to return to the club, and when he had, it was only because of the darker urges that he'd learned to manage in recent years. He never would've seen himself as a submissive, but as it turned out, he was. At least when it came to Luke.

That didn't mean he didn't have some vivid fantasies about being anything *but* submissive. His interests these days revolved around the three of them, nothing more. Although they continued to push the boundaries with one another, there were still a few that Luke had refused to breach. Those were the fantasies Cole continued to have, the ones he counted on coming to fruition at some point.

The club couldn't offer them what they could find together, just the three of them. One of the biggest draws of the club had always been the voyeuristic aspect. On any given night, one could come and enjoy enough visual stimulation to last an entire week. Since that didn't appeal to him, outside of watching Sierra or Luke, or both of them, Cole had no desire to visit.

The familiar snap of a whip and Mistress Serena's following command caused Sierra to jump, which in turn had Cole releasing her hand and folding her into his arms. With his chest pressed against her back, he could easily wrap his arms around her and rest his hands over her protruding belly. When she took his hand and moved it over her stomach, he grinned the moment he felt what she was trying to show him. A small, rounded ball protruded slightly from her stomach, probably a knee or an elbow he'd been told.

Their daughter was undoubtedly an active one, especially now. He didn't know what it said about him that he gladly would spend the day with his arms wrapped around Sierra, his hands molded to her belly as he felt the precious child moving inside. He couldn't wait for the day he held her in his arms.

"Want to see the rest of the place?" he whispered against her ear, making sure she could hear him over the thunderous boom of the sound system.

She nodded her head, but didn't move away from him immediately, so Cole waited until she was ready. They continued to watch Mistress Serena for a couple of minutes before Sierra took his hand and led him away from the glass room.

With a protective hand on her back, Cole followed Sierra up to the second floor, then stayed beside her as they traversed the narrow walkways that formed a square with glass rooms on one side and rows of seating on the other. They didn't stop to linger, and when they reached the stairs once more, Cole held his arm out, signaling for her to head back downstairs.

"What's up there?" she asked, and he read her lips more than heard her words because, for some reason, the music was blaring tonight. Or maybe he was just getting old, he thought to himself.

Leaning down so that his mouth was close to her ear, he whispered some of the not so erotic fetishes that took place up there. When her face paled, he knew she wasn't going to want to pursue it any further. Taking her hand, he led the way down the stairs, taking his time to walk beside her.

When they reached the ground floor once again, Cole noticed Samantha and McKenna, along with Tag and Logan, now standing near one of the bars, laughing and talking. Considering they weren't partaking in any of the action the place had to offer, Cole knew it was going to be a short night. For that, he was grateful.

Rather than moving to join the others, Sierra surprised him when she turned around and headed toward the glass enclosed rooms, specifically the one that Mistress Serena was still in.

He had to admit, the scene was rather intense, but nothing that Sierra wouldn't have been used to already, considering there were many times where she opted merely to watch him and Luke. In this particular scene, there were two men, and it appeared that everything they'd done thus far had led up to what was about to happen.

Kneeling on the floor in front of one of the men was a pretty blonde woman, her hands tied effectively behind her back while the taller, dark haired man stood in front of her, driving his cock deep into her mouth. The woman seemed perfectly satisfied, and the man appeared to be hovering on the edge of implosion, the pained look on his face reflecting his need for release.

Cole noticed that the man's ass was red, probably from the flogger Mistress Serena was wielding at the moment. Apparently she must've retired her whip and opted for something a little more personal. Not that he'd ever seen her use a whip on anyone.

"Bend over." Mistress Serena's voice echoed through the room and out to the floor of the club, heard clearly although the music was loud.

When the man didn't move fast enough, Mistress Serena brought the flogger back down on his ass, causing him to clench his teeth together, but he didn't cry out as he continued to focus on the blow job he was currently receiving. He did, however, slow his pace and managed to ease over so that he could reach the back of the chair sitting just behind the kneeling woman.

"Have you ever been fucked by a man?" Mistress Serena asked, and the other man standing beside her grinned.

"No," he groaned, still trying to force his cock deeper into the blonde woman's mouth.

The flogger landed again, this time on the other side of his ass, and he couldn't stifle the cry of pain that time.

"No, what?" she asked forcefully.

"No, Mistress," he answered, his body relaxing slightly, his legs appearing to strengthen once more.

"Don't you dare make him come," Mistress Serena ordered the woman. "He doesn't come until I give him permission to."

The woman didn't respond verbally. However, she did appear to acknowledge the instruction, her movements slowing somewhat. The man didn't seem pleased with the change in tempo.

"You." Mistress Serena acknowledged the other man. "On your knees. Behind him."

The other man quickly knelt, offering a "Yes, Mistress" as he did.

"Now, it's up to you to prepare him for your cock," Mistress Serena told the man on his knees. "I want to watch while you lube his ass with your tongue."

Cole was fascinated by the scene in front of him. It wasn't something he hadn't seen before, but for some reason, it seemed to sate an urge he'd been having in recent months. He practically could envision himself on his knees, Luke standing in front of him as he buried his tongue in his ass, preparing him for his cock. He knew it wasn't something Luke would agree to, but that didn't stop his mind from conjuring up the image.

When Luke's body heat pressed up against his back seconds later, Cole was tempted to turn to him and bury his tongue down his throat. What he did was stand absolutely still and try to pretend that he was not in any way affected by what was happening inside the glass room.

Keeping his gaze on Mistress Serena, who was now standing in the center of the room, the flogger hanging limply by her side, Cole waited just like everyone in the audience to see what she would do next.

"Reach between his legs and squeeze his balls," Mistress Serena instructed the kneeling man. There wasn't a second of uncertainty as the man on the floor slid one hand between the other man's legs, cupping his balls while he continued to ream his ass with his tongue.

Cole's dick swelled in response to the scene. *Fuck.* This was part of the lure. It was like watching porn, live. Only there weren't any fake moans and groans to go along with the action, nor were the scenes choreographed in any way. The only thing that was premeditated was the way in which Mistress Serena set up the scene so that the audience had a perfect view of everything that was going on. She didn't disappoint this time either.

When Sierra moved closer against him, Cole glanced down, gently squeezing her to reassure her that he was still there. He did his best to keep his growing erection from pressing into her back, but if she kept moving closer, he wasn't going to be able to avoid it.

Luke stood just to his right, his body heat a vivid reminder that his lover was also watching what was happening in front of them. Cole wondered whether Luke envisioned the three of them up there in the same situation. He seriously doubted it would play out the same way in Luke's mind as it did in his though.

For the next few minutes, Mistress Serena continued to ask the standing man questions, easing the kneeling man's head back with her fingers threaded into his hair when he didn't respond appropriately, before pushing him back between the man's ass cheeks. This seemed to go on forever before, finally, Mistress Serena instructed the other man to stand.

Cole didn't need to watch to know what was going to happen next. In fact, he preferred not to. It was suddenly getting extremely warm in the cavernous club, and if he had his way, the three of them could go home and pick up where the scene left off.

"You ready to go?" Surprisingly it was Luke who posed the question to Sierra and she glanced up at him, nodding her head before turning in Cole's arms.

Both relief and disappointment twisted inside of him as he turned to follow Sierra and Luke away from the area. He didn't want to watch because he didn't want to be reminded that his own fantasy had little to no chance of ever coming true. On the other hand, he was relieved because at least for now, he'd be going home to the welcoming arms of the two people he loved most. And no matter how this played out, Cole would consider himself the luckiest man in the world.

That is until the moment came when Luke finally succumbed to what they both knew was inevitable.

Chapter Two

Much to the credit of the club and the particular scene with
Mistress Serena, by the time Cole arrived home he was just a little
edgy and even more than a little horny. The visuals that continued
to play on a loop in his mind consisted of Luke experiencing what
it was like to succumb to Cole's more alpha urges. Then again, the
fantasy wasn't a new one, but tonight it was especially persistent.
Not that he expected Luke to give in to that much temptation
tonight, but his dick had some ideas on what would work to satisfy
them both.

Calling it an early night had been the right call because as
soon as they drove out of the parking garage of the club, Sierra
started yawning. She was not the type to complain, but Cole could
tell by the look on her face that she was exhausted and ready to be
off of her feet.

When they walked in the house, Sierra was the first to turn
to them, informing them both that she was going to bed. Cole
wasn't going to ask any questions, and based on Luke's concerned
gaze, he wasn't either.

Bear, Luke's German shepherd, arrived in the kitchen just in time to follow Sierra as she retreated toward the bedroom. Ever since the three of them had moved in together, Bear had gone from being Luke's dog, to being Sierra's protector. He was by her side whenever she was in the house, with the exception of when they went to bed because Luke insisted he not sleep in bed with them. Hell, Cole was more than glad not to have the one hundred pound dog to contend with. It was hard enough with three people, no matter how large the bed was.

They weren't alone but for a few seconds when Luke peered over at him, a seductive grin tipping his full lips. "Upstairs."

Considering how subdued they'd been on the drive home, Cole was a little taken aback at the abrupt command, but he didn't waver from his stance just a few feet away. Daring Luke had become second nature for Cole, and he knew Luke expected it as well.

"You heard me." The look on Luke's face said he was as affected by their evening at the club as Cole was.

Without question, Cole fell into his normal submissive role, nodding his head while his dick lengthened and swelled behind his zipper, an ever present throbbing that he knew would be sated if he could maintain some semblance of patience. That was asking a lot at this point. He had no intention of arguing with Luke. Not tonight.

It wasn't often that they took the opportunity for alone time together, although they were both quick to jump when Sierra offered an invitation for a one on one moment. Granted, those times were rare, but these even more so. The three of them had made it clear that they much preferred their threesome moments, although alone time with one or the other was certainly a nice change of pace.

Cole managed to ascend the stairs without rushing. His cock was hard enough to hammer nails which added some slight discomfort, and he was anxious to free his throbbing cock. Once he was at the top of the stairs, he opened the double doors that led to the large room they used specifically as a playroom. Literally.

The room didn't contain much more than a massive bed and a sofa, although they did have some second hand bondage equipment that Luke had garnered from one of the abandoned apartments at the club. Luke had taken possession of the items, but they didn't make a habit of using them. In fact, it had been far too long since they'd actually used the playroom at all. Considering Luke was fond of morning sex, they generally opted to succumb to their desires, just the three of them, long before they even climbed out of bed.

Cole was thrilled by the idea of him and Luke stealing a few minutes alone together. Tonight.

He didn't have to wait long for Luke to join him. He was staring at the various toys on the wall when he heard the door close with a click. Without turning around, Cole tried to pretend his body wasn't flashing with a heat so intense, he wasn't sure he wouldn't pass out.

"You want me to use one of those on you?" Luke asked.

The heat of Luke's body infused him as he moved up against his back, the ridge of his erection pressing against his ass. Although he was sure Luke was teasing, Cole wasn't sure he would be able to answer that. Aside from a couple of spankings that Luke had given Sierra, they'd never engaged in that sort of activity. Bondage – mostly for Sierra's benefit – was as far as they ventured.

"Answer me," Luke stated demandingly, a powerful combination of power and passion in just the two words.

Cole nodded his head, not expecting his own answer.

Luke's arms came around Cole's waist, his palm rubbing forcefully against the ridge of his cock behind his jeans. He didn't suppress the groan this time, enjoying Luke's rough touch. He loved when Luke got worked up to the point he was forceful with him. It didn't happen nearly as often as it used to though.

"You want to be spanked?"

The question sounded strange to Cole's ears, and he had to give that some thought. He'd never actually been into pain, even for the sake of pleasure. Thinking about Luke bending him over and using his hand, or even one of the items on the wall, against his ass made his dick throb.

"Do you like when I redden Sierra's sweet little ass?" Luke asked, grinding the heel of his hand harder against Cole's cock, making him moan. "One of these days, I might have to do that. Bend you over and redden your ass before I plunge my cock in deep."

Cole shivered at the thought.

"But, right now, I need you." Luke's admission sent a tremor through Cole's entire body. If only Luke knew how much he needed to hear those words these days.

"Turn around," Luke commanded and Cole turned obediently as Luke took a step back. "I want to feel your mouth on my cock."

It would seem they were on the same wavelength.

Unable just to do as Luke told him without some sort of hesitation, Cole met his gaze, making sure his lover saw the opposition in his eyes. He didn't voluntarily submit to Luke. Neither of them would get off on that. His defiance was his way of pushing Luke and all those months ago, it had worked to bring the two of them closer together.

"I'm going to bury my cock deep in your throat. Then I'm going to bend you over and bury myself so deep inside of you, I'll be the only thing you know."

He just wondered whether Luke realized that was the case even when they weren't intimately together. Cole loved Luke to the depths of his very soul.

"Knees," Luke said, abruptly moving closer and fisting his hand in Cole's hair.

Cole gave in to him, lowering himself to his knees at Luke's feet. He knew he had to give in because it was what they both wanted and truthfully, he wasn't quite sure how much longer he could torture himself by withholding. He also knew that Luke wouldn't be able to force him if he didn't. Cole was physically stronger than Luke. They both knew it, but Luke controlled every part of him and Cole willingly gave himself because he wanted Luke with a passion that defied logic.

Once on his knees, Cole looked up into wicked hazel eyes glimmering with lust, waiting for the next command that he could defy.

"Take my dick out."

Cole paused briefly before doing as he was told, unbuttoning Luke's jeans and lowering the zipper, making sure he brushed the back of his hand over the steely length of him.

"Fuck."

Cole barely heard the word, but he felt the emotion behind it. Luke might be holding himself back most of the time, but when he did give in, Cole could hear the affection in his words.

With Luke's jeans pushed down over his hips, Cole stroked Luke's smooth, warm cock slowly, not wanting to rush this. They didn't share this type of intimacy often, and he didn't want to waste a second.

"Take me in your mouth."

Cole met Luke's eyes before he used his tongue to lave the engorged head, his hand wrapped firmly around the base.

"Oh, fuck," Luke growled.

That's exactly what Cole was thinking as he used his mouth to explore Luke's impressive erection, sucking, licking and teasing while Luke kept his hands firmly entwined in his hair.

Every now and then there was a sharp tingle that shot from his scalp down between his legs as Luke held him still, thrusting into his mouth. It seemed as though Luke wasn't looking to rush this either by the way that he paced himself.

"Stop!"

Cole reluctantly released Luke's cock from his mouth, looking up at him expectantly.

"I want to come inside of you."

Cole knew what that meant. Despite some of the more graphic images that were flitting through his mind, that was precisely what he wanted as well. He wanted to feel that connection that the two of them had when they came together. Sex for the sake of sex between them was a thing of the past. No matter who was topping who, there was more to this than just physical gratification and although Cole needed that, he needed Luke's love more.

When Luke instructed him to stand up and strip, Cole did as he was told while watching Luke remove his clothes as well. The sight of the man's well-honed body made his mouth water. Luke was by far the most beautiful man Cole had ever met. Even with his gruff and abrasive nature, Luke made Cole crave more.

As Luke began to stalk him, Cole backed up slowly, not giving in immediately. The smirk that tilted Luke's mouth made Cole's breath hitch. God, he wanted to feel his hands on him. All over his body. He wanted to taste Luke's kiss and to feel the passion that was often repressed when it came to the two of them.

The bed was at the back of his knees by the time Luke approached. Cole watched as Luke used one hand to grasp the back of his neck, pulling him closer until their mouths crashed together, a volcanic eruption igniting in his belly, lighting up all of his nerve endings as Luke's tongue plunged inside. Cole couldn't resist, he sucked Luke's tongue before using his own hands to pull Luke against him, their erections pressing together.

Luke's moan exploded in his mouth and Cole swallowed every breath, wanting to be closer. He wanted Luke to give in to him, but he knew it wouldn't happen today.

The kiss intensified as Cole waited for Luke to make the next move. As much as he wanted to look Luke in the eyes when they came together, he didn't expect that to happen either. The pent up energy he felt coming off of the man was going to result in hard and fast. At this point, Cole was ready to explode just from the brush of Luke's skin against his own so he couldn't complain.

"Turn around," Luke demanded when he broke the kiss. "Get on the bed."

Cole didn't say anything as he turned away from Luke, slowly moving onto the bed, anticipation like a fire in his gut. He just wanted to feel Luke.

There was movement and then the bed dipped as Luke crawled between his spread legs. The warmth of Luke's hand nestled between him and the mattress had Cole shifting to give him better access. As Luke stroked him with one hand, Cole felt the invigorating chill of lubricant as Luke prepared him using two fingers. Before he knew what was happening, Cole was thrusting against Luke's fingers, using his own hand over Luke's to stroke his cock faster.

"I want to feel you come. I want to shove my dick in your ass and feel you come on my hand."

Yes. Fuck yes. Cole didn't say the words out loud, but he groaned his agreement as he felt his release building.

Luke stopped suddenly, but returned as his cock penetrated his ass, forcing a gasp from him. He was so fucking big. Cole continued stroking himself while Luke slowly slid in deeper before covering his body with his. The warmth of Luke's breath was against his ear, one strong hand gripping his hip while the other returned to his aching dick.

"You're so fucking tight. So. Fucking. Tight," Luke panted and groaned and the words penetrated Cole's lust filled brain, punctuated by the impact of his hips. He wasn't going to last.

"Fuck me, Luke. Take whatever you want from me," Cole told him, not wanting the moment to end but needing more.

"Do you like when I'm buried in your ass?"

Cole nodded, holding his breath as he tried to keep from coming. He knew when Luke started talking, he wasn't going to be able to resist. It's what Luke did. He spoke to him, telling him what he wanted and what he needed while encouraging Cole to answer his questions. The deep, grumble of Luke's voice sent chills down his spine. He loved this man. Whole heartedly loved this man and had come to cherish these very rare occurrences.

"So goddamn tight! Fuck." Luke continued his verbal litany as his hips continued to pound him from behind.

Cole counteracted the thrusts with his own, sending Luke deeper inside of him as Luke's body warmed every inch of his skin, starting from the inside out.

"You're gonna make me come," Cole ground the words out, accepting the fact that he wasn't going to be able to hold out much longer. It felt too good. Too perfect. "Fuck me harder."

Luke's hips rammed him, his heaving breaths loud in his ear and Cole used his hand to guide Luke's over his cock.

"Come for me, Cole."

Sonuvabitch. The combined sensation of Luke's cock grazing overstimulated nerve endings, his palm stroking him roughly, and the searing heat of his body against his back melded together. Simmering, churning. While his mind tried to process everything at once, Cole lost the ability to refrain, coming hard and fast, triggering Luke's almost violent eruption inside of him.

Dropping to the bed, Cole absorbed the impact of Luke's weight as he came down on top of him, both of them fighting to draw in air, their bodies coated in sweat.

"One of these days, I'm gonna be too old for this," Luke announced with a laugh as he rolled to his side.

"Not if I have anything to say about it." As far as Cole was concerned, age was just a number, and although he might not be able to gear up for another round as quickly as he used to, he damn sure wasn't planning to cease their intimate activities anytime in the near future.

"Come here," Luke's voice lowered, his tone losing the humor it'd just contained seconds before. Cole rolled to his side, facing Luke, his eyes immediately taking in Luke's disheveled hair, his lean, muscular build and wondered if he'd been wrong about his recovery time.

Luke reached up, sliding his hand into Cole's hair, pulling him closer. Their mouths met briefly in a kiss that sent a different sort of sensation fluttering through his insides. This man had the ability to cause sensory overload with just a look, but when he kissed him like that, gentle and soft, Cole was suddenly reduced to a jumble of emotions.

As long as Cole had known Luke, he'd never sensed that he could open himself up completely, but these rare, intimate insights into his soul made him realize they were still moving mountains. He knew it wasn't easy for Luke, which was why he latched on to these moments, storing them in his memory banks so he could reflect back on them when his doubts seemed to inundate him.

"Mine," Luke breathed against his lips and Cole answered by sliding his tongue in deep.

Cole was able to recognize that Luke had a different way of showing his love, his inability to say the three worlds that Cole longed to hear freely. There were just times like this when he wished he didn't need to hear it.

Chapter Three

"Please tell me that you know what you're doing,"
McKenna's concern was evident even though she was trying to
disguise it with a strangled laugh.

Cole couldn't resist the urge to roll his eyes. Luckily, he
was looking away from her so she didn't see his frustration.
Seriously? It was a baby crib. How hard could it possibly be to put
together? And who appointed his stepbrother's fiancé as his
watchdog?

"Again, why didn't you ask your man to put this
together?" Cole still wasn't sure how he got nominated for the job,
but he'd been told – twice already – that he needed to get it put
together quickly because the baby shower was supposed to
commence in just a couple of hours and he had to be out of sight
by that time. Someone dropped the ball, obviously, and if it
weren't for the fact that this was for Sierra – well, technically this
was for him as well – he'd have said no thanks.

"He was supposed to," McKenna clarified as she paced the
floor behind him. "Something came up, and he had to go to a
meeting. If I remember correctly, it was your lover who called that
meeting."

Cole grinned. Yes, it was true. Luke did have Tag jumping through plenty of hoops these days. Every time he turned around, Luke was coming up with another idea on what he wanted to do with the club, but changing his mind just as quickly. He wasn't sure at the moment what the last one had even been.

"I really wish you'd sit down," he told her, not bothering to look up from what he was doing. "You're going to wear a hole in the damn carpet."

"You don't have carpet," she retorted, laughing.

At least she was smiling again. It was almost funny how out of sorts McKenna, Ashleigh and Sam were as they ran back and forth through the house trying to get everything ready. Somehow they'd managed to score his house as the location for the baby shower, but it'd been a little tricky. Luckily, Sierra's mother was just as much a part of this as the others, only her job was to keep Sierra busy today. Cole had offered to be the one to keep her busy, but he'd been told to stop thinking with his dick. He smiled at the thought.

As soon as McKenna's heels clicked out of the room, Cole busied himself with finishing up. As much as he loved Sierra, and as eager as he was for the baby to be born, he did not want to be involved in this little estrogen-fest.

For the next fifteen minutes, Cole worked diligently while the women busied themselves in the other room. He was grateful for the reprieve. At least he had managed to steer clear of Sam for most of the day. The woman was a nervous wreck. He couldn't imagine how the others were managing to deal with her at the moment. Maybe he'd be lucky and he'd get to finish his little project in peace and then disappear before anyone noticed.

"Where does this go?"

The sweet voice from the doorway told him that he was not so lucky.

Turning around, Cole saw Ashleigh staring back at him, holding a bolt in one hand and a confused expression on her face.

"It's an extra piece," he assured her.

"Are you sure?"

No, he certainly was not. Cole couldn't help but laugh. It was either that or storm out of the house and tell these high maintenance women to put it together themselves. Not that he actually would do the latter, but it sounded good.

"I'm sure, Ash. Now, get back in there and help Sam."

Ashleigh nodded her head, but he could tell she still didn't believe him.

Picking up the bolt, Cole turned to stare back at the crib he'd just put together. Scratching his head, he tried to figure out just where he could've possibly gone wrong.

Ten minutes later, Cole was tightening the last bolt –
again. He'd just pushed back to his feet when he felt the presence
of someone behind him. Turning slowly, he noticed Alex
McDermott standing there with a huge grin on his face.

"What the hell are you smiling at?" Cole asked, an
answering smile splitting his face.

"Nothing," Alex said with a chuckle that belied his
answer. "I was just called over to supervise, but now that I see
you're finished, I think this calls for a beer."

Supervise? Cole would've laughed if the underhanded
scheme was even remotely funny. "I'm thinking more like a six
pack. Have you heard from Tag and Luke?"

Cole followed Alex out of the small room that Sierra had
set up as the nursery and down the main hall to the living room.
When he walked in, he stopped abruptly, staring at the mess of shit
hanging from every possible place they could reach.

Lord, he was so glad that Luke would be responsible for
the cleanup and not him. That was the deal. He put the crib
together, Luke signed on for cleanup. Even if he didn't know it yet.

"They're going to meet us at the club in forty five minutes.
Logan's on his way now."

Thank God they had managed to get out of having to attend the baby shower. At one point, Sam tried to convince them that this was a couple's baby shower and that he and Luke needed to be there for Sierra. For once, the men managed to win that argument when they practically boycotted going. Needless to say, Sam probably wasn't all that happy with them, but, if Cole had to guess, Logan more than made it up to her later that night.

"Mind if I catch a ride with you?" Cole asked as he continued staring around the overly decorated living room, streams of pink and white ribbons everywhere.

Yep, he was definitely not going to clean this mess up.

~~*~~

"Put your damn phone down," Luke growled. "Leave that woman alone and let her enjoy the damned baby shower."

Cole glanced over at Logan and grinned. The man had been glued to his cell phone for the last twenty minutes, and by the look on his face, it was clear he was texting Sam. Or knowing them, sexting.

"Screw you," Logan laughed. "You're just jealous because yours is too busy opening presents to want to have anything to do with you. Or him." Logan grinned, glancing over at Cole.

"Well, you better enjoy this while you can, that's all I can say. Before long, you'll be pulling diaper duty, and there'll be no running out of the house for a beer with the guys," Alex said before downing the rest of his beer.

"And what the hell do you know about diaper duty? Aren't you supposed to be planning a wedding?" Cole countered.

"I think Ashleigh's got that one covered. She asks my opinion, I nod, and she goes on about her business. It's not like she'd care if I disagreed with her anyway."

"I'm still trying to convince McKenna to run off to Vegas," Tag chimed in.

"Bullshit." Luke didn't even bother to hide his opinion behind a cough the way Logan did which incited a round of laughter at the table. "That's not how I heard it. I was told McKenna wanted to run off to Vegas, but you insist on a real wedding."

Cole wanted to see his stepbrother get out of that one. There was no way Tag could deny that he was the one who insisted they have a normal wedding. Whatever the hell normal meant.

Cole happened to know that Tag was getting a little antsy about when they were going to get married. They had yet to set a date, and even though Tag said he hassled McKenna about it – good naturedly of course – she hadn't committed to anything. Cole was pretty sure they didn't have a valid reason for the delay, aside from Tag being so busy.

"I noticed you two were hanging at the club last Tuesday," Logan commented, his eyes intensely focused on Tag.

That caught Cole's attention, and he turned to stare at Tag, fighting the urge to smile. He lost. That was a fascinating tidbit of information if he did say so himself. Considering Tag was as possessive toward McKenna as a man possibly could be, hearing that he was hanging out at the club made Cole wonder whether he might be reconsidering some of his rigid rules.

"Does that mean y'all are looking for something more?" Luke asked, suddenly looking somewhat interested in the direction the conversation was headed.

"We're always looking for something more," Tag replied snidely, and Cole sensed a wealth of hidden meaning behind that statement.

Over the last few months, the five men had managed to meet up at least once a week. It seemed as though they all had the relationship thing in common, which somehow equated to some sort of bond – or so Sam and Sierra tried to tell them.

Cole would admit, they'd become pretty close during that time, and they liked to razz each other about their relationships. Tag wasn't any different, with the exception that he seemed to be in denial these days.

Logan had a point though, Tag and McKenna did seem to be venturing out more these days, and into other areas that Tag hadn't been keen on previously when it came to her.

"Are you looking for a third?" Luke asked, ever the inquisitive one.

"Let's just say we're experimenting. At the moment, I'm not sure where it'll lead, but we're not ruling anything out right now."

The few conversations that Cole and Tag had shared over the last few months went beyond their regular casualty, which was a little surprising. In fact, they'd become closer in a sense, more like brothers should be, and Cole certainly wasn't complaining. He found it easy to talk to Tag, and it appeared that the feeling was mutual.

During one of their more open discussions, Tag mentioned that McKenna had convinced him that he was being too restrictive on their sex life, although he didn't agree for the most part. Cole figured it had something to do with the fact that Tag had been a third in several relationships, including Logan's in the past, yet he'd closed himself off to the possibility once he met McKenna. As it turned out, McKenna was questioning his logic. According to Tag, McKenna had talked him into going to the club on the infamous Tuesday nights just to see where things led.

"What about you? You going to cross over to the dark side one of these days?" Luke asked Alex and Cole noticed the look of utter relief on Tag's face. Apparently the man was happy to have the conversation redirected.

"Not on your life." Alex's response came out easily and based on the expression on his face, he didn't intend to share his woman with anyone.

Cole knew Ashleigh felt the same, although he'd been privy to a few bedtime stories that Sierra had forced him and Luke to listen to, and holy fucking hell, the woman could write a sex scene that would blow your fucking mind.

"How is she going to keep coming up with material if you're not experimenting?" Cole asked, grinning. These days, he lived to get Alex riled up, mainly because it seemed Alex had it in for him.

"Who says we're not experimenting?" Alex sipped his whiskey and stared back at Cole shooting him a look that said "don't push me".

The table erupted in laughter, everyone joining in, including Alex.

A deep voice from behind them echoed through the empty bar, and Cole immediately recognized the significant drawl of one of the Walker brothers. "Whatever it is, I'm just glad we didn't have to hang out for long,"

Cole glanced over his shoulder in time to see Kaleb and Zane Walker heading their way.

"Kaleb. Zane," Luke turned slightly in his chair. "So glad you boys could join us."

"Yeah, well, I thought for a minute we weren't going to get out of there in time. Zoey threatened to make us hide out until it was over," Kaleb said as the two men took a seat at the table.

"Can I get you guys a beer while I'm up?" Tag asked, standing from his chair and grabbing his empty beer bottle.

"Might want to make that two," Zane said, sounding defeated. "The only thing I know, I'm just damn happy that ain't my house. Whoever has to clean that up is gonna to be hatin' life later."

Another round of laughter.

"So, what the hell do they do at a baby shower anyway?" Cole asked, Zane's comment reminding him of the condition the house was in when he left. "Oh, and I'm not cleaning that shit up, man. It's all on you," he told Luke, grinning as he said it.

He meant every word.

Chapter Four

"Oh my goodness!" Sierra exclaimed as she walked into her house, stunned nearly speechless by the outrageous display of giant helium balloons and floating pink and white streamers that decorated the living room as well as the entryway.

Grabbing hold of her mother's arm, Sierra stood motionless, her mouth hanging open as she tried to take it all in while fighting back tears.

Hormones, she told herself.

"Surprise!" Sam squealed, sounding like a little kid who'd just pulled a huge prank. Sierra's smile widened.

"I can't believe –" Sierra let the sentence hang because she didn't quite know how to finish it. She couldn't believe a lot of things, one of them being what her friends had done.

Unable to stop a tear from trickling down her cheek, Sierra smiled at Sam, unable to find the words. When Sam cupped her face, wiping away the tear with her thumb and smiling down at her, Sierra had to swallow to hold back the rest of them.

"Did you really think I wasn't going to have it put together in time?" Sam asked, grinning.

"Come on in here, girl!" Ashleigh called from the other room, and Sierra turned to see Ashleigh, McKenna, Lucie, Zoey, V, and another woman whose face she couldn't place right away, scattered in a semicircle around the living room.

There, on a table that stood in front of the massive stone fireplace were more gifts than Sierra had ever seen in her entire life, all sporting shiny wrapping paper and pretty pink and white bows. Another flood of tears threatened as the women all began to rise, taking turns hugging her as she moved closer into the room.

"I'm so glad the two of you are here," Sierra said to Zoey and V as she hugged them both. "I can't believe you drove all this way."

"Honey, we wouldn't miss it," Zoey said with a huge grin.

"Did Kaleb let you drive by yourselves?"

"Are you kidding?" Zoey laughed. "I just barely got him out of here a few minutes ago."

Sierra smiled. She still couldn't believe how much trouble her friends had gone through. For her.

"I can't believe you guys did this," Sierra laughed, sounding almost hysterical, even to her own ears.

"Oh, girl. You don't know the half of it. We've got games to play so why don't you sit down and put your feet up," Ashleigh said, placing her hand on Sierra's arm and leading her to a chair that looked as though it had been specifically placed so everyone could see her.

Sierra took her seat while Sam disappeared into the kitchen. She listened as her mother introduced Deanna, Logan's receptionist and close friend of Veronica's. That's when she recognized her.

"Thank you for coming," Sierra smiled back at Deanna.

"Honey, I've been begging your mother to let me come for months. Then again, I thought we were going to have to tie Sam up just so she'd quit working so hard."

"Well, it's beautiful. I –" Once again, Sierra didn't know how to say the words. What her friends had done for her was beyond what she expected.

"We've got food and drinks, non-alcoholic of course, so ladies, help yourselves," Sam called from the kitchen.

Ashleigh leaned over, smiling from ear to ear. "So, did we really surprise you?"

"You have no idea." Sierra still couldn't believe it. For some reason, she hadn't expected a large baby shower, maybe something small and intimate, maybe one or two people, but certainly not all of the women who were there.

When everyone was back in the living room, plates in hand, Sam brought one for Sierra, and they sat around chatting for a few minutes about how they'd managed to pull one over on Sierra good. She couldn't help but laugh at how excited Sam was that she did.

"I take it from all of the pink and white that you're having a girl," V stated.

"Well, that's what the doctor tells us anyway," Sierra said with awe. She was still a little stunned by the fact that she was going to be a mother. The feeling was so incredible, a beautiful little life growing inside of her.

"You better get your rest while you can," Lucie chimed in. "Let me tell you, girls are hell on wheels."

"Are you kidding? Haley is a perfect little angel," Sam added, grinning.

"I would've agreed with you at one point, but her daddy is doing a fantastic job of corrupting her."

Kane, Haley's father, hadn't been a part of Haley's life for the first few years because he didn't know he was the child's father. Back when Sierra was dating Luke and Cole, Lucie was going through a rough time, and she finally decided she needed to break the news to him. None of them had been the same since, and it was a sight to see.

"Well, I could tell you some stories about Sierra from when she was a little girl," Veronica added with a grin.

"Mom, don't you dare!" Sierra feigned discomfort with the subject. She didn't have any problems with her mother telling her stories. She'd heard them more than once, and she was pretty sure Sam probably had too by now.

"I want to know what games we're gonna play," Ashleigh added in.

Sierra smiled, taking a sip of her punch and smiling at the handful of women. She couldn't have asked for anything more than this.

Two hours later, Sierra was nearly dead on her feet, although she wasn't exactly *on* her feet. Sitting on the couch, her feet propped up, she closed her eyes and relived everything that had happened over the last couple of hours. There'd been some games, one of them actually involved them trying to guess how big around she was by using ribbon. To her surprise, McKenna had almost been spot on in her estimate. Then there was some sort of diaper game with smashed candy bars that they had to guess. She could've lived without that one, but it had been entertaining.

Not only did they have a lot of laughs, there were a few tears. Each gift that Sierra opened had her crying, which she tried to hide stoically. She was pretty sure there wasn't a single thing they needed to buy at this point because the ladies had thought of everything, right down to the crib, which she was told Cole had put together. She made a mental note to thank him later.

Now that the house was quiet, she wasn't sure what she was going to do with herself. Bear probably felt the same way because he was now lying in front of the couch and she was pretty sure he hadn't lifted his head once since the women left.

After Sam insisted she clean up the mess so Sierra didn't have to, she waved her off, telling her friend that she would have the men do it when they got home. Most of everything was cleaned up anyway, except for a few decorations that remained streaming across the living room.

The baby shower had been astounding. More so was the fact that she had felt so loved with all of the women in the room. Every single one of them, her mother included, understood the dynamic between her and Luke and Cole and not a one of them judged her in any way.

Surprisingly, no one even asked whom the father was. She knew it was probably on their minds, but she appreciated the fact that they respected her enough not to ask. It wasn't that they were keeping the information from their friends and family, but they weren't offering it up either. If someone asked, she would probably tell them. Not that it really mattered because as far as she was concerned, they were both the father. And, more importantly, her baby was going to be blessed with more love because of it.

~~*~~

"Honey," Cole whispered, gently touching Sierra's arm, trying to wake her without alarming her. She wasn't fond of being woken from her naps, and she generally startled easily, and her confusion was downright adorable.

He and Luke were surprised to find her sound asleep on the couch when they walked in, the house in much better shape than when he left, although there were still a few decorations that needed to come down. The most overwhelming part now was the abundance of baby things that were piled in one corner. Luke had certainly lucked out.

"Hi," Sierra said sleepily, peering through heavy eyelids with a smile on her face. "You're home."

"And you're asleep."

"Sorry, I must've dozed for a few minutes. What time is it?"

"Eight-thirty," he told her, watching as Luke began rummaging through the pile of baby things. Cole grinned at the man's confused expression, obviously just as clueless as Cole was about what all that stuff was for. "Did you have fun?"

"Oh, Cole. It was unbelievable. We had so much fun. Did you see all the stuff we got?"

"What in the he—, er… world is this?" Luke asked, obviously still working on his profanity.

Sierra sat up straighter and Cole moved over, giving her space. "It's a diaper Genie."

"Because a regular trash can won't do?" Luke asked, staring at the box.

Sierra didn't bother to try and explain, she merely laughed.

"Have you had dinner?" Cole asked, turning his attention back to Sierra.

"No, but I don't think I could eat a thing. After the cake and ice cream, I think I'm pretty well done for the night."

Cole nodded, then glanced over at Luke. "You want me to make you something?"

"If you're making yourself something, then sure."

Cole smiled up at Luke, wondering if the man even realized how bewildered he looked. Cole certainly knew how he felt. With a baby on the way, the baby shower pretty much signifying that they were heading down the home stretch now, it was beginning to get real.

As he walked to the kitchen, Cole wondered whether the anxiety actually would get better or worse once the baby was born. The conversations over the course of the evening hadn't done anything to alleviate the stress he was feeling either. When Kane showed up, he'd showered them with various stories about Haley and quite frankly, Cole was petrified.

For now, he was just grateful for something to do to take his mind off of the stories and the nerves and the gifts. The last thing he wanted was for Sierra to realize how nervous he truly was. There'd be plenty of time for that later.

Chapter Five

Luke was up with the sun the following morning, which was way too early in his opinion. After the events of the night before, and getting home to find his house a complete and utter disaster, – at least in his opinion – he should've been too tired to get out of bed. That didn't appear to be the case because no matter how hard he tried, he couldn't keep his eyes closed.

With so many things on his mind he had tossed and turned most of the night so finding any peace within his dreams wasn't going to happen. With Sierra still sleeping soundly beside him, Luke decided to get up so she could rest a little longer.

Sneaking out of bed and into the kitchen required stealth that a man of his size didn't have, but he tried. He was thankful that he knew his house so well because his thoughts were still on the fritz and he was practically moving around while lost inside of his thoughts entirely.

As with most morning's, Luke's first thought was about the club and the current turmoil it was in, and he knew he couldn't give one hundred percent until he had a cup of coffee. He wasn't a big fan of the stuff, but he'd learned in recent months that the caffeine did wonders to clear the fog from his brain.

Not that coffee was going to make him come up with some brilliant plan to counteract the result of his actions. If it would, he'd have been in much better shape long ago. After closing the doors on the fetish club, he had taken a substantial hit from all angles, financially being the least of his worries, although with a baby on the way, it was another factor that was beginning to weigh heavily on his already overloaded brain.

He would be the first to admit that he was prone to rash decisions. He just couldn't help but feel that this one wasn't rash. After finding out most of his members were nothing more than sanctimonious assholes who felt as though he actually owed *them* something, he'd decided enough was enough.

So, that left him in the rebuilding phase, only he wasn't exactly sure what that meant for him yet. With Kane Steele now handling the memberships, he was getting much more in depth than ever before, digging even further into the member's background – those that still remained – which meant remarkably little escaped him, and it was probably easier to get into the White House than it was to get into his club these days. But even he knew Kane was not going to be able to make that a full time job.

Unfortunately, Luke was at a standstill on what to do from here, which meant his brain was working overtime. He was at the point he just wanted someone else to take over, to make the damned decisions, to figure out what the best approach to take was. For the first time in his life, Luke was about ready to relinquish control to someone else.

"Mornin'," Cole greeted from his seat at the breakfast bar as Luke moved into the kitchen.

He allowed his gaze to drift over the taut, firm muscles of Cole's bare back and as with any morning, Luke appreciated that he was able to wake up to someone as incredibly sexy as Cole. The man had the ability to turn him on like a fucking switch and this morning was apparently no different than any other.

"What are you doing up?" Luke asked, forcing his thoughts from sex and back to what his plans were for the day.

"Alex asked me to go meet with Carson Throckmorton this morning," Cole answered, sipping his coffee. Luke felt Cole's eyes on him, which didn't help the current state he was in.

"What time?"

"Ten," Cole said as he stood from the bar stool before carrying his cup back to the sink and rinsing it. "What are your plans for the day?"

Luke wasn't quite sure what his plans were. He knew he needed to go to the club. He needed to have a conversation with Serena, better known as Mistress Serena, before Trent Ramsey made another appearance. From what he heard, the two of them went toe to toe the night they'd allowed the Walker brothers to visit the club. It hadn't been a good run in either, or at least that's the story he'd gotten. With Serena, he had absolutely no idea. The woman was in a league all her own, and for a man who didn't get scared easily, she sometimes freaked Luke out.

"I'm going to talk to Serena and Kane today." Luke
needed to talk to Cole, but he wanted to do it at the club, he just
wasn't sure how to go about bringing up the subject yet.
Convincing his lover to quit his full time job and come help him
manage the club wasn't an easy conversation to instigate. He
wasn't sure how Cole would take the request, so he kept putting it
off.

"Well, once I'm done with my meeting I'll come back and
keep Sierra company." The grin that split Cole's too handsome
face quickly forced the weariness from his brain and got his blood
pumping. That mischievous glint in Cole's eyes said he had
something much more compelling than an afternoon of meetings
planned.

"Speaking of," Luke began, glancing down the hall to their
bedroom, checking to see if Sierra was awake yet. "You think
she's doing all right?"

"Why?" Cole looked perplexed as he turned to face him,
standing just a few feet away. "I don't know, I'm sure it's the
pregnancy," Luke admitted, turning away to face the counter
again. Luke knew Sierra was more fatigued than usual, she'd told
him as much. But for some reason he wasn't sure that was all it
was with her.

Cole's intoxicating scent drifted his way, and Luke damn near dropped his coffee. He wasn't sure what the hell was going on with him these days, but he couldn't seem to get enough of him. They both had too much to do today for him to get something started. He damn sure wouldn't survive not being able to finish it. After the last time the two of them had been alone upstairs, Luke had been hoping for a repeat.

Only he was hoping for something a little different.

Maybe.

Shit.

"Are *you* ok?" Cole's smooth, rich voice slid around him at the same time his warm hands pressed against his back.

Luke let out an involuntary hiss at the feel of those smooth, yet callused fingers against his skin. When Cole leaned in closer, tucking his chin in the crook of Luke's shoulder, pulling his head back slightly, he damn near saw stars. He was getting bolder these days, and Luke would be damned if he didn't love the hell out of it. He just wanted to give in to Cole, to give in to whatever the man wanted to take from him, only he feared that's not what Cole wanted.

Luke had his own fears as well, but they revolved more around giving too much of himself away. Those demons were still lingering, still fresh in his mind, even if Sierra and Cole had managed to alleviate the worst of his fears over the last several months.

But he also feared that by taking, or rather giving in this case, what he needed, he would be taking something away from Cole. He knew by the way that Cole reacted to him just how much he expected Luke to be the dominant one. And for the most part that's what Luke preferred as well. It was only recently that he'd started thinking about something else.

Something more.

Cole nipped his earlobe and Luke growled, reaching behind him and gripping Cole's head, holding him close and absorbing his body heat against his back. *Fuck.* This was two seconds from getting out of control, and the feel of Cole's thick cock pressing against his ass wasn't helping matters at all.

"You don't have time to start this," Luke warned, but Cole didn't pull away.

To his shock, Cole tilted Luke's head to the side until their mouths hovered close together. The feel of Cole's bare chest against his back, his strong hand planted in the center of Luke's chest, the other holding his chin firmly had his entire body gearing up for what he knew would come next. Only his natural reaction was to control it, so why he didn't try to pull out of Cole's arms, he had no idea. Sliding his hand through Cole's hair, he allowed the man to bite his lower lip before sucking it into his mouth.

"Fuck." It was Cole's turn to growl, the vibration in his chest sending a torrent of pleasure coursing through Luke's veins, which in turn had all of his blood heading south.

"Don't do this," Luke warned, reaching for some measure of sanity. He couldn't let Cole take control. It wasn't in him to let anyone take control. He didn't care if he trusted Cole with his life, he still wasn't about to let him see him weak.

"You want it," Cole whispered. "You know you do."

Luke didn't respond. He remained stone still, feeling Cole's breath feather over his lips. *Fuck.* He wanted to kiss him senseless and then bend him over the fucking table and take him like a mad man. That's how hot Cole made him.

"See, that's where you're wrong," Luke growled, gripping Cole's hair tighter. "I won't deny wanting you," Luke managed to turn slightly, "but never mistake who's in control here."

Cole let go, taking a step back but still meeting his stare. Luke turned fully to face him, then stalked him across the kitchen like a jungle animal set free, only Cole didn't back up. He was exerting even more of his dominance than Luke was used to. Like usual, he didn't succumb to Luke's demands. At least not at first.

"Just remember, you started this," Luke smiled, leaning in and biting Cole's lip the same way he'd done to him seconds before. "And I'm going to finish it."

"I'm counting on it," Cole said, kissing him briefly before turning and walking out of the room without looking back.

Rubbing his cock through his jeans, Luke trailed Cole with his eyes until he disappeared around the corner. *Sonuvabitch.* It was going to be a long fucking day.

~~*~~

"Did you notice that Dylan's here again?" Luke asked Logan as they stood in his office at the club staring down at the small group growing bigger by the minute.

Club Destiny was popular on Friday and Saturday nights, but in recent months, Monday's had become quite busy. Probably for the fact that Luke made Monday's karaoke night despite Logan's extreme distaste for that decision.

Logan joined him beside the window and glanced down at the bar. Luke watched as Dylan held up a hand motioning for Lucie to bring another drink. From where he stood, it was clear that the man wasn't drinking water. Whatever it was, he was doing doubles, and he was rapid firing them as soon as Lucie handed them over.

Luke couldn't help but think that Dylan's day was going about as shitty as his own. Not only had Trent postponed their morning meeting to the evening, Luke had the pleasure of sitting in a room with a decidedly unhappy Domme for the better part of an hour. Serena didn't talk often, but when she did, it was hard to get her to stop. He didn't mind for the most part because he truly needed to know what was going on between her and Trent Ramsey.

As it turned out, after sixty minutes of continuous chatter on her part, Luke had learned nothing.

"Something wrong with him? Besides the obvious?" Luke asked, watching as Lucie handed Dylan another glass, nearly half full with clear liquid. It didn't take long for him to down that one. He had to be feeling good and numb by now. When he called Lucie over again, this time she had the proper sense to ignore him momentarily and shoot a glance up at the window. Luke knew she couldn't see him, but he could see her.

"You want to go talk to him?"

"Not really, no," Luke admitted.

It wasn't that he didn't want to talk to Dylan, but he knew the man was going through a tough time right now. The anniversary of his wife's death was never an easy day, and although Luke didn't want Dylan to pass out cold on his bar floor, he knew someone had to go talk to him.

"Fine," Logan said, turning to walk away.

"Hey," Luke called to Logan, turning to face his identical twin brother. "Why the hell are you here anyway?"

The grin Logan tossed at him said Luke wasn't going to like the answer.

"I heard you were supposed to meet with Trent. I knew by your mood when I walked in that it hadn't happened yet." Logan didn't look nearly as pleased with himself as the words came out.

"He should be here any minute. You might want to go talk to Dylan, or I'm tempted to force you to hang out with us."

"Oh, hell no. Give me the drunk guy any day," Logan responded at the same time there was a knock on Luke's office door. Before he could call out to whoever it was, the door opened and in walked Trent. Somehow Logan managed to slip out of the room without even having to talk to him.

Bastard.

Luke had been expecting Trent for a while now, and like usual, the man seemed to keep his own schedule, the rest of them be damned. Ever since the night he gave a tour of the club to the Walker brothers, Trent had been pacing like a caged tiger. It was clear he had something on his mind.

"What brings you slummin'?" Luke greeted Trent with the question as he moved closer to his desk. He wasn't sure he wanted to sit just yet. At six-foot-five-inches, Luke was by far a small man; however, it was interesting because even though Trent was probably an inch or two shorter, he was larger. Strangely, he was bigger both in size and personality. It explained why he was in the industry that he was in.

"Slummin'?" Trent laughed, his deep, raspy voice sounding oddly jovial and putting Luke's back up.

What was he up to?

Luke, Logan, and Trent went way back. Although Trent was five or six years younger, the three of them had somehow forged a friendship prior to Club Destiny's inception. Theirs was one of those friendships that coincidentally happened – right place, right time and all that. The three of them shared the same unique appreciation of adult clubs and many years later, here they were.

With the help of Trent's and Logan's capital, along with almost every penny Luke had in savings at the time, the club had been born. Going into it, the three of them knew they had bigger dreams than just creating a public bar.

Their intention was to create and expand a fetish club into something much bigger than what Club Destiny even was today. Considering recent events, they seemed to be moving in the opposite direction which had obviously pulled Trent out from behind the scenes.

"You bring the paparazzi with you?" Luke asked before deciding to drop into his chair. Hell, he wasn't intimidated by Trent, and if the man wanted to loom over him like he had all of the control in this situation, he'd let him.

"Let's hope not," Trent sighed, finally taking the seat across from Luke. The more days that passed, the calmer Trent became at least in comparison to that first phone conversation they'd had when Trent insisted Luke open the doors to the club once more. He hadn't been happy when Luke told him that wasn't going to happen. At least not yet.

"How'd you manage that?"

Trent held up a baseball cap and a pair of sunglasses.

"Does that normally work?" Luke asked, laughing.

Trent Ramsey was one of the hottest actors on the scene at the moment. Being a hot commodity didn't allow for much anonymity; therefore, Trent had never out and out shared his interest in the club only because of the fact he didn't want to bring the press down on them. Luke was pretty sure that was going to be a thing of the past now that Trent had decided to jump back into the game so to speak.

"Most of the time, yes," Trent answered. "It helps that I sent a decoy out early this morning, and I'm pretty sure they're hot on his tail by now."

"I'd tell you I'm impressed with your evasive skills, but I'd be lying," Luke said sternly, working to get them to the topic he knew Trent came to talk about. "If you came by to insist that I reopen the club, it's not going to work."

Trent's handsome features changed from lighthearted to serious in the blink of an eye.

"When?"

"When what?" Luke decided to play ignorant. He'd had more than his fair share of these conversations with Trent in the last few months. He didn't want to have another one. Not today, not tomorrow, not ever.

Club Destiny was his fucking club, and he made the decisions on whether the doors remained open or not. With Logan standing behind him on his choice, Luke knew he could make any decision he chose. Without a doubt, he knew his brother, as well as Sierra and Cole, would support him regardless of whether they agreed with him entirely or not. And between him and Logan, they still owned the majority of the shares.

"How much longer are you going to keep the doors closed?"

"Don't know." Since he had wiped out all of the previous members with the exception of a few, Luke wasn't sure it actually would matter whether he opened the doors or not at this point.

"I think we need to put a plan together. We can't keep them closed forever. We've got an opportunity to take this to the next level," Trent said seriously. "It's time we amp up our game."

"We don't have any competition in this, remember? It's a private adult club. How the hell do you propose we do that? Advertise?" Luke could see it now: a billboard shining bright over one of Dallas' main thoroughfares letting the great city know about the fetish club equipped with its very own dominatrix.

Not gonna happen.

"Not exactly what I was thinking."

"Then what *were* you thinking?"

In all honesty, Luke had given significant thought to what he wanted to do with the club. He didn't go into this business to manage a night club, but that seemed to be where he was at the moment.

With the fetish club seemingly nonexistent for the time being, he was spinning his wheels trying to come up with a plan. He'd even hired Kane Steele full time to work on growing their membership, but until Luke figured out what he wanted to do with the club, Kane couldn't do much of anything more than conduct background checks and extensive research on the applications they were receiving. He had to be getting bored at this point, Luke knew.

"How are we going to fare against the Alluring Indulgence resort? Are they our direct competition?" Trent asked.

Luke watched Trent intently. He seemed to be fixated on the Walkers new resort, which amused him somewhat. Until now, Luke hadn't tried to figure out exactly why Trent was so concerned about an adult resort being built three hundred miles south. Considering Luke was also an investor in the resort, he didn't see a conflict of interest for himself; however, stepping into Trent's shoes for a minute, he could certainly see the potential for concern.

"It's not the same concept. They're going all out with their resort concept. You know, spa, hotel, convention center. That sort of thing. Their clubs will be the only thing we have in common, but since they have yet to design them that I know of, I seriously doubt they'll be our competition. On top of that, they're three hundred miles away."

"I heard Travis nixed the hotel idea," Trent added, twisting his hulking body around in the wooden chair across from Luke. The way he continued to tap his sunglasses against his thigh was slightly annoying. It also was a tell for Trent's anxiety level.

"He didn't nix it entirely. He just opted to change the floor plan so to speak. He's not building a hotel, rather adding single, standalone bungalows in lieu of. He thinks it'll give the guests more privacy."

"Not a bad idea, I have to admit. Have you thought about broadening our scope?"

"Broadening how?"

"The resort concept is a brilliant idea."

Luke knew Trent was hinting at something, but he was being evasive as usual. Was he interested in expanding on what they had?

Luke tended to subscribe to the "if it's not broke, don't fix it" concept. Since their doors were closed, it was obvious something had gone awry, but he wasn't sure he wanted to start with a different concept. Interesting thought though. He'd have to talk to Cole and get his input. He valued Cole's opinion as well as Sierra's over anyone else because he was confident they had his best interest in mind.

"I'm not sure I'm interested in going that route right now," Luke admitted honestly.

"What if we disconnect the two and let Kane take over running the show here?" Trent asked.

Luke thought about that for a moment. He liked the idea.

He openly would admit that Trent was the most creative of the three of them when it came to the direction they wanted to take the club. In fact, it had been Trent's proposal to implement the general public bar in order to take some of the interest off of the adult portion of the club. Luke had been left to implement the idea, which he did, and until recently, they hadn't had any significant road bumps along the way.

"What's your biggest concern?" Trent asked when Luke didn't answer his earlier question.

Luke narrowed his eyes at Trent, trying to gauge where he was taking this conversation. "With what?"

Luke wanted Trent to get to the point and he wasn't interested in putting himself totally out there just yet. Not until he had a chance to talk to Cole.

"Let's start with the members. I know you eliminated most of them, and it's obvious the more we try to keep the club hidden, the more we're going to risk as far as memberships being leaked. What if we go the route that the Walkers are going?"

"You mean not keep the membership secret?"

"Yes, in a sense. It's not like we'd have to broadcast who belongs to the club, but if we make sure applicants understand we aren't risking our own necks up front, maybe we'll get a different type of clientele."

The idea had merit. Luke had specifically closed the doors to his club because the members were more interested in protecting their own asses than helping to ensure Luke's family weren't thrown to the wolves. As far as he was concerned, Cole and Sierra came first and foremost before anyone else. He'd protect them and his brother with his life if he had to. And they knew it, which was why his family had supported him in his decision.

"Let me think on it," Luke said. "I like the idea, and I think it'll be easier to manage that way, but it will also expose us publicly. What does that mean for you? If we go public, where do you stand in all this?"

Trent had always been silent, and his association with the club was buried deep. So deep, Luke was almost certain no one would be able to link the two.

"Well, if you go public, I go public," Trent replied.

Luke expected to hear concern in Trent's tone, not the shit eating grin beaming back at him tenfold. From the looks of it, Trent was actually fond of the idea and Luke couldn't help but wonder just what he was going to get out of this.

Chapter Six

To think that this was what his life had come down to. Only fifteen minutes in and Cole didn't question whether this was about to take the same turn as the majority of other meetings he'd gone on for Alex in the last few months. Just like the others, it appeared that his boss was setting him up for failure. Thankfully, Cole only had to drive less than twenty miles for this head on collision.

Cole stared back at the uptight man sitting across from him, pelting questions at him left and right, practically begging Cole to prove to him that CISS was the best security firm in the state. It was the same song and dance, just different office and different asshole. What the hell was Alex thinking?

Mr. Carson Throckmorton was not the nicest person that Cole had come in contact with lately. In fact, he was getting damn tired of the man's condescending attitude, and he was about ready to walk out the door. This was well out of his job scope, and as far as he was concerned, Alex could deal with this shit.

Instead of getting up and leaving, Cole smiled and continued with his spiel, informing Mr. Throckmorton of their proven success rate as a corporate security firm. He'd gotten rather adept at the whole pitch, but he was growing more and more irritated as the days passed. This wasn't his job, it was Alex's job. Except, for some reason, Alex continued to delegate these shitty assignments week after week.

He was supposed to be the guy who came in after the deal had been made so he could get a decent feel for what would best protect the company. Throckmorton was nothing more than an arrogant show off who wanted people to believe he was bigger than what he was, and honestly, Cole was getting tired of the bullshit.

"And you're going to guarantee –"

Carson's voice brought him back to the present and Cole stared at him, trying to figure out what he was saying. That's when the words sank in. *Guarantee.* Right. Figuring he was about three seconds from losing his temper, Cole stood, putting his hands out in front of him, signaling his surrender, and staring down at the creepy guy who'd been shunning everything he tried to tell him for the last half hour.

"Mr. Throckmorton," Cole dropped his hands and glanced over at the door, then back, "it's clear that you're not interested in what my company has to offer you, so rather than wasting any more of your time, or mine, I think we can safely conclude this meeting."

"That's it?" Mr. Throckmorton asked incredulously. It dumbfounded Cole at how obtuse some people could be.

"As far as I'm concerned, yes. You and I both know there are no guarantees in this world, and I'm not going to sit here and shed blood to try and prove to you that we are who we say we are. Nor am I going to risk the possibility that we can't please you. I think it's in both of our best interest if you go with the other choice of security firms. I'm sure they'll be able to suit your needs just fine."

Cole turned on his heel and moved to the door of Mr. Throckmorton's office. He didn't bother stopping when the asshole began to tell him exactly what he thought of his attitude.

Quite frankly, Cole didn't have it in him to deal with a lot of shit these days. He was too busy elsewhere to bother with it. It seemed like Alex McDermott was sending him to these asinine meetings at least once or twice a week, and for some reason, he wasn't handling them well.

It was almost like CISS had too many hands in the pot, even if they were apparently one man down for whatever reason. Jake, the young man Dylan had hired to handle the residential sales, was getting restless being under Alex's thumb all the time, considering he'd certainly had more free rein when Dylan was at the helm. Cole couldn't blame the kid. Dylan didn't take a turn for the better like they all thought he would shortly after Nate, Dylan's son, graduated from high school. From where he stood, Dylan was digging himself deeper and deeper into depression, and he seemed to be chasing the demons with alcohol which somehow had left Cole picking up the slack.

He was pretty sure he'd get an earful from Alex after Mr. Throckmorton gave him a call.

He really didn't care.

As Cole was walking out of the office toward his truck, his cell phone rang, and he almost laughed. Glancing down at the caller id before answering, he noticed that it was Sierra and not Alex as he expected.

"Hey. Everything ok, baby?"

"Absolutely perfect," Sierra replied sweetly, her cheerful tone immediately making Cole feel better. "I wanted to see if you could meet me for lunch."

Cole glanced at his watch. He didn't even realize it was after noon. "I'd be glad to. Want me to pick you up? Or do you want to meet me somewhere?"

Cole loved these impromptu lunch dates with Sierra. Since her business was still growing and she had decided to work out of the house, they had more time to spend with her these days, although they generally revolved around an hour or two at lunch. Granted, he was hoping one of these days they'd have the opportunity to spend more time together, all three of them. Life seemed to be getting in the way of that dream though.

"I'll meet you. Where are you at?" Sierra answered.

Cole explained where he was and which direction he would be heading. They worked out where to meet and what time before Sierra hung up.

Rather than wait for Alex to call him and chew his ass out, Cole called his boss from the truck on the drive to the restaurant.

"I didn't expect you to call so soon. I figured you'd need some time to cool off. Didn't sound like it went well?" Alex stated in lieu of a greeting when he answered the phone.

Apparently Cole wasn't as quick as Mr. Throckmorton.

"That would be one way to look at it."

Pulling out of the parking lot, Cole aimed his truck for the restaurant he was to meet Sierra at while Alex's voice reverberated through the Bluetooth speaker in the truck.

"Can't say I blame you."

Cole's eyebrows shot skyward. Did Alex expect him to walk out on the asshole? If so, why the hell had he set him up like that? He was trying extremely hard to look at the situation from Alex's perspective, but the more and more he found himself in situations like this one, he couldn't help but wonder what was actually going on with Alex. If the man was in his right mind, he wouldn't be dealing with this type of shit either.

"Getting burned out already, Cole?" Alex asked.

The question took him by surprise, and he wondered whether that was actually the case. Was he getting burned out? He hadn't thought about it like that, but yeah, he might just be. Seemed rather unexpected since Cole hadn't worked for Alex for long, but considering he'd been self-employed for most of his life, working for someone else wasn't doing it for him.

Especially when he seemed to be taking over the role of salesman instead of what he'd originally been hired to do.

Rather than answer the question because he wasn't sure he wanted Alex to know the truth just yet, Cole opted to redirect back to the original subject. "I don't appreciate being sent to slaughter. There was no way that asshole was going to be satisfied with our services, no matter how I tried to convince him," Cole explained, feeling a rare burst of anger penetrate his bloodstream. For some reason, he felt set up.

"Sorry about that," Alex began, "I don't disagree. I'm sorry I didn't warn you ahead of time. Things have been a little crazy lately."

Cole detected something in his boss' tone, and from what he heard, Alex wasn't telling him the whole story.

Instead of questioning Alex, Cole opted to put the conversation on the back burner for a little while. It would give him time to cool off, which he desperately needed. He had no desire to be pissed off when he was looking forward to lunch with Sierra. He'd rather be preparing for the conversation he was hoping to have with her. It seemed as though she were trying to give him and Luke more alone time these days, but he didn't quite understand why. For the last few nights, when he finally made it to bed, Sierra had been fast asleep. He knew she was tired from the pregnancy, but he couldn't help but wonder if something else was bothering her. At least he would have the opportunity to ask her.

"I'd appreciate some warning in the future. It's done and over with. I won't try and convince the man, and as far as I'm concerned, our services aren't right for him anyway." It felt like déjà vu. Cole was pretty sure he'd said the same thing to Alex about the last dozen sales calls he'd gone on.

"Agree." Alex paused, and Cole waited patiently for him to continue. "I'll catch up with you later."

The abrupt end to the conversation took him by surprise, but Cole disconnected the call and focused on driving. Only five more minutes and he'd be with Sierra. A little alone time with her was just what he needed at the moment.

~~*~~

"Are you all right?"

Sierra's blunt question surprised Cole a little as he finished eating, having spent the last half hour trying to conjure up enough courage to ask her basically the same question she just spouted.

For the most part, neither of them had talked much, aside from discussing what they'd done that day and how their afternoons were lining up. Based on her question, Cole hadn't been as effective at hiding his pent up frustration nearly as well as he thought he had. Focusing on her was easy, but his conversation with Alex kept pricking at him, leaving him with more answers than questions.

"Fine, why?" His answer didn't sound exactly truthful, even to his own ears, but he wasn't sure what else to say. It wasn't like he was going to burden Sierra with his problems at work. The goal was to keep her as stress free as possible these days.

"Well, aside from the fact that you've been quiet almost the entire time we've been here," Sierra replied, a small smile on her lips as she sipped her water.

"Quiet?" Cole laughed. If anything, he felt as though he'd been talking too much.

Sierra's smile grew, and Cole's heart constricted. He loved when she smiled, even if it was one of those small ones that said she was still worried but she wasn't going to push him to talk. She had learned early on not to push because, between him and Luke, they very rarely shared much emotion.

"How's work?" she asked after the waiter returned to the table to clear the plates away.

"I'd prefer to talk about anything but work," he said hastily.

"Ok."

"Sorry. Things aren't going that great right now, and I'm not sure what Alex is up to."

"Ashleigh told me she's worried about Dylan."

"I'm thinking that might be it. He's been sending me out on these ridiculous sales calls, when in reality he should be the one handling them."

"Well, it makes sense if Dylan's not pulling his weight at the office. Have you talked to him about it yet?"

Sierra was always the sensible one. Talking to her, even briefly, often had Cole rethinking his reactions to certain situations. This was one of them.

"No. Not yet." *Shit.* He really needed to talk to Alex. Hell, he probably should make a pit stop and have a conversation with Dylan while he was at it. "Luke mentioned that Dylan's drinking again."

"Yeah. It seems he's gone a little overboard this time. Ashleigh mentioned that he broke up with Sarah a couple of weeks ago. Something about needing some space."

Cole didn't know Sarah personally, but he'd met her at Nate's graduation party. He was also familiar with her because she was Jake's aunt, and it was because of her that Dylan actually hired the kid to come work for CISS.

Cole knew that Alex had previously had a conversation with Dylan back when he first came on at CISS. Dylan's grief over losing his wife eight years prior was still very much alive and churning inside of him. They all thought he was progressing, moving forward, but it appears he was suddenly back tracking.

"What if Dylan can't cut it at work? Are you going to be satisfied handling the commercial sales?" Sierra's question was the same one he'd been asking himself for the better part of the last month, and one he really didn't have an answer for. He'd always been loyal to his friends. Often sacrificing his own happiness for the sake of others. For some reason, he had difficulty doing that these days.

"Is there something else you'd rather be doing?" Sierra asked, apparently thinking he didn't intend to answer her.

Cole cocked his head slightly, staring into the crystal blue eyes that captivated him to the point of distraction. She was absolutely, beyond doubt, the most beautiful woman in the world. Inside and out. He grinned at her, and when she blushed, he realized she recognized her double entendre as much as he did.

He lowered his voice and responded to the unintended question so that only she would hear. "You, baby. I'd much prefer to be doing you. Always you."

Sierra's sexy laugh sent a blast of heat straight to his groin, and he fought the urge to fidget. When her hand moved down to her belly, as though the baby was moving and she was trying to cuddle her, he grinned even more. Cole could've watched her all day, the way her face softened when the baby kicked made him smile.

It was a reminder of how fortunate he was these days. To have Sierra and Luke, not to mention a precious gift on the way, Cole had to remind himself not to let the small things get to him. In just a few short weeks, the three of them were going to be parents. The idea of it all still took his breath away.

Not to mention sent his nerves rioting.

"What happened to you the other night?"

The night they had come home from the tour at the club, Sierra chose not to join them, and at the time he figured she was tired, but as he sat here with her now, he wondered if it was something else. It wasn't like she was dodging his questions, but she did seem as though she had something on her mind.

"I was tired, and I knew that you and Luke needed some time together."

"And you didn't feel like watching?" Just the thought made his cock swell behind the restrictive confines of his jeans.

Cole couldn't deny how fucking hot it was when Sierra watched the two of them. It was the best of both worlds for Cole. It was even better when she joined them, but that had happened less and less over the last few weeks. She claimed it was the pregnancy, but Cole couldn't help but wonder.

Sierra smiled again, this time her face brightening. "I love watching the two of you. I sometimes think that the two of you might want to be alone, though."

Cole reached over and took Sierra's hand in his, twining their fingers as he stared back into those brilliant blue eyes. "Honey, you know it has never been like that. It's always been the three of us. The way it should be."

He was a little surprised they were having this conversation in such a public place, but he realized they hadn't had much time just to sit and talk recently. With all that was going on with the club, entertaining the Walker brothers, Sierra's new prospective clients, and Alex sending Cole on sales calls while Dylan was out, at least one, if not all three of them, was usually working late. Luke was even more wrapped up in trying to figure out the future of Club Destiny, which resulted in exceptionally little time at home.

"I don't want you and Luke to drift apart," Sierra stated, and Cole's stomach churned. Did she know something he didn't? Was Luke unhappy? He hadn't noticed anything different about their relationship.

"Why would you say that?" When Sierra looked away, Cole released her hand and tilted her chin until she looked him in the eye, moving his chair closer to hers.

He knew he wasn't able to hide his own insecurities exceedingly well, but he hadn't expected Sierra to be worried about anything. The one constant in their relationship was her. Both he and Luke made it a point to ensure she was always taken care of. And yes, there were times Cole wanted more. More from Luke, more from Sierra, but he wasn't about to disclose as much.

"The two of you are always doting on me. I don't think an hour goes by without one or both of you calling to check up on me. And yes, maybe it's because of the pregnancy, but I sometimes feel as though the two of you don't get enough time alone."

Alone? Cole wasn't under the impression they were looking for alone time together. They weren't separate couples. They were in this together, the three of them as a whole. Sure, Cole wouldn't mind stealing a few minutes with either of them separately, but it was the times they were all three together that he felt most complete.

"Luke and I are close, baby. I'm not looking for anything more than what we already have." But now that Sierra had planted the seed of doubt in his mind, Cole wasn't sure that Luke might not be looking for something different.

He and Luke were getting closer, both on a personal as well as a professional level. They had finally developed a level of trust that was critical to the success of their relationship. And maybe Luke wasn't always shouting his love, but that was what Cole had come to expect from him. Sure, he'd like a little reassurance from time to time, but he accepted Luke for who he was. Changing him wasn't in the cards, nor did Cole want it to be. He wouldn't have stuck around if he truly thought Luke didn't love him.

Maybe this could be chalked up to hormones. Cole knew they were all a little antsy these days, both fear and anxiety from becoming new parents were intensifying as the weeks progressed. They had yet to have a full conversation about some of the logistics, such as the baby's last name, which Cole knew was inevitable. Biologically, and on record, there could only be one father. The subject alone had presented some conflict in their relationship early on.

Thanks to his conversation with his stepbrother, Tag, Cole had attempted to address the issue with Luke. He was told not to be ridiculous in so many words; however, he could see some concern in Luke's eyes. Not that the man ever would admit as much.

"I love him, Sierra, just as I love you. I don't expect things to be easy between us. This isn't a traditional relationship. We have to expect a few bumps along the way."

"Yes, there will be bumps, I know that," she argued. "That doesn't mean that you and Luke have to drift apart."

"Did you lie about being tired the other night just to push us together?"

Sierra looked away again, and Cole knew the truth. She was trying to get them closer.

He wanted to tell her that the alone time wasn't going to be what brought him and Luke closer. He couldn't bring himself to admit that there was a connection they'd yet to make and in Cole's eyes, it was a piece that would likely change them both forever.

"So, you're telling me I shouldn't worry?" Sierra asked, sounding both distraught and a little relieved.

"That's exactly what I'm telling you." Cole smiled. "This isn't temporary. We're in this for the long haul. Right now, we all need to be focused on the baby. I'm pretty sure the rest will work itself out."

At least Cole hoped it would.

Chapter Seven

One week later...

Cole couldn't pinpoint what the issue was, but over the last few days, he'd come to one conclusion: he had to talk to Alex. He needed to confront the man and try to get them on the same page because at the moment, he feared they were reading from different books.

Ever since Alex set him up on that debacle of a meeting with Carson Throckmorton, the man hadn't been acting like himself. He was vague in his direction, and even somewhat standoffish. As much as Cole wanted to believe that Dylan was the only reason for all of the changes taking place, something told him that wasn't the case.

Walking into the office of CISS, Cole peered in the small section that Jake and Nate had commandeered as an office that they both shared during the few times they weren't out in the field. Neither of them were in. Not surprising.

Cole continued, stopping to peek in Dylan's office. He wasn't in either, but that was to be expected. He hadn't seen or heard from Dylan in at least a few weeks, even though Cole had left him a couple of messages in the last few days, suggesting they get together to talk. Based on what everyone was telling him, he shouldn't have been surprised at Dylan's avoidance.

After giving the situation a lot of thought, Cole realized what was going on with Alex probably wasn't entirely work related. Considering the man was about to get married to Dylan's sister, the whole situation was a little more personal than he had anticipated. Even if Alex wasn't admitting as much.

As he continued to the next office, directly across from the one that Alex had assigned to him, Cole stopped. He could hear Alex's voice, and based on the long pauses and one sided discussion, it was clear he was on the phone. The door was open so Cole poked his head in, wanting to let Alex know he was there. Just when he was going to escape to his office until Alex was finished, his boss waved him inside.

Hesitantly, he moved forward, foregoing the chair opposite Alex's desk. He opted to lean up against the wall just in case Alex ended up needing more privacy for the phone call. Not to mention, there was no telling how the conversation he intended to have was going to go, and Cole wasn't interested in staying long if Alex opted to avoid his questions as had become his M.O.

"Thanks. I'll talk to you tomorrow," Alex said to the person on the other end before returning the phone to its cradle. "Hey." Alex spared him a quick glance, taking a deep breath, looking both tired and agitated.

"I can come back if you need me to." Cole didn't like that idea, but he didn't want to barge in on Alex if he wasn't prepared to talk either.

"No, it's fine. Take a seat. You make me nervous hovering above me like that," Alex stated, his attempt at humor falling flat.

Cole took a seat in the chair across from Alex, resting his hands on his stomach and crossing one ankle over the opposite knee, hoping he appeared more relaxed than he felt.

"What brings you in?"

"Oh, you know, I just figured it was time you and I talked," Cole said calmly.

"About?" Alex sounded genuinely surprised.

"First of all, you're both frustrated and pissed off. Maybe I'm wrong, but I've known you for quite some time. It's obvious something's wrong."

"Fuck." Alex's frustrated exhale was followed by him leaning back in his chair and thrusting his hands through his hair.

"Problems?"

Alex didn't immediately respond, instead turning to face the picture window behind him, offering up a fairly decent view of the Dallas skyline in the distance. Without getting an answer, Cole knew there were issues. Thankfully, he and Alex had been friends for a while, so he felt fairly comfortable asking the difficult questions, but in doing so, he knew he might risk affecting their working relationship. Since Alex was doing a fine job of the latter all on his own, Cole decided to take his chances.

"What the hell's going on?" Cole broke the silence after a couple of minutes, figuring it was now or never.

"It's Dylan," Alex said after a long pause.

"What's Dylan?" Cole knew Dylan had been having problems with depression brought on with his wife's death over eight years before, and from what he learned recently, it wasn't getting any better. There for a short while, Dylan appeared to be on the mend somewhat, even dating Jake's aunt, Sarah. But lately, after having taken two steps forward, it appeared Dylan was in the process of taking twenty steps back. He'd become an almost permanent fixture, bellied up to the bar at the club as Luke was to tell it.

"He's drinking. A lot." Alex turned to face Cole and the concern on his face said it all. There was no misunderstanding the look in his eyes.

"How bad?"

"Bad."

"Have you tried to talk to him about it?" Cole knew Luke hadn't because he'd asked him recently. Luke wasn't known for his emotional, heartfelt conversations, and quite frankly, Cole was pretty sure Luke avoided them at all costs.

"A few weeks ago, maybe. I tried talking to him, but as you can see," Alex motioned with his hands as though signifying the fact that Dylan wasn't there, "he's not talking to me much anymore."

"Did you ask him if he had a drinking problem?"

Alex glared back at him, seemingly offended by the question. "I did. And just like I expected, he told me that he was fine and that it wasn't any of my business."

"Have you talked to Sarah?" Cole had never spoken with her, but since she was the only one who had gotten fairly close to Dylan recently, he figured it was worth a shot.

"No. Ashleigh did though. She didn't have much to say, aside from the fact that Dylan called it quits. She said they hadn't gotten that close, but she was worried."

From Cole's perspective, it sounded like Dylan was definitely trying to hide a drinking problem. He wondered how far back this problem went.

"I know you're pissed at me," Alex added, turning to face him once more, "and I don't blame you. Dylan's not coming into the office at all these days and as much as I want to send Jake out on his own, I'm just not that comfortable yet. He's handling most of it, but I still need someone a little more… mature, I guess is the right word."

"Has Ashleigh tried to talk to him?" Cole avoided the obvious, choosing not to confirm or deny Alex's assumption about his anger. Yes, he was pissed. But Alex and Dylan were friends, and they both deserved the benefit of the doubt.

Alex's face fell as he appeared to prepare his answer. Cole didn't try to rush him, figuring he'd get the information sooner or later.

"Ashleigh's pregnant," Alex finally blurted, sad green eyes peering up at him.

Cole sat up straight, an impending sense of fear lodging in his chest. He would've expected Alex to be shouting the news from the rooftops. Unless, of course, there was a problem. He couldn't bring himself to ask anything else, so he waited, not so patiently for Alex to continue.

Sierra and Ashleigh had forged a friendship almost since the moment they met, and it was surprising that she didn't know about the pregnancy. Or if she did, she didn't mention it to him. Cole didn't think she knew because he couldn't imagine her keeping something like that from him and Luke. Then again, if there were problems, maybe Ashleigh had asked her not to.

"She's not very far along, but she's had some spotting and some cramping. The doctor told her that everything's fine. For now. As you can imagine, she's scared." Alex paused, swallowing hard. "I'm scared."

Cole wasn't sure he was breathing. He couldn't even imagine what Alex and Ashleigh were going through. He'd been a nervous wreck since they found out that Sierra was pregnant and up to this point, things had gone exactly as expected.

"Does Dylan know?"

"Are you kidding?" Alex pushed up out of his chair. "You don't know how many times I've wanted to tell him, to beat him over the head and let him know that his sister is petrified that she's going to lose our baby, and he's not helping the situation. I can't do it to him, man. He's hurting. When I try to put myself in his shoes, try to imagine what it would feel like to lose Ashleigh, I'm not sure I'd be in as good of shape as he's in now."

Cole couldn't argue with Alex's logic. If he put himself in Dylan's shoes, he wasn't sure he'd be sane even eight years later.

"Has anyone tried to talk to him? Maybe someone who knows him better?" Cole knew that Logan was probably the closest to Dylan, but he had no idea whether anyone would be able to get through to him at the moment.

"Logan's tried. He succeeded about as well as we did. Ashleigh's refusing to get married until Dylan is better, but hell, I'm not sure that'll ever happen."

Cole sympathized with Alex. He knew the man was ready to get married, and the fact that they were expecting meant he was probably even more anxious. They were already planning, down to the details from what Cole had heard, but it sounded as though Ashleigh might just push it off if Dylan kept going down this path.

If the three of them had already tried talking to Dylan, Cole wasn't sure anyone would be able to get through to him, but he couldn't imagine not trying. Clearly Dylan didn't want to talk, but sometimes people had to do things they didn't want to do.

"Do you know why he broke it off with Sarah?"

"No clue. It doesn't sound like she knows either. That, or whatever happened between them was enough to make her want to keep quiet. A few weeks ago, they got into an argument, and Dylan walked out on her. I heard that much from Jake. Although she told Ashleigh they weren't that close, I get the impression that she's taking it hard."

Cole knew Jake was highly protective of his aunt. The woman had practically raised him after her sister realized she didn't want kids – unfortunately that was *after* Jake was born. Sarah was several years younger than Jake's mother, but she had stepped up to the plate, along with Jake's grandmother, from what Cole remembered. According to bits and pieces of conversations he'd heard, Sarah had been married at one point, although he wasn't sure what had happened there, but he knew she didn't have any children of her own.

If he thought it would do any good, he'd be willing to talk to Dylan, but of all of them, he knew him the least. They worked together closely when McKenna Thorne was going through some issues with the man who blackmailed Luke and Logan, but it wasn't like they'd actually had any personal conversations. And since Dylan wasn't returning his phone calls, it was pretty clear that Cole wasn't high on his list of people to talk to about anything, much less his problems.

"So, this is the reason you're piling all of this shit on me?" Cole spoke his mind clearly, doing his level best to keep everything he'd just learned in mind.

It was clear that Alex had a lot on his mind lately, and between the pregnancy and Dylan going off the grid, it made sense that Alex was leaning on him.

Alex nodded but didn't say anything.

"Why didn't you tell me?" It was one thing for Alex to need help, it was entirely different for him to pile the shit on Cole when he wasn't expecting it.

Another shrug from Alex.

Cole hated that he'd walked in here fully intending to lay into Alex for being so damn selfish, when it turns out that Cole was the one being selfish. He wasn't fond of the idea of moving forward in this capacity, almost positive he was going to burn out quickly, but from what he'd learned in the last half hour, it wasn't like he had much of a choice.

"I need you to explain it to me, Alex. I'm barely hanging on here. In the past week, I've been tempted to tell you to shove this job up your fucking ass and just leave you high and dry. At the very least, I deserve an explanation. I'm not fond of being kept in the dark."

The stunned look on Alex's face told Cole that he'd pretty much laid his feelings on the line there.

And for the first time in a long time, he wasn't worried about offending anyone else.

Chapter Eight

With the day pretty well shot to shit after the meeting with Alex, Cole opted to head home. If he was lucky, Luke and Sierra would be there, and he'd have a chance to have dinner with them both. For some reason, after the conversation he had with Alex, he felt the need to be close to them.

Due to their schedules, they didn't get to have a lot of down time these days, but he was hoping today would be different. If they didn't learn to slow down a little, it was likely they were all going to burn out at some point, not just him.

Based on the last real conversation he'd had with Sierra over lunch, he was pretty sure they were rapidly heading in that direction without even realizing it. It occurred to him that they'd somehow managed to stop talking like they used to and that worried him on more than just one level. As much as he tried to convince himself that this was just one of those instances where life gets in the way, and you wake up to realize that the important things were left behind, Cole was worried they were taking some very valuable things for granted.

Maybe his conversation with Alex had affected him more than he thought.

When he walked in the back door, he found Sierra sitting at the kitchen table, a mess of things cluttered in front of her. Leaning down, he kissed her on the top of her head before making his way to the refrigerator where he retrieved a beer and returned to stand beside her.

"Luke here yet?"

"No," she said, not looking up from the pattern she was looking at.

"Did he say when he'd be here?" It was painfully clear already that he wasn't going to be getting Sierra's full attention tonight.

"Late. He told us not to wait up for him."

Cole nodded his head and turned to walk out of the room. It was clear she was busy, and Luke obviously was too. It wasn't like he didn't expect it. There was so much going on at the club, and Sierra had been working with a new client for the last week which kept her plenty occupied.

Foregoing the living room where he normally would find a way to pass the time, Cole went out on the back patio with his beer. The days were shorter, and the sun was going down quickly, but it was still warm for January, so he figured he might as well enjoy it while he could.

Cole had never been big on being cooped up in the house, always preferring the outdoors. That's part of why he liked his job with Alex because he was always on the go and very rarely stuck inside. Would that change if Dylan went off the deep end and Alex was forced to make some significant changes, he thought to himself.

He had just sat down when his cell phone rang. He glanced down at the screen to see it was Luke and promptly answered. "Hey."

"Hey back," Luke greeted, sounding unusually upbeat. "Why don't you and Sierra come down to the club for dinner? I can't get away, but I'd like to see you."

Cole's stomach tightened, and a chill ran through him. The times when Luke said so much in one instance were few and far between. For him actually to ask to see them was even more infrequent than a sentence with more than ten words in it.

"Will do. I just walked in the door, but I'll talk to Sierra and we'll head that way."

"See you then," Luke said and the phone disconnected.

Cole finished his beer and then went back in the house to find Sierra in the same spot, only this time there were more patterns and swatches spread out before her.

"Luke wants us to come down to the club for dinner. You up for it?"

Sierra stopped what she was doing and looked up at him for the first time. He knew instantly that this wasn't going to go the way he had hoped it would.

"I can't. I really need to get this together. I've got a meeting first thing in the morning, and I need to have the design laid out."

Cole nodded his head, pretending to understand. Once again, life was getting in the way, but there wasn't anything he could do to change it. Figuring he had nothing better to do, and Sierra would be working for at least a couple of hours, he decided to go down to Club Destiny to see Luke by himself.

Before he left, he kissed her on the cheek, once again not getting a response from her, but he tried his best not to think about it.

Oh hell, who was he kidding? He didn't think about anything else.

~~*~~

When Cole walked through the door at Club Destiny a half hour later, something deep inside of Luke loosened. Just seeing him calmed the frayed edges of his nerves. Too bad he was currently in the middle of a dramatic conversation with Mistress Serena, which meant he couldn't go downstairs to greet him.

"Give me a sec," Luke stated to the woman pacing the floor in front of his desk. He needed to let Cole know that he'd just be a few more minutes.

Shooting off a quick text, he continued to watch Cole through the window, noticing the moment he received the message. Rather than going to the stairs, Cole turned and headed to the bar and Luke couldn't help but notice the way Cole's shoulders appeared to deflate instantly.

"Sorry," Luke turned his attention back to Serena and waited for her to continue. She'd spent the better part of the last half hour giving him a piece of her mind. Apparently she didn't take too kindly to Trent Ramsey sticking his nose in her club, which, much to Luke's surprise, he'd been doing as of late.

Not that Luke cared that Trent was suddenly taking an interest in the club, but he'd have preferred the man talk to him first. As for Serena, well, she was being just a little dramatic. At least in his opinion.

"I don't want him there," she stated adamantly, turning to face him with her hands on her hips.

Luke stared back at the woman, forcing himself not to smile. He had a pretty decent idea that there was something going on between her and Trent, although she might not even be aware of it. It seemed that the man was sparking a reaction in her and based on what he knew of Trent, he was probably doing it on purpose. He got the impression the two of them didn't care much for one another. Not that it surprised him. There was no way in hell that the two of them would make a good pair because they were both the dominant, type-A personalities that would absolutely clash if they were to go head to head. Sort of like now.

"I'll talk to him," Luke told her. "I can't make any promises though. You know as well as I do that he's a member of the club as well as an owner. If he wants to weigh in, you're just going to have to humor him for now."

Serena's incredulous laugh made the hairs on the back of his neck stand up. Quite frankly, Luke wasn't sure why Trent would be trying to piss her off, unless of course, he just wanted to see her like this. Luke, on the other hand, did not want to have to have these conversations on a daily basis. Considering the club was closed for the time being, he wasn't even sure how the two of them were even having this type of contact.

"I will. I'll talk to him," Luke reassured her, moving toward the door, hoping to give her a hint.

Serena followed him, but she didn't say another word. A single grunt was all he got as she made her way through the doorway and toward the doors that would lead down to the bar. Grabbing his phone, Luke quickly sent Cole another text.

Figuring he probably had a couple of minutes, Luke took a seat at his desk and pulled up his email. By the time Cole finally arrived, he was in the middle of sending a response to one of the reports Kane had provided on a recent application.

"Give me just a minute," he told Cole when he walked in the door. "I've got food being sent up in a few minutes."

Cole didn't respond, and Luke didn't look up. He finished typing his email and hit send before turning in his chair to face the one man who had the ability to distract Luke like no one else.

He still remembered the days when he tried to convince himself otherwise. The times when he managed to suppress the deep rooted desire that sparked inside of him whenever Cole was near. He much preferred the way things were between them now, the way just seeing Cole, being in the same room with him even, managed to shift his seemingly sideways world back on an even keel.

"Is Sierra doing ok?"

Cole had called on his way over to let Luke know that Sierra was working against a deadline on an important project. He wasn't all that fond of the idea of her at home alone, but he was glad that Cole had come down to the club. During their brief phone conversation, he had sensed something in his lover's voice that concerned him.

To his surprise, Cole didn't turn to face him when he finally spoke. "She's busy."

There was an edge to Cole's tone that caused Luke to stand, slowly moving closer. "Have you heard any more about Dylan?"

"No. Alex hasn't said anything else, but I do know he hasn't been in the office either." For such an impersonal answer, Luke sensed that Cole's irritation level was rising, but for the life of him, he didn't understand why.

"Is that why he has you running your ass off these days?"

He had noticed how much Cole was out and about lately, and they'd had a brief conversation about a week ago after Cole mentioned he'd called Alex on it. Although Cole didn't share much about what he and Alex talked about, Luke was under the impression things were better. Or at least that's what he thought. Based on Cole's body language and the edge in his voice, he was beginning to wonder whether he'd imagined it.

It didn't escape him that Cole didn't answer his question.

He moved closer until he was standing directly behind Cole, letting his chest brush against his back, noticing the rigid way his muscles flexed when their bodies touched.

There were days that Luke found this was enough, just being close to Cole after the exhaustion of the day was like a balm to his ever increasing anxiety. Between him and Sierra, the two of them managed to keep him on a level playing field and he had reached the point that he didn't know what he'd do without either one of them. Despite the constant concerns waging a war in his brain, Luke looked forward to those rare moments when he could let down his guard. That only seemed to happen with Cole and Sierra.

"Are you ok?" Luke asked, gripping Cole's arms with his hands.

Damn.

He felt the tension in Cole's rock hard biceps, saw the strain in his shoulders. But even then, Cole made him burn from the inside out at the mere feel of his body beneath his fingertips. The feeling still took him by surprise most of the time.

Although Luke had come to terms with what he wanted, it still seemed somewhat surreal that a relationship like the one he had with Sierra and Cole actually could work. There were times when he knew they were all confused about what they were supposed to do, about what emotion was the right one or the wrong one, but at the end of the day, Luke knew whose bed he wanted to be in. And that was the one that belonged to Cole and Sierra.

Cole turned, facing him, his cobalt blue eyes swirling with something Luke couldn't pinpoint. He waited to see if he would say anything, but in typical Cole style, he didn't. It dawned on Luke that, in recent days, there hadn't been a lot of talking going on between the three of them. Not that there was much time to talk, but it seemed to be getting worse.

Unable to resist the urge, Luke reached up, sliding his hand on the back of Cole's head, twining his fingers roughly in his silky blonde hair, pulling him closer, never taking his eyes off of him. The tension between them was palpable, but then again, it usually was.

"Talk to me," he whispered.

The way Cole held his gaze, Luke knew he was expecting something entirely different from him. As much as he wanted to take him right then and there in his office like he'd done on more than one occasion, he sensed that Cole needed something more.

It might not seem like it most days, but Luke didn't miss the obvious. It wasn't like he was oblivious to the fact that they weren't spending a lot of time together, but he thought they'd reached a point where they were learning to live day to day without the reassurance that even he seemed to need from time to time.

It wasn't easy for him, but he was making an effort. Luke was working to ensure that both Sierra and Cole understood just how committed he was to the relationship, and not just the sex portion. Or at least he thought he had been.

Cole pulled away, stalking to the other side of the room, thrusting his hands through his already ruffled hair. Luke waited, anxiously awaiting a single word from Cole. This wasn't like him. He wasn't the one who normally retreated, yet here he was, closing himself down when Luke least expected it.

As his own walls began crashing into place, – a conditioned response – Luke found his temper was getting the best of him. "What the fuck is the problem?" he barked, unable to control the anger that surged inside of him.

He'd been working on this side of himself, the part of him that feared losing everything he had and moments like this brought out the worst in him. He didn't know what to expect, didn't know even what to think and with Cole not talking, he knew he wasn't going to get anywhere.

"Are there issues between us?" Cole finally asked, and Luke simply stared at him.

Was that a trick question?

"What the hell are you talking about?"

"Sierra mentioned it. She said she thought something was coming between us."

It was Luke's turn to thrust his hand through his hair as he turned his back on Cole. "I don't know what the hell you're talking about." He had an idea, but he didn't want to bring it up at the moment. This wasn't the time, and it damn sure wasn't the place to have this conversation.

It just so happened that he and Sierra had been talking the other night about the baby and Luke might've said a few things he shouldn't have. It couldn't be helped. He was worried. Confused even. He still didn't understand the dynamic of their relationship, and sometimes he couldn't even picture how their relationship would work once the baby was born. How were people going to react? Were they going to wonder how two men could be fathers to one child? What about Sierra? Would people look at her funny? Would they treat her differently because of the situation they were in?

It wasn't like Luke had any experience in this and although they'd made a commitment to one another, it still felt shaky at times. Like they were hovering on the edge of a cliff, and one wrong move would send them crashing to the rocky edges below. The last thing he wanted was to be impaled with a jagged edge piercing his heart.

"So you want me to talk, but the second I ask you a question, you shut me out as well?" Cole blasted him, his voice edged with anger and frustration, the same mix that was welling up inside of Luke at a rapid rate.

This was a strange conversation and one that Luke honestly wasn't prepared for. He was seeing an entirely different side of Cole from the laid back man he was familiar with. Something was obviously bothering him, and he was lashing out, but Luke couldn't seem to control his own emotional reaction.

"It's a two way street here, Cole. You brush off my question, acting like it's impossible that I actually do care whether something is bothering you. But you don't answer me. Is it fair that you ask me to pour my fucking heart out, yet don't think I deserve to hear it once in a while?" Luke was fast approaching destructive.

"*Hear it?* You're telling me I don't tell you that I love you enough? Is that what you need to hear? You need me to announce it to the world, Luke? I fucking love you. I love you with everything that I am, and if I recall correctly, I tell you repeatedly. Can you even remember the last time you told me that you loved me?" Cole's voice was loud, the deep rumble reverberating off of the freshly painted walls.

Cole's question shocked Luke, and as he took deep breaths, turning away from him again, trying his best to rein in his temper before it got too far out of hand, he tried to remember the last time he had told Cole that he loved him.

Fuck.

"That's right. It's going to take you a while. So, I'll leave you to think about it." When he turned to look at Cole, Luke's heart ceased its steady beat for a moment or two. As he stood there, gearing up to say something, he was met with Cole's back as the other man walked right out the door.

This was not how he wanted his fucking night to go.

Damn it.

Chapter Nine

Luke should've gone home right after his blowup with Cole. He knew that. He didn't though.

Instead of doing what was necessary to right the wrongs, Luke had sat his ass in his office, staring at the walls and wondering just what the hell was going on. Why was this so damn hard? Were they making it harder on themselves? The only person who seemed to be grounded in the relationship was Sierra. Even with so much going on, she seemed to be the only one thinking rationally.

It wasn't like he could fault Cole for expressing himself because he'd obviously managed to keep it all in, the same way Luke was managing his own feelings these days.

During Luke's conversation with Sierra the week before, he'd pelted her with his insecurity. He tossed out question after question on how they were going to handle this relationship once the baby was born. To his surprise, she had simply looked up at him with those crystal blue eyes and smiled. She told him that she had absolutely no doubts. Their love was stronger than the three of them, and if they relied on it, they'd get through anything.

Luke wanted to believe her. He wanted to think that the gut reaction to the pregnancy was just his insecurities manifesting into something morbid. Why was it that he always had the worst case scenario in mind?

As he pulled into the garage of his house, Luke took a deep breath, held it. He was going to have to confront Cole. They were going to have to talk this out. They had to. They both needed more than what they were currently getting, and it was up to them to decide how to make it better. Because that was the only option.

At least as far as Luke was concerned.

As he made his way inside, Luke glanced around, noticing that all of the lights were off which meant Cole and Sierra would be in bed. There were too many nights that he came home to this. Maybe Trent was on to something with the idea of Kane managing the night club. It would free Luke up to be with his family more.

His family.

That thought had warmth churning in his chest. Sierra and Cole were his family. And soon, they'd be bringing a child into the mix. Even though that thought worried him because he still couldn't picture himself as a father, it made his heart soar at the same time.

Bear appeared in the doorway and Luke knelt down to pat him before he disappeared into the bedroom for the night.

"Hey, boy. You keeping things under control around here?" His question earned him a lick on his hand and Luke ruffled the hair on Bear's back before pushing back to his full height. "Keep an eye on things out here, boy. See you in the morning."

Trying to be as quiet as he possibly could, Luke opened the bedroom door, his eyes taking a few seconds to adjust to the room illuminated by the muted light of the moon through the blinds. When it did, he shut the door and disappeared into the bathroom.

After brushing his teeth, Luke undressed quickly before going back to the bedroom. With as much stealth as he could muster, Luke slid into bed naked, easing one arm over Sierra's hip. Neither Sierra nor Cole had moved from the position they were in when he came in, so he spooned up behind her, his hand searching until he reached Cole on her other side. Not wanting to wake him, Luke couldn't help gently squeezing Cole's thigh, wanting him to know that he was there.

The darkness surrounded him as he lay there, listening to Sierra's soft breathing, her petite body warm against his. Cole wasn't making a sound, which meant he was awake. Luke couldn't bring himself to say anything, no matter how much he wanted to.

Just when he was going to attempt to give in to sleep, Sierra rolled onto her back, her hand sliding over his arm.

"I need you both," she whispered. "Right now."

Luke opened his eyes to look at her, her black silky hair spread out around her, highlighted by the streams of moonlight creeping through the blinds. He watched as she pulled Cole onto his back with a gentle hand, looking over at him.

"Come here, baby," she whispered to Cole and Luke's heart skipped a beat.

These were the moments that Luke looked forward to. The moments he dreamed about. The three of them together, the world shut outside of their bedroom door, nothing to intrude on their time together. The moments when everything that plagued his mind during the day could be drowned out by the mind numbing pleasure that only these two could bring him.

Cole rolled over onto his right side, now facing Sierra who was between them, and Luke met his gaze, seeing the same frustration still lingering there, even in the darkness. She rolled onto her side to face Cole, and Luke eased up closer to her yet again, pressing his cock against the rounded curve of her ass.

He watched as Sierra slid her hands over Cole's jaw, pulling him closer as he propped himself up on one arm. His eyes were closed as he kissed her, their lips melding together softly as though they were trying to feel out the moment. Luke ran his palm over the outside of Sierra's thigh, then over to Cole's hip, letting his fingers graze his warm skin. God, he loved touching them. The differences between them were significant, and his body knew every one of them, but his heart knew them to be the same.

When Cole's hand moved over the top of his, Luke stared back at the man, waiting for him to open his eyes. He was still kissing Sierra as he linked their fingers, moving Luke's hand down until he was brushing over the velvety length of Cole's massive erection. A breath stuttered in his chest as Cole wrapped his hand around the length of him before stroking slowly. Cole continued to guide Luke's hand with his own, squeezing firmly as they both stroked his length in tandem.

A growl tore from Cole's chest as he separated his mouth from Sierra's, both of them looking over at Luke. Sierra managed to turn toward him, kissing him the same as she had Cole, and Luke tried his best to keep the kiss gentle. With his hand still stroking Cole's cock, he had a hard time focusing on the gentle part.

He needed them.

The three of them lay there, gently fondling one another while Sierra somehow managed to keep the intensity to a minimum. Luke wanted to be inside of her. His want was quickly morphing into need.

"Inside me," she whispered against his mouth when the temperature in the room elevated several degrees as their bodies began to burn with the passion they shared for one another. "I need to feel you inside me. Now."

At first Luke thought she was talking to him, but when he opened his eyes, he noticed she was pulling Cole up against her back, forcing Luke to move his hand. He occupied himself by lifting her leg up, allowing Cole more room to slide between her thighs from behind. Luke propped himself up on one arm, glancing down between her legs as Cole slowly slid inside of her, another groan tearing from his chest.

"Oh, yes. That feels so good. Make love to me, Cole."

Luke felt his blood pressure spike as he watched, his eyes locked with Cole's as the man continued to slide gently in and out of Sierra's beautiful, slick pussy. They'd adapted to her growing belly over the last few weeks, adjusting their positions and eliminating a few just to ensure they didn't hurt her. Double penetration wasn't an option, but that didn't stop Luke from thinking about it.

The vision caused him to growl, and when Cole hooked his arm beneath Sierra's thigh, Luke let go, cupping her chin as he kissed her mouth lightly before trailing his lips down her body, over the soft swell of her breast, her ribs.

She was facing him so he couldn't reach her the way he wanted. Repositioning himself, he moved down lower on the oversized bed until he could align his mouth with her sweet pussy, watching as Cole's cock slid in and out of her, fucking her slowly, his labored breathing evidence that he was quickly heading for the edge. Using one hand, Luke cupped Cole's balls, gently kneading, reveling in the soft moans as his lover tried to hang on.

"Cole!" Sierra moaned, leaning into Cole more, offering Luke a better angle as he propped himself on one elbow, his fingers sliding between Sierra's soft, swollen folds until he gently grazed her clit.

"Oh, God!"

Luke leaned forward, swiping his tongue from the top of her slit, down to where Cole was sliding in and out, his tongue easing down Cole's shaft when he retreated from her body.

"Fuck!" Cole groaned.

Luke continued to tease them both with his tongue, tasting their combined flavors, ignoring his own throbbing erection as he tried to focus on sending Sierra over the edge.

When Cole's hips began pumping faster, Sierra's moans getting louder, Luke flicked his tongue relentlessly over her clit until she was screaming their names over and over, her orgasm ripping through her.

"Don't come yet," Luke demanded, lifting his head to meet Cole's gaze. "Not yet."

They both held on to Sierra as she came down from her climax, but it didn't take long before she was glancing between them both, a bright smile on her face.

As if she knew what was about to happen, Sierra eased out from between them, moving to Luke's side of the bed as he crawled over Cole, his hand stroking slowly as he crushed his mouth down on him. Luke might not be the most outspoken when it came to his emotions, but he let Cole feel everything he was feeling in the kiss. Stroking his tongue over Cole's tongue, slowing as he did, he felt the moment Cole gave in.

Cole's hands came up to cup his head, holding him close as their tongues dueled, leaving Luke breathless and anxious to be inside of him.

The sound of the drawer on the bedside table closing had him pulling back, resting his forehead against Cole's, their breaths mingling. Luke eased Cole's legs apart with his knees until he was kneeling between them. Lifting his head, he stared down at the man he loved as Sierra's soft, smooth fingers slipped between them, preparing Luke for what came next. The cool brush of her fingers had his cock jumping, his body hardening even more.

"I need to be inside of you," he whispered to Cole, wanting to express himself, but not sure how. "I want to feel you. All of you. And when I'm inside you, I want your eyes to stay open. Watching me as I fuck you."

Cole didn't say a word, nor did he move. There was no acknowledgement other than the way his dark blue eyes locked with his. Luke felt the tension in Cole's body, and as Sierra moved back, Luke guided his cock until he was lined up with Cole's ass, sliding the tip in slowly.

Sierra moved up closer to them, her fingers sliding into Cole's hair as Luke continued to stare down at him. He didn't thrust hard or fast, although he wanted to. Instead, he maintained a painfully slow rhythm as he pushed forward, guiding himself in deep.

A strangled groan tore for Cole's chest and his eyes closed.

"Open them," Luke demanded. "Watch me. Feel me. Right here. Right now. Me and you." Luke couldn't stop the words from spilling forth as he impaled Cole completely, the warmth of his body enveloping him. "You feel so fucking good."

Cole's hands tightened on his face, his mouth forming a hard line as he tried to thrust upward, to take Luke even deeper. Luke wouldn't allow him to control the movements. Not this time.

"Fuck me," Cole groaned. "Luke. Fuck. Please fuck me."

The plea in Cole's tone was nearly his undoing. Luke pulled back, forcing Cole to let go of his face as he sat up, lifting Cole's legs to allow for a better angle. He never broke eye contact with Cole, willing him to feel everything he was feeling.

He maintained a steady rhythm for as long as he could manage. When Cole began stroking his own cock faster, Luke knew they were both about to stumble right over that proverbial edge that they were white knuckling with both hands.

Increasing the pace, Luke looked down, watching as he tunneled in and out of Cole's tight, hot ass, the heat of his body wrapping around him, pulling him deeper. So good. It was always this good.

"Come for me," Cole pleaded. "Come inside of me."

Luke's eyes moved back to Cole's holding his gaze as he thrust his hips faster, harder until he was hanging on the edge, barely able to hold himself back. He wasn't going to come until Cole did.

"Oh, fuck! I'm coming!" Luke watched as Cole's cock jerked in his hands, the hard ridges of his abs tightening even more as his body tensed.

"I love you," Luke said the words as his body stilled, spilling himself deep inside of Cole. "Always love you."

Chapter Ten

"I talked to Trent yesterday." Luke's words drifted lazily across the living room, causing Cole to glance his way from his spot on the sofa.

The day had gone by without incident, much to Cole's relief. After his blow up the night before in Luke's office, he'd felt guilty for voicing his feelings the way that he did. It wasn't like him to release his pent up frustration like that, but lately he'd been unable to hold it in.

"About?"

Now that they were home, he and Luke were both lounging on separate couches, staring up at the television screen as a baseball game played without the benefit of sound. Surprisingly, Luke was home early, and Sierra had insisted that the two of them hang out while she made dinner. Cole's attempted argument was quickly squashed. Hoping that she would let him make dinner so she could put her feet up for a while, he had tried to change her mind, but she refused him.

"I think he wants me to take the club in a different direction."

That got Cole's attention, and he sat up straight and turned to face Luke. "What direction?"

Cole didn't know much about Trent Ramsey, but he did know the back story on how he'd come to be a silent partner in the club. His friendship with Luke and Logan was one of those that formed by happenstance and had solidified over the years, probably mostly due to their similar interests. Cole actually liked the guy, although Luke was a little standoffish when it came to Trent. Due to the man's career, they didn't see him much, which didn't seem to bother Luke in the least.

Cole wasn't sure whether it was something all Hollywood actors had in common, but Trent was certainly outgoing and didn't have a problem sharing his ideas. From the little that he did know, Trent was immensely devoted to his work and was pursuing some more behind the scenes activities as it related to movies as well as taking his fair share of the big screen. He was, at least according to Sierra and the other ladies, definitely at the top of the hot list.

Luke sat up and grabbed his beer from the table. "He mentioned breaking the night club and the fetish club apart."

Cole tossed the information around in his head for a second. It actually wasn't a bad idea. "And then what?"

"I think he's a little intimidated by Alluring Indulgence. He's worried they are direct competition."

"Did you tell him there was enough space in Texas to occupy both of you without concern?" Cole asked with a chuckle. He didn't see the competition aspect that Trent seemed to be so bothered by. They were adult sex clubs, and each of them would draw certain types of people even if they were similar in many aspects.

"I tried. He doesn't listen."

"Well, I don't see it," Cole admitted after taking a long pull on his beer. "They're a resort and, at least from what Travis mentioned the last time, they're going the whole by invitation only route. Who knows with that guy though, he could change his mind tomorrow."

Luke grinned and Cole leaned forward, setting his empty beer bottle on the table before leaning back into the soft, brown leather, crossing one ankle over the other knee. "What do you think? Do you want to break them apart?"

"I don't see the downside of it," Luke admitted, his tone turning hesitant. "It would free me up from late nights, which I'd really like. I'm confident that Kane could run the place without me."

"I'm assuming you would completely separate the two? As in relocate the adult club?"

"I'm thinking that's the best idea. Do you see another option?"

Cole appreciated the fact that Luke had started talking to him more about the club. They'd always had brief conversations from time to time, mainly because Cole had been a member from the start, and also because they'd been involved in a few threesome opportunities over the last couple of years, prior to Sierra, which meant they'd established a sort of friendship. Even before Luke accepted the fact that he was bisexual, Cole had developed feelings for the man. Knowing that Luke trusted him, even if Luke sometimes didn't trust himself, meant something to Cole.

"Do you intend to keep it similar to what it is now? The same setup? The apartments and the separate fetish club?"

"Don't know. I haven't been able to wrap my head around how it would be. Aside from the fact that we don't have many members anymore, I'm not sure what I envision."

Cole liked the idea of having more time with Luke. He knew Sierra would feel the same. And with the baby on the way, it was perfect timing. He wasn't sure about relocating the club because that would be expensive. They'd have to start completely over with designing and building. Although, separating completely from the night club would offer them a little more options as to how they structured it.

"Are you looking to go the resort route?"

Because they had invested in Alluring Indulgence Resort, they'd discussed the concept, but Cole didn't think Luke was looking to replicate it.

"No," Luke said brusquely, sitting up straight and leaning forward so his elbows rested on his knees. "I'm not signing up for that type of headache. The Walkers are a lot younger than I am. I have no desire to start over at this point. Not that much anyway."

"I agree," Cole said, still considering what Luke was proposing. "What if we strip out the apartments and move to a large commercial building. We wouldn't need to stay downtown because we wouldn't be catering to the nightclub scene anymore."

"The same concept?"

"I think so. The Club was doing well," Cole said, realizing he didn't want to make Luke feel as though he'd made the wrong decision in closing the doors. "I think it was more than time that we did something drastic to shake things up a bit. Weed out the few that managed to get through that we'd have preferred not. This works. And it gives us a chance to revamp the membership rules."

Luke stared back at him, and Cole fought the urge to squirm under the scrutiny of his penetrating hazel eyes. He didn't know why, but he wanted Luke to listen to what he had to say. Hoped that what he shared made sense.

"See, that's another reason I love you," Luke said gruffly.

Cole's heart did jumping jacks in his chest at the words. Until last night, Luke hadn't shared how he felt as far as saying "I love you" for quite some time, and now he was handing it out freely. He hated getting his hopes up, but when Luke opened up like this, Cole couldn't help but believe in the happily ever after that he still doubted despite the reassurance both Luke and Sierra had offered him.

"Why's that?" he asked, pretending the words didn't tilt his entire world sideways and make his heart swell to three times its normal size.

"Because you get it," Luke began, setting his beer on the table as he pushed to his feet. Cole kept his gaze trained on the beautiful man who was now moving his way, and he feared his palms might actually begin to sweat.

The way Luke stalked toward him made him feel as though they'd just met, like the chemistry between them was just as combustible as it had been that first night at Logan's house when Luke had finally taken what Cole had been offering for far too long.

He remained sitting upright, even as Luke leaned over him until Luke forced him to fall back onto the couch. He was fixated on Luke's hungry stare, practically daring the man to take what he wanted. It wasn't like Luke didn't know that Cole would give him anything, do anything for him, but when the man took what he wanted, it only exacerbated the intensity between them.

Luke slid one knee between his spread thighs and when he leaned closer, grinding his rock hard thigh against Cole's cock, he wasn't sure they were going to be in any kind of mood for dinner in the next few minutes.

"Look at me," Luke demanded and Cole realized he'd closed his eyes, focusing on the feel of Luke's entire body hovering above him. The heat, the weight of him, it all made his head spin and his cock throb.

Opening his eyes, he gazed up into those sexy green-brown eyes, seeing the spark of lust glimmering there.

"Unbutton your jeans," Luke instructed as he leaned in closer, brushing his lips firmly against his mouth.

Cole sucked in a breath, trying his damnedest not to give in and beg Luke to kiss him hard. Instead, he eased his hands down to his jeans, deftly undoing the button and lowering the zipper as Luke stroked his iron hard flesh with his thigh. Fuck, if Luke kept this up, Cole wasn't going to last until whatever Luke had in store for them.

The only sound was that of Sierra banging around in the kitchen and his own ragged breaths. Luke appeared to be in total control as his tongue darted out, grazing his bottom lip. Cole was desperate, anxious for Luke to take exactly what he wanted, but having no idea what that might be.

"Push your jeans down," Luke said, tilting his head slightly, aligning their mouths until there was barely room for a breath between them. "All the way down."

Cole maneuvered as best he could with Luke's large frame leaning over him, sliding his jeans down over his hips until they bunched at his thighs, his cock springing free, jutting upward as though begging for Luke's attention.

"Now tell me what you want."

Cole wanted everything. More than he ever could tell Luke. He wanted to see Luke vulnerable beneath him, his legs spread wide while he slid deep inside of him, using his teeth to nip him as he made love to him slow and easy. He wanted to see Luke sprawled out on all fours, his ass taking Cole's cock deep as he fucked him hard and fast.

A bead of sweat formed on his forehead as he tried to contain the fantasies, desperately trying to remind himself that Luke wasn't a bottom. Although Cole had never mentioned it, he didn't need to make the request to know that Luke would never give in.

"Tell me, Cole. Tell me what you want." Luke's palm slid over his straining cock, his grip painfully tight as he slowly stroked him. Cole's balls immediately tightened, threatening to explode long before he got a chance to consider what he wanted from Luke that his lover would be willing to give.

"Fuck," he growled, barely able to contain the urge to thrust into Luke's hand. "Touch me." Those were the only two words that came to mind. At this point, he didn't give a shit what Luke did, as long as he didn't stop touching him.

Luke leaned in closer, grazing his lips over his jaw and Cole held his breath. The heat of Luke's callused hand gliding firmly over his cock and the warm breath against his ear had him biting his lip to keep from crying out.

"Do you want me to suck you into my mouth?" Luke asked, his words merely a whisper against his ear. "Or just stroke you until you come in my hand? Which do you prefer?"

Cole wasn't sure he could answer. Just the thought of Luke's mouth on his dick was making him thrust his hips upward, trying to increase the friction.

"Tell me," Luke barked, his tone demanding, proof that he was losing his patience.

"Suck me," Cole whispered. "Put your mouth on me. I want to fuck your lips." Cole knew his tone contained a demand of his own, but that's what he suspected Luke wanted.

As much as Luke wanted to be in control, Cole knew he needed him to be firm, not to give in. He might pretend to be submissive, but it was only for Luke's benefit. If the tables were turned, he knew damn good and well Luke would be screaming his name.

Fucking hell!

Luke didn't hesitate as he resituated himself between Cole's thighs, yanking his jeans down below his knees, his broad torso forcing his thighs apart as his mouth came down on his cock. Cole slid his hand into Luke's hair, staring down at the man swallowing his dick, lapping at him until he wasn't sure he could breathe from the intensity of it.

"Fuck yes. Suck me harder," Cole ordered, applying the slightest amount of pressure to Luke's head, holding him until the head of his dick was pressing against Luke's throat. "That's it. Just like that."

Cole didn't want it to end. He wasn't ready to come yet, but Luke wasn't giving him much choice. If he had a say, he'd sit there and watch Luke bathe his cock in heat for hours, fucking his skilled mouth for all he was worth. Unfortunately, Luke had other ideas in mind as he used one hand to squeeze his balls, the other to grip the base of his dick, sliding him deep as he swallowed hard.

"Oh fuck! Fucking hell!" Cole threw his head back as his orgasm ripped loose, his entire body going rigid as he came down Luke's throat.

By the time the world stopped spinning, Luke was once again kneeling over him, his mouth just inches away.

"One of these days, you might just ask for what you really want," Luke whispered, and slammed his mouth down on his. Cole reached up, gripping his head, pulling him close as he thrust his tongue inside, tasting himself in Luke's mouth.

One day, Cole might just ask.

He just hoped like hell Luke knew what he was committing to.

Chapter Eleven

"How did you talk me into this again?" Luke questioned Cole, not necessarily expecting an answer.

"I'm pretty sure Trent is the one who convinced you, not me," Cole answered, his eyes on the road as they headed south on the interstate to some God forsaken little town that supposedly had a property for sale that Trent felt would be the perfect place for the club.

Only Luke hadn't decided what he was going to do at this point. It did seem as though Cole was onboard with the idea of splitting up the nightclub and the fetish club, but no matter how much he wanted to move forward with a new club, it still felt like starting over. He was too fucking old to start over at this point. Hell, he was going to be a father in just a few weeks, which meant he clearly didn't have time to be worried about getting a club off the ground.

"Is someone meeting us there?" Cole asked, checking his blind spot in the mirror before changing lanes.

Hell, they were almost there. "Supposedly." Luke didn't know much about this guy, but Trent had vouched for him. Some prominent land developer who obviously had more money than sense. According to the information he received, this guy was looking to invest in the club. Luke hadn't even known he was looking for investors, but Trent obviously was.

"This guy got a name?" Cole asked, and Luke realized he was just trying to make conversation.

So, his foul mood *was* apparent.

It wasn't necessarily that he was in a bad mood, he just was too tired to deal with this shit at the moment. He'd rather be at home, a place he had finally managed to spend more than an hour at a time in the last two weeks. After convincing Kane to fill in more at the bar, handling most of what Luke had been handling, he'd found some free time on his hands. Better yet, he was finally getting to spend time with Sierra.

Unfortunately, Alex had been running Cole all over the fucking state, which meant he wasn't home nearly as much as they'd all like. Luke was just about to the point he was going to have a talk with McDermott. If he were smart, he'd just have a conversation with Cole. If Luke was going to take on a new venture, he would much rather do it with Cole by his side. Permanently.

"Boone," Luke answered, glaring out the window. "Where the hell is this place?" Cole chuckled, and Luke turned to look at him. "What the fuck are you laughing at?"

"You. You need to calm down. We're just going to check it out. It doesn't mean you have to buy the place. Who knows, it might be just what you're looking for."

"I'm not willing to make any decisions until Logan can see it," Luke told him. He'd tried to get Logan to meet them, but his twin had an urgent meeting he had to attend. As if Luke believed him. He wasn't an idiot. He had heard Sam in the background and Luke knew what type of meeting Logan was going for. One that required him to be naked.

"Is that it?" Luke asked a few minutes later when they pulled into the parking lot of an ultra-modern commercial building surrounded by rolling hills. It looked almost like a compound with the eight foot stone wall surrounding the place, equipped with its very own electronic gate.

"If the address you gave me is correct, this is it." Cole drove the truck up to the electronic keypad and entered the code that Trent had supplied them with that morning.

Moments later, the intricate wrought iron gate slid open, allowing them to enter.

There was a sleek, black Lexus parked in the small visitors parking in the front and Cole pulled up in the space next to it.

"What do you think so far?" Cole asked as they exited the truck and moved around to the front of the vehicle.

Luke wanted to say he was impressed. Considering the entire building was made of glass, he had to wonder exactly how this would work for them, considering they were in the business of being discreet. Windows, at least in his opinion, did not do much to keep curious eyes from peering in.

"I'm not sure the glass is going to work," he admitted, realizing his bad mood had followed him out of the truck. When he started to move toward the building, he was pulled up short when Cole gripped his arm, effectively stopping him.

Luke turned to face his lover, waiting as patiently as he could for the tongue lashing he was sure to get. When Cole leaned in, pulling him close and pressing his lips to his, Luke inhaled slowly.

"Keep an open mind," Cole whispered. "This decision is entirely up to you. Don't forget that. I'll give you my opinion, as always, but you know I support you, regardless."

Cole's words soothed him, his lips did as well. With his gaze pinned on Cole's, Luke forced a smile and a nod. He knew Cole supported him, just another in the long list of reasons why he was in love with the man.

"Let's get this over with," Luke barked, doing his best to remember Cole's words.

When they reached the main entrance, Luke opened the door, allowing Cole to enter first, and braced himself for what was to come. He wanted to have an open mind, but more than that, he wanted to have a conversation with Cole. Asking the man to go into business with him, officially, was the only thing he could think about. Before he could act on that, footsteps sounded on the concrete floor, and Luke looked around at the vast, empty warehouse space until he noticed the source of the sound.

Coming toward them was a man. A rather imposing figure, dressed head to toe in one of those expensive ass suits like Tag Murphy favored. This man reeked of money and power.

When the man reached them, he held out his arm and Luke immediately returned the gesture, shaking the proffered hand.

"Xander Boone," the man said by way of introduction.

"Luke McCoy," he replied and then Cole did the same.

"Trent's told me a lot about the two of you," Xander stated firmly in a no-nonsense rough baritone that echoed through the cavernous warehouse space. "What do you think?"

Luke almost made a smart ass comment, but he held it in, letting his gaze roam the area and then back over Xander. Standing at six-foot-five in bare feet, it wasn't every day that Luke met a man taller than him. Xander probably had an inch or two on him, and he was built more like a professional athlete than what one would expect of a business man. Luke wasn't bulky the way Cole was, but Xander had some serious bulk beneath that fancy ass suit. His dark brown hair was perfectly styled, his light green eyes gave nothing away, and his strong, square jaw reflected no tension. All in all, Xander was an impressive man and clearly used to being in charge when it came to business. Intimidating almost.

Almost.

"Trent said you were looking to sell this place," Luke began, glancing around.

From where he stood, Luke liked what he saw. It was a warehouse that had essentially received a modern overhaul. The floors were stained concrete, dark, chocolate brown with cream marbled through them that had seen a significant amount of wear over the years. The walls were constructed of glass windows. Top to bottom and on all four sides. In the center of the space was a square box of cement block walls that he assumed contained the restrooms since there weren't any other enclosures within the warehouse.

"I previously leased it out to a call center, but they went out of business and went bad on the lease. No surprise there. I'm in the process of letting go of some of my properties, and I figured this would be a good one. As you probably noticed, it's a little far out."

Luke did notice that. In fact, it was quite a ways from their house, which meant that Luke would be spending a significant amount of time traveling if they did purchase it. He wasn't sure how he felt about that idea.

"Only one floor, although I don't think you'd have issues adding another, or even an additional section on top of that structure," Xander stated, referring to the enclosed area Luke had been checking out.

"How much did Trent tell you about what I'm looking for?" Luke had to ask the question because he had a feeling this guy knew more than he would've expected.

"Enough," Xander stated, meeting Luke's gaze head on. "I'm aware of the fetish club. I needed to know in order to find an appropriate property."

"Then you'll understand my concern with all of the windows," Luke added, moving farther into the space.

Plenty of ideas ran through his head, and he wished Sierra was there. He fully intended to get her help if they decided to move forward with another club. She knew what he liked, knew what he was looking for, and now that she had been to *The Club*, she could understand what he had in mind.

"The exterior windows are mirrored. They're also backlit with fiber optics, which means when the shutters close," Xander lifted a remote and hit a button, "from the outside, it will appear that there are lights on inside. It affords complete privacy, which I expected to be important."

Definitely important, and an intriguing concept. The electronic shutters slid into place, blocking out all natural light at the same time the overhead lights clicked on with a gentle hum.

"What do you think?" Luke asked Cole, turning to face him.

"I like the concept," he stated noncommittally.

That's what Luke was looking for from Cole. He knew if Cole didn't approve, he would've said as much. However, his statement told him that he could see this working for them.

"I'll need to bring my brother by to see the place before I will consider anything more." Luke turned, giving the area another once over.

"Here," Xander said, holding out a set of keys along with the remote. "Feel free to stop by whenever you want. Let me know what you think, and I'll stop by the club to pick them up when you're ready. If, at that time, you feel as though this place'll work for you, I'd like to talk about a few other things as well."

The three of them were quiet for a minute as Luke took the keys and moved around the perimeter of the warehouse trying to envision how this would work.

"I'll send over the specs, and all the information that I have on the property for the two of you to review. Just let me know one way or the other," Xander added, sounding as though he didn't care which way Luke's decision went. Not much of a salesman, that was for sure. Or quite possibly, better than most.

Deciding he'd seen enough, Luke turned toward the main door, falling into step beside Cole. He would call Logan to let him know. At this point, if this decision was going to go in Trent's favor, Luke liked the idea of the space. His only concern was the location. He'd have to talk that one out with Sierra and Cole. Then again, this wasn't his decision to make. They were just as much a part of his decisions these days.

He was lucky in that regard, because, until them, he'd had no one to answer to.

He much preferred it this way.

Chapter Twelve

"Luke?" Sierra said when Luke grumbled a greeting.

"Baby? Are you ok?" Luke asked, and Sierra heard the panic in his tone, which made her smile. He'd clearly been expecting this phone call.

"That depends," she replied, gripping the door handle of the Escalade as Cole drove.

"On?"

"Whether or not you're ready to be a daddy."

"Are you fucking serious?" Luke's growl sounded a lot like Cole had just a short while ago when she told him she was pretty sure the baby was coming. "Where are you?"

"Cole is taking me to the hospital," she answered, gripping the door handle and holding a protective arm across her protruding belly instinctively. "You might want to hurry."

Sierra wasn't sure she'd ever been in so much pain in her entire life. She was grateful that Cole was by her side, holding her hand as they rushed to the hospital while she listened to Luke on the other end of the phone. She could tell he was in a panic, and she honestly didn't want to worry him, but knowing Luke, he wouldn't listen to her anyway.

"Baby, I'm on my way now. Don't hang up." Luke's desperation was palpable, reverberating through the phone. "How far apart are the contractions?" he asked.

"Three minutes," she told him calmly.

Cole glanced her way, announcing loudly in hopes that Luke would hear that they were less than that at this point, but she managed to cover the phone as she laughed. She didn't need Luke having a wreck on his way to the hospital. He sounded as though he were running as it was.

The contractions were actually about two and a half minutes apart, but her water was still intact and she hoped that it would remain that way until they reached the hospital. Cole had calmly called the doctor, informing her of the status of the contractions, and they were told that if they made it to less than three minutes and they were consistent, to go on over to the hospital. Sierra smiled as she remembered how Cole paced the floor, asking her every few seconds whether she was having another one.

She wondered whether it was normal to be scared. Or maybe she was just anxious. Either way, her heart was beating like she'd run a marathon when in actuality, Cole had practically carried her to the car. But, there was a nervous flutter in her tummy to go along with the rapid thump in her chest, so she was pretty sure she was just nervous.

Luke's voice came back as he yelled at Kane. Sierra only could imagine what the other man was thinking at the moment.

"Baby, are you there?" Luke asked.

"I'm here," she whispered, gritting her teeth as another contraction took hold. "Please hurry, Luke."

"Don't worry, baby. I'll be there in five minutes."

As it turned out, five minutes were actually more like ten, but Sierra stopped counting as soon as Cole pulled up to the emergency room doors, leaving the truck running as he practically leaped out of the vehicle while it was still in motion. Sierra tried not to laugh, which wasn't all that difficult with the pain from the last contraction still fresh in her mind.

By the time they made it to labor and delivery, Luke was by their side, sweat dotting his forehead and his beautiful brown-green eyes appearing slightly dazed and confused.

It wasn't until she was situated in a hospital bed, hooked up to machines that Luke and Cole both finally managed to calm down. Well, that was only partially true. It was after the nurse gave Luke a glare that pretty much told him not to push his luck, or she'd be happy to escort him right out of the room. Not that he would've allowed it, but Sierra knew Luke realized his hysteria wasn't going to benefit any of them.

Ten long, incredibly painful hours later, Sierra was holding their baby girl against her chest.

It no longer mattered that the doctor had opted to get her rest in between checking in with the nurse on her progress, only having shown up twice during the long, drawn out process throughout the night.

All of the pain, both from the contractions and the giant needle they shoved in her back – an epidural they called it – were a thing of the past.

The fact that Luke had turned a not so attractive shade of green there for a few minutes or that Sierra had nearly broken Cole's fingers during the last push weren't important anymore.

The perfect tiny body lying against her breast was now the only thing that Sierra could focus on. She was beyond perfect. So tiny, yet she had her daddy's temper and no qualms about expressing herself, and not at all happy about being extracted from her warm little cocoon.

Cole and Luke were both standing at the head of the bed, one on either side, each leaning over to peer down at their little girl. Sierra was pretty sure her heart wouldn't be able to expand much more than it was already without bursting.

The next few minutes were a blur of movement, the nurse taking the baby, cleaning her up as the doctor finished the process of taking care of things down south. Cole and Luke both opted to follow the nurse, standing there like two kids in a candy store, eyeing the one thing they'd longed for more than anything.

With heavy lids, Sierra tried to stay awake, but the exhaustion was quickly pulling her under. The last thing she saw right before she gave in to sleep was Luke pulling Cole up next to him, their fingers cautiously linking between them. Sierra's heart took a major tumble one last time before she fell asleep with a smile on her face.

~~*~~

Cole felt the breath rush from his lungs the instant Luke's hand made contact with his. The last ten hours had been a complex mix of so many emotions, Cole wasn't sure which way was up at the moment. Having Luke by his side suddenly helped ease some of the weight that had been steadily growing heavier on his chest for the last few hours. That and the fact that their baby girl was just as perfect as he imagined she would be and according to what he could tell, based on the reactions from the doctor and nurses, healthy as well.

He and Luke silently stood side by side, watching as the nurse handled the baby like she'd done it a million times, using random instruments to check her, suction her nose and mouth, as well as clean her. In truth, Cole wasn't sure what he expected to see when the baby came out, but he had to admit, he felt a little like Luke looked for a brief second. That's when reality broke through, and it dawned on him that their baby had officially made her presence in the world.

He remained right where he was, glancing over to see that Sierra had given in to sleep, and he couldn't blame her. She'd been so strong, stronger than any of them probably expected. Then again, she had to deal with him and Luke. Cole smiled, remembering the way Luke had nearly launched from nervous father-to-be to neurotic in a few seconds flat.

That wasn't the case now. He was pretty sure they were all a little shocked, sobered by the fact that they were parents, and the only thing that mattered from here on out was the baby girl with her little eyes closed, her tiny fingers and toes all perfect and entirely hidden from view inside the security that she had found nestled in a pink blanket right there in the bassinette.

"We're going to take her to the nursery while mom rests for a few minutes. We'll bring her back as soon as she's awake. The two of you are welcome to come visit her," the nurse told him after she finished putting the hospital bracelet on, checking Sierra's, then Luke's and Cole's before wheeling their daughter out of the room.

Another nurse was caring for Sierra, and Cole suddenly needed a little air. Moving back across the room, he kissed her on the forehead lightly before disappearing out the door, not looking back to see that Luke was following him. By the time he reached the main entrance to the hospital, he was pretty sure he was shaking and on the verge of hyperventilating.

Within a minute of being in the fresh early morning air, he was feeling only slightly better.

"You all right?" Luke asked, moving in close and not giving Cole the space he tried to convince himself he needed.

Looking at him, Cole tried to force a smile. He felt like an overemotional wreck. "I will be."

To Cole's complete amazement, Luke pulled him in close, palming the back of his head as he forced him to lean against him, chest to chest, forehead to forehead. God, the man's simple touch was enough to ease the undercurrent of tension he'd had to endure thanks to his nerves.

He loved this man.

The sound of a throat clearing caught their attention, but Luke didn't pull away abruptly. His voice came as a whisper between them, "she's perfect. Everything's perfect."

Cole pulled back, looking directly into Luke's eyes, and this time his smile wasn't forced. She *was* perfect. For just that brief moment, everything was right in the world.

"I come bearing gifts," Logan announced, moving closer to where Cole and Luke stood off to the side of the main entrance. Cole turned to face him at the same time as Luke, then they both were pulled into a hug, followed by solid thumps on the back as Logan congratulated them each in turn.

Seeing that Logan had brought cigars, Cole merely laughed. He was suddenly grateful for the distraction because the emotional whirlwind he'd just endured had been enough to put him on his ass and he wasn't sure he wouldn't be laid out right there on the ground if it hadn't been for Luke. Glancing over at his lover, he managed to exhale, forcing himself to release all that he'd held in. He was right, everything was perfect.

Half an hour later, Cole was standing beside Luke as they peered through the glass window of the hospital nursery. They'd endured endless congratulations from Logan and Tag, and now they were showing off their daughter, letting their brothers see exactly how perfect their baby girl truly was.

"Damn, bro. It's a good thing that little girl looks like her momma." Logan's laugh echoed through the hall, causing Cole to grin. He was right, she did look like her mother, a tiny little thing with a head full of black hair.

"I was thinkin' the same thing," Tag added, standing beside him, another thump on the back made Cole grin.

Ever since he'd managed to let go of the tension, he found he couldn't stop smiling. The euphoric feeling had suddenly taken over, and he was more than happy to stand right there with Luke beside him, a grin much the same as his own on his handsome face.

"Shouldn't you be taking care of your wife?" Luke asked, giving Logan a hard time.

"What do you mean by 'take care of'?" Logan smirked. "We already had to find a way to pass the time for a few hours."

"Nope. Don't want to hear it," Luke laughed and the rumble hit somewhere deep inside of Cole, making him relax even that much more.

They'd done well.

"You hanging in there?" Cole asked Luke when the silence descended around them, wondering if the same roller coaster of emotions was on a wild ride inside of him as well.

"Yeah. You?"

"Barely," Cole whispered. "It's still a little surreal."

"Is she as perfect as she looks?" Luke asked, sounding as though he didn't mean for the words to slip out.

"She is," Cole reassured him and their hands touched, their fingers linking together between them again as they both stood in awe.

"Like I said, just like her momma." Logan once again chimed in.

"So, what's it feel like to be an uncle?" Luke asked, seemingly filling the time with idle chatter.

"It feels like I'm gonna get to give you a hard time about a lot more now. A girl, huh? I hope she gives you two a run for your money."

The conversation continued around him, but Cole didn't participate much. He smiled when it was expected, but he was more content to stare at their baby girl.

Hannah.

For the last six months or so, they'd tossed around so many names, Cole had a hard time keeping up, but the moment their daughter took her first breath, Cole knew she was their Hannah. Ever since they laid her precious body on Sierra's chest, he had known his life would never be the same.

For months, he'd been preparing for this day, secretly wondering whether it would be awkward for him and Luke, knowing that only one of them had created her. Thankfully, from the moment she made her appearance in the world, none of his insecurities seemed to matter. Only her. It was a blessed relief from all of the confusion he'd been facing lately.

Now, with Luke's hand in his, Cole felt the security of the love he'd embraced so many months before. He had a hard time even remembering why he worried so much.

"You think Sierra's ready to see us yet?" Luke asked, glancing over at him.

He nodded his head, glancing into Luke's hazel eyes, seeing the pure joy on his lover's face. "Let's get her some flowers first," he told him, squeezing his hand before pulling away.

To his absolute shock, Luke grabbed his hand, linking his fingers with his once more and turning to face him completely. "Don't pull away from me," Luke demanded and Cole felt the tension in his words.

Their relationship had taken a turn in the last few weeks, probably because Cole had revealed more of himself than he truly expected to. He loved Luke with every piece of himself, and he accepted Luke and his inability to say how he felt, but there were times it got to be too much. Right this minute, seeing this side of Luke, the man who didn't hide his true feelings, even in public, sent his heart soaring higher than he thought it could possibly go.

Squeezing Luke's hand once more to let him know he wasn't going anywhere, they released one another and turned toward the gift shop.

Three hundred dollars and practically every gift the tiny gift shop had to offer later, Cole and Luke were once again heading back to the labor and delivery floor where Sierra was.

After gently knocking on the door to announce their presence, Luke pushed it open, and they both moved forward. To Cole's surprise, Sierra was sitting up in bed, Hannah cradled in her arms as mother and daughter stared back at one another. Cole's breath lodged in his chest. He wasn't sure he'd ever seen anything as perfect as the picture they presented.

When Sierra's eyes met his, a brilliant smile tipping her perfect lips, Cole couldn't contain his own grin.

"Hey, baby," Luke greeted Sierra as he moved around to the far side of the bed standing beside Sierra's mother Veronica while Cole moved to stand on the opposite side of the bed, closest to the door.

"Never better," Sierra said sweetly, cupping the back of Hannah's tiny head and looking up at Luke.

Cole's heart swelled as he stared down at his girls, then back up at Luke. A few hours ago, they'd been standing in the same place, holding her hand as she tried stoically to suffer in silence. To his amusement, that hadn't lasted very long after the contractions began to increase in their intensity. No matter how tough he or Luke thought they were, it had been brutal to watch.

But when Hannah was born, Sierra's tears of joy streaming down her face as they laid her against her chest, the weight of the world lifted. Mom and baby had made it through without complications. It was as though the final piece of the puzzle was now in place, completing the three of them in ways they hadn't expected.

Cole watched as Sierra stared down at Hannah, the baby's pretty blue eyes roaming briefly before her lids slid closed as she dozed. Their baby girl, so utterly perfect, was the little piece that solidified what they had started so many months ago.

"So, how does it feel to be fathers?" Veronica asked, glancing back and forth between him and Luke. At this point, Cole had no idea how to explain the feeling.

"It's a bit surreal at this point," Luke admitted honestly, and Cole met his gaze.

"Well, I'm going to leave the four of you alone to bond for a little while. Xavier is on his way over, and I told him I'd meet him in the lobby. We'll be back soon."

Cole watched as Veronica kissed her daughter on the forehead, then her granddaughter before slipping out of the room.

"Do you want to hold her?" Sierra asked, sounding understandably tired as she looked between him and Luke. "Not that I want to give her up, but I will." The smile on her face lit up the entire room, and Cole couldn't hold back his answering smile.

Even though the elation of Hannah's birth hadn't worn off, and he hoped it never would, Cole couldn't help but wonder whether Hannah actually would change the way he and Luke reacted to one another. Up to this point, it didn't even appear to be an issue, but his fears still lingered down deep. He knew Hannah's birth had changed him, and he was pretty sure it'd changed Luke as well, maybe more so, he just wasn't sure how yet.

When Luke leaned over Sierra, smiling down at the baby in her arms, Cole felt a pang in his heart. Seeing Luke with a baby, their daughter, was heartwarming.

Cole watched as Luke took the tiny bundle, the strong, powerful man looking infinitely softer with a baby in his arms.

Cole could've sworn he noticed a fleeting moment of uncertainty flash in Luke's green-brown eyes, but if he did, Luke quickly masked it.

Part Two

Seven weeks after the birth of their daughter...

Hannah Gabriella Ackerley

Chapter Thirteen

"Good morning," Luke whispered close to Sierra's ear as she snuggled beneath the blankets, covered almost to the top of her head.

"Mmmm, what time is it?" she asked.

Luke smiled as he glanced over at the clock on the bedside table. "Six thirty." He knew he needed to get out of bed and into the shower, but he had a difficult time pulling himself away from Sierra's soft, warm body.

Sliding his hand down beneath the blankets, Luke traced the gentle curve of her waist, then over her hip, gently squeezing her thigh.

"You know what that means, right?"

"It means I get to sleep for a few more minutes?" Sierra asked sweetly, followed by a startled laugh when Luke squeezed her thigh, tickling her in the process.

Glancing over, Luke noticed that Cole had woken, probably from Sierra's laughter. He wasted no time rolling over and successfully trapping Sierra between the two of them. Her eyes had yet to open, but Luke saw the smile on her face and enjoyed the way she pushed her bottom against his hips.

Not willing to let the opportunity pass, Luke ground his erection against the sweet curves of Sierra's ass, growling low in her ear.

"Don't you have somewhere to be?" Sierra teased, but Luke got the impression she genuinely was hoping for a couple more hours of sleep. He knew she wasn't going to get them because any minute now Hannah was going to wake up demanding her breakfast.

"I do. I've got to go to work, but I can always spare a few minutes for the two of you," he answered her, pressing his mouth against the hollow between her neck and shoulder.

Cole had yet to push too far, probably trying to work his way through the fog of sleep, but Luke saw the hunger reflected in his midnight blue eyes. Reaching over Sierra, Luke gripped Cole's naked hip and pulled him closer.

A sudden whimper sounded on the baby monitor that lived on the bedside table alongside the clock.

"Three minutes," Luke warned Sierra. He knew they had about that much time before Hannah made her presence known throughout the entire house.

Sierra had already roused even more now that she knew sleep was not about to come again for a little while anyway.

"Three minutes, my ass," Sierra laughed. "You're insatiable."

True. Luke didn't disagree there, but he deserved some credit. Both he and Cole had been deprived of Sierra's sweet body for the last seven weeks thanks to her doctor's orders. The little minx had waited until they were all dead on their feet the night before to let them know that the doctor had given her the go ahead to have sex.

Despite his body's baser urges, Luke hadn't been able to keep his eyes open. For the last week, they'd been learning about diapers, formula (more so than anything else) and car seats and endless other items required to care for Hannah properly. All the while, taking care of a very grumpy, extremely colicky baby, and by the time they managed to get her to sleep, the three of them were ready to pass out themselves.

Hannah's persistent wail streamed through the monitor and Luke rolled over onto his back, grumbling as he did. He wasn't sure how much longer he'd be able to put off burying himself inside of the woman now crawling over him to get to her feet.

"Damn woman," Luke groaned as she straddled his hips, teasing him ruthlessly. "Do that again and you'll find my cock buried deep in that sweet pussy without even a please to go along with it."

Cole laughed and pushed up out of the bed before he disappeared into the bathroom. Luke knew damn well that Cole was going through the same withdrawals as he was. They were taking the term blue balls to the extreme these days.

What he didn't understand was how their little hellcat was managing to turn them away so easily. She'd been like kindling for the last week of her pregnancy, ready and willing to go up in flames at just the slightest touch from either one of them. It seemed as though Luke's impromptu decision to give Cole a blow job on their couch while she was making dinner had flipped a switch inside of her.

Needless to say, ever since Hannah was born, they'd managed to refrain, forced to pleasure her orally a time or two, but mostly they'd been holding out. At this point, Luke was well past the point of frustration.

Luke watched as Sierra grabbed her robe, effectively covering her sweet, naked body, and disappeared from the bedroom. With effort, he manage to sit upright, his feet touching the floor as he tried to get his bearings.

He had things to do today, but the only thing he wanted to do was to wait right there until Sierra was back. Unfortunately, he couldn't do that, so he glanced up at the bathroom door, hearing the shower turn on.

His curiosity almost got the better of him. He could only imagine what was going on behind that closed door.

~~*~~

Cole stood beneath the hot water, waiting for it to clear the fog from his brain.

His dick was as hard as a steel pipe, and the firm grip he had on it wasn't helping matters much. The teasing he'd endured for the last few days was beginning to take its toll on him. Sierra had dealt the final blow the night before when she'd told them that the doctor had given her the ok for sex, but then they'd all been too tired to do anything about it.

Now here he was, his dick in his hand and at the point he didn't care how he found relief. His balls ached. He closed his eyes, tipping his head down beneath the spray as he absently stroked his cock, wondering how much longer he could take this. Letting the heat of the water ease some of the stress from his shoulders, he tried to relax.

The sound of the bathroom door opening caught Cole's attention, but he kept his eyes closed. If Luke wasn't careful, Cole was going to take him by his hair and shove his cock down his throat at any second. He wasn't sure where the aggression was coming from, but he was past the point of caring about the boundaries of their relationship.

If he couldn't bury himself in Sierra's sweet body soon, he was ready to indulge in the next best thing.

With his eyes closed, he allowed his mind to drift, imagining the feel of Sierra beneath him, Luke's warmth at his back. For a second or two, it felt almost real, but he was scared to open his eyes for fear it'd just be another daydream. It was almost like Luke was right there with him, his warm body pressed up against his back, dragging a ragged groan from him.

He knew where this would lead and as much as he wanted Sierra's smooth thighs wrapped around his hips, or the delectable taste of her pussy coating his lips, he needed to bury his cock in someone. He didn't have a preference at this point.

Considering Luke had never succumbed to the idea of Cole topping him, he knew he was going to be left holding his dick. Like usual.

"Turn around," Luke demanded and Cole found himself doing as instructed. Backing up against the cool tile, Cole stared back at the sexy man standing before him. When Luke gripped his throbbing erection, Cole damn near cried out.

"I don't know how much longer I can take this," Cole bit out. "I need to be inside of her."

Admitting his need didn't bother Cole anymore. Maybe it was the pent up sexual tension, or possibly just all of the events of the last two months churning together into one giant ball of stress in his chest. He'd slowly managed to open up with both Sierra and Luke over the last couple of months, more and more each day, but he'd yet to ask for the one thing he truly wanted. As it was, lately Cole felt as though he needed to tread lightly with both Luke and Sierra. Not that either of them had given him a reason to, but his insecurities were a tangible thing once again.

Luke's mouth slammed against his, stealing his breath and thankfully, causing his wandering thoughts to evaporate just like the steam that was filling the bathroom. Grabbing the back of Luke's neck, Cole pulled him close, holding him tighter against him as their bodies scraped intimately together. *Fuck.* He longed for these moments when he could steal a few minutes with Luke. These were as few and far between as the three of them together, and Cole missed those moments even more.

"I want to make you come," Luke growled the words.

Cole wanted that more than anything else. He wanted to grip Luke's hair, then ram his cock down his throat. That was as dominant as Luke allowed Cole to get with him, but that didn't stop the needs from building.

When Luke went to his knees, Cole damn near came in his own fucking hand. The water continued to cascade down over him, his rough grip almost enough friction to take care of matters himself, except the image of Luke on his knees in front of him had him biting his lip, the sting giving him something else to focus on.

"I need your mouth on me," Cole bit out.

He'd taken to being more explicit with his needs when he and Luke were alone. Maybe it was the fact that they'd been deprived of Sierra for so long, but Cole sensed Luke needed that as much as he did these days.

Gripping Luke's thick, dark hair in one hand, Cole pulled him closer, reveling in the rough growl that tore from Luke's chest. When his lips wrapped around the sensitive head, Cole held his breath, focusing on the heat of Luke's hungry mouth.

"Suck me. Take me deeper," Cole groaned, trying to hang on just a little while longer so he could revel in the sensation. He was well aware of how rare this moment was.

Luke continued to suck and lick, his hand gripping the base of Cole's cock roughly as he stroked in earnest.

"Fuck!" Cole wasn't going to last. Just envisioning his cock in Luke's mouth was more than he dreamed of. Having the man on his knees, eager to please him drove him absolutely fucking wild.

The grip on his cock became tighter, squeezing until his release was barreling through him and a rough growl tore from his chest.

Cole forced his eyes open as his muscles slowly relaxed. Glancing around, he realized he was still in the shower.

Alone.

Sonuvabitch! These fucking daydreams were going to kill him.

Chapter Fourteen

Sierra sat in the oversized rocking chair in Hannah's room, holding her daughter as she smiled down at her sweet, round face. She was still in complete awe of the precious little girl who was quickly approaching two months old.

For some reason, she'd somewhat expected the novelty of a new baby in her arms to have worn off by now, but that wasn't the case. The complete opposite. Each and every time she looked into Hannah's sparkling blue eyes, touched her soft little hands, smelled her sweet baby scent, Sierra fell in love a little more.

There was no other way to put it. Hannah was perfect.

Over the last few weeks, Hannah's eyes had lightened from the newborn baby blue to almost crystal blue like her own; however, they had a fascinating cobalt blue ring around them, similar to Cole's. Hannah's hair was still dark, although it wasn't as thick as it had been when she was born. Aside from the dark hair and the lighter shade of blue eyes, Hannah looked just like her daddy.

She had Cole's slightly dimpled chin, his nose, and his eyebrows but thankfully, it appeared as though she wasn't going to get his height. Sierra could only hope that she wouldn't be quite as short as her mother.

"I'll see you later." Luke's hushed voice distracted Sierra, and she glanced up to see the handsome man looking down at her from the doorway of Hannah's room. When she smiled up at him, he moved in closer before leaning down to press a gentle kiss to Hannah's forehead.

The kiss he shared with her after that lacked some of the gentleness he was known to show his daughter, and Sierra sensed the hunger building inside of him. She knew what he was feeling because she felt it just the same.

"I'm taking Hannah to see my mother today, just in case you wonder where I am," she told him.

Watching him closely, she tried to read Luke's expression. He seemed somewhat detached these days. She didn't think it had anything to do with her or the baby, but she wasn't sure. There were so many things going on with the club and the changes that were underway, Sierra had a hard time keeping up.

Ever since Hannah was born, Sierra hadn't had much time to take on new clients and even after they all agreed to purchase the new building for the future club, she hadn't had any time to devote to getting the new design mapped out either.

"I'll be at the club most of the day. I'm gonna meet Logan for lunch. I'll try to get off early, but no promises. I think Xander's stopping in today, and I need to talk to him."

"We'll see you tonight then." Smiling up at him, Sierra watched as Luke disappeared from view.

Xander Boone, the newest partner in the club, was a force to be reckoned with, but Sierra liked him immensely. Being that there were now four partners – Luke and Logan still the majority shareholders – it was getting interesting, to say the least. The new club, which she had insisted they figure out a name for other than "The Club" was going to be amazing. Considering the amount of work it was taking to get it ready, there wasn't any other option.

As it turned out, Trent Ramsey, the once silent partner in Club Destiny, was far from silent these days. He officially stepped up to the plate to help fill in while Luke spent much needed bonding time with Hannah. Although he was unquestionably a public sensation, they were managing to keep the paparazzo at bay by not announcing the location of the new club just yet.

According to Luke, they weren't going to be able to keep it a secret much longer, which meant it was going to be any day now.

Ever since Luke had closed the doors on the fetish club, thanks to some of the member's unsavory business dealings coming back to bite Luke and Logan in the ass, Trent had been a prominent part of their lives. He wasn't happy with the choices, but he seemed to understand.

At first Luke wasn't thrilled that Trent had opted to come out of hiding to offer his two cents, but being that Trent did own close to a third of the club at the time, he'd had to deal with him. Lately, it seemed as though the three of them – Logan still opting to remain behind the scenes because of his position at XTX – were working together nicely.

Just in the last few days, Luke had started working a lot more. Spending less and less time at the house, usually coming in after Hannah was asleep for the night. According to him, it wasn't going to last long, but the logistics of the club were being mapped out, and he would be damned if he would be left out of it. Sierra couldn't blame him, but she was beginning to wonder whether he was just coming up with excuses to stay away from the house.

Realizing Hannah had fallen back asleep, Sierra placed her back in her bed before tiptoeing out of the room. She probably had enough time to take a shower and grab some breakfast before Hannah would be up again. By then, Sierra should be ready to head over to her mother's. She needed a distraction, and she couldn't think of anything better than her mother at the moment.

~~*~~

The instant Sierra walked in the front door several hours later, Cole could do nothing more than stare at her. He'd been sitting on the couch, minding his own business, working on his computer, but the instant he sensed her presence, he was hypnotized by the sight of her.

Seven weeks ago she had a baby, and he was pretty sure that every single day since the first day he met her, she had gotten just that much more beautiful. And now... well, he still couldn't take his eyes off of her.

"Where's Hannah?" he asked, noticing Sierra's arms were empty.

"At my mother's," she replied sweetly, a mischievous gleam in her eyes that Cole could see from across the room.

At her mother's?

Cole was somewhat surprised, although a little relieved that Sierra had decided to give Veronica a little time alone with the baby. As much as he missed Hannah every second that he was away from her, he knew Sierra was in need of a little break from time to time. He had been relieving her as soon as he got home in the evenings, but there had been a few days, especially in the last couple of weeks, where Alex had sent him on some crazy ass mission to dredge up business farther north than was their usual market.

Veronica had gently, although firmly, announced her desire to spend a little more time with her only grandchild, but Sierra had seemed nervous. Cole knew it had nothing to do with Veronica, and everything to do with Sierra wanting to keep Hannah close, so he was happy to see she'd finally decided to take Veronica up on her offer.

"Come here," he told her, moving his laptop to the coffee table. When Sierra got close enough, he pulled her down onto his lap gently, sliding all of her jet black hair back behind her and holding it in one fist. "You all right?"

Sierra laughed as she snuggled against him. God he loved how she felt in his arms. He had gotten used to her cuddling up to him or to Luke or both of them at the same time, and he found he missed her when she wasn't right there with him. These moments had occurred even less since Hannah was born, but it seemed as though all of them were trying to incorporate a few more hours into an already busy day and that never seemed to work the way they hoped.

"I'm fine. She's fine," Sierra said, sounding as though she were trying to convince herself more than anything.

"Well, I can think of something to take your mind off Hannah not being here," he whispered, nuzzling her neck and inhaling her sexy, lavender scent.

"I'm thinking that sounds just about perfect right now," she whispered back, her hand touching his cheek as she pulled his mouth closer to hers.

Cole couldn't resist pressing his lips to hers as he pulled her closer, tightening his grip on her hair just slightly. Almost eight weeks had gone by since the last time he'd been buried inside of this woman, and he wasn't sure how much longer he could wait to feel her velvet heat surrounding him again. Even after the evil trick his mind played on him in the shower that morning, he was still brutally aroused and in desperate need of burying his cock inside of her.

"Where's Luke?" she asked, pulling back and looking at him.

"At the club." Cole watched her closely, wondering what she was getting at. As far as he was concerned, there were two ways this could go.

"I was thinking we could surprise him," she smiled, and Cole's cock made sure she felt exactly what that idea did to him.

That was the second way, and he loved the idea.

"Right now?" He was all for taking her to the club, he just wasn't sure whether she'd be able to walk after they were finished with her. The thought made him smile.

"I can't think of a better time," she said, but when he moved, Sierra made no effort to get off of him.

Instead, Cole found himself flat on his back on the couch, Sierra straddling his hips and her mouth fused with his, her pussy grinding down along the ridge of his erection. She was so damn sweet, so damn responsive, he wasn't sure they were going to make it out of the house if she kept this up.

When she took his hand, easing it between their bodies, Cole felt the smooth, hairless lips of her cunt, and he damn near jolted up off of the couch. She was naked beneath that little frilly skirt, and he'd be damned if he didn't wish his jeans would dissolve so he could slide right up inside of her.

"I need you, Cole," she said between kisses.

"I'm here, baby. Whatever you need." Cole would never be able to deny Sierra anything. "But if we go now," he told her when she began trailing kisses down his neck, "we have a chance at surprising Luke." He was pretty sure he was torturing himself at this point because, in three or four seconds, he could easily be inside of this woman.

Sierra leaned up on her forearms, smiling down on him. "Ok, but you have to do one thing for me."

The seductive tone of her voice told Cole she had only one thing on her mind. Not that he could blame her because it had been a damn long time.

"Anything, you know that," he told her as he sat up, still holding her close.

"I want you to tease me in the car."

Holy fuck!

~~*~~

Sierra couldn't believe what she said to Cole a few minutes ago while they had been making out like teenagers on their couch, and she was surprised either of them had been able to make it out of the house afterward. She was so damn horny, she didn't know what to do with herself, and she only hoped that surprising Luke would help to alleviate that growing ache that hadn't been satisfied in nearly two months.

The idea had come to her that morning while she was at her mother's house, both of them cooing over Hannah. It had been a tough decision to leave her, but Sierra knew there was no one she trusted more than her mother, besides Cole and Luke, to watch Hannah while she was gone for a couple of hours.

Veronica had gone so far as to turn one of her extra bedrooms into a nursery, so Sierra knew how much her mother was looking forward to having Hannah all to herself for a little while.

"Please tell me you are still naked underneath that skirt." Cole's voice was dark and rich and laced with more than a little hunger as he drove down one of the back roads that would lead to the club in downtown Dallas. He was taking the long way apparently.

"What do you think?" She'd been prepared for this since she woke up that morning.

Her hormones were totally on the fritz, and she hadn't been able to do what she intended when the three of them were still in bed that morning because Hannah woke up, letting them all know she was clearly ready for breakfast. Now... well, now they had some time and Sierra was so overcome with lust, she could barely breathe past the ache that filled her.

Sierra didn't have to do anything besides sit back and relax because Cole was obviously just as eager as she was. His big, warm hand drifted up her thigh, lifting her skirt as he went along. He kept his eyes on the road, but he was definitely focused on her.

When his fingertips teased the inside of her thigh, Sierra instinctively pushed her legs farther apart, wanting to encourage him to continue. He didn't disappoint.

"Are you wet already, Sierra?" Cole's deep rumble filled the interior of the car.

"So wet," she assured him. She was pretty sure he didn't understand how much she needed both of them right then. "Touch me, Cole."

Sliding his hand farther up her leg, Cole teased her clit with one long finger, rubbing circles over the swollen nub. God, she needed to be fucked. None of the sweet lovemaking they'd insisted on for far too long because of her "delicate condition". Their words, not hers. She wanted down and dirty, up against the wall, take what you want fucking. She smiled inwardly, realizing she probably sounded a lot like Sam at the moment.

Yes, maybe she sounded like a total freak, but Sierra didn't care. They hadn't had sex in so long, and now she wanted to do nothing except spend the next two hours with her men buried to the hilt inside of her.

Cole continued to tease her slowly, never penetrating her fully, but using his finger to torture her clit. In his defense, she had asked to be teased; she just didn't realize it was going to be so brutal. Sierra wanted to come. She wanted to ride his fingers until her body came apart at the seams.

A few minutes later, they were pulling into the underground garage of the club, and she sighed. She was ready to leap out of the car and run inside at that point, leaving Cole to catch up with her.

She didn't.

Sierra waited patiently for Cole to come around and open her door for her. She'd learned the hard way that both Luke and Cole were adamant about opening doors for her. They insisted, and the couple of times she had done so herself, they had punished her. Exquisitely.

By the time they reached the second floor of the club, noticing that Luke wasn't downstairs, Sierra was shaking with need. Even her clothes were causing her pain as they brushed against her hypersensitive skin. Based on the smirk on Cole's beautiful face, he knew it too.

Cole rapped his knuckles on the closed door to Luke's office and waited for him to answer. When he did, Sierra was surprised she didn't plow over Cole's much larger body in an attempt to get inside. The second they were over the threshold though, she stopped suddenly, her jaw nearly dropping to the floor.

Luke's magnificent body was sitting on the couch in his office, completely naked, his cock in his hand. The gleam in his eye said he knew she was coming, and he was prepared.

"You texted him," Sierra said, glaring at Cole accusingly.

Cole shook his head and chuckled.

"Come here," Luke demanded and his tone was rough and insistent, not an ounce of the patient man she'd gotten familiar with lately. The sound alone made her pussy throb in anticipation. It had been too long.

For most of her pregnancy, Cole and Luke had treated her like she was made of glass. Never wanting to push her too far, never wanting to let go completely – even when she begged. Well, they didn't have any excuses now.

She heard the door lock engage as she moved across the room toward Luke. There was no hesitation in her movements.

She needed this more than she needed air.

Chapter Fifteen

Luke watched as Sierra moved closer. She was a woman on a mission, and he fought the urge to grin. He knew what she wanted, hell, what they all wanted, but he hadn't expected either of them to show up at the club. He happened to be watching one of the closed circuit cameras when Cole pulled into the parking garage, so he had managed to turn the tables on their apparent attempt to surprise him.

It hadn't taken long to remove his clothes, and his cock had taken notice of what the intent was probably before his brain relayed the message.

"Stop," he insisted, his eyes glued to Sierra.

She was so damn beautiful. Her glossy black hair was even longer than when he met her, thanks to the prenatal vitamins she told them. Her ice blue eyes were bright with the lust he could feel crackling in the air around her. Sierra stopped just a foot away from him, her eyes locked between his legs where he continued to stroke his cock slowly. His entire body was rigid, his muscles refusing to relax as he anticipated what it meant that they were here in the middle of the day.

It felt like he'd been hoping for this moment for an eternity and now that they were both right there with him, he refused to hold back. He glanced back at Cole, willing the man to move forward with just his eyes.

When Cole took another step closer, Luke couldn't hold back his demands. "Strip. You," he said, turning his attention to Sierra, "come here and turn around."

Once Sierra was close enough, she turned to face Cole on the other side of the room, and Luke pulled her down onto his lap, making sure his erection was pressed intimately between her legs. Damn, she wasn't wearing panties. *Fuck!* She was so fucking hot! At this rate, he wasn't going to have even the stamina of a teenage boy.

"Tell me what you see," he instructed Sierra as they both sat watching Cole remove his clothes as though he didn't have a single care in the world. The man didn't appear to be in a rush and Luke was a little in awe of his patience, especially knowing what was about to happen.

"Perfection," Sierra whispered, her ass grinding against his thighs.

"Don't move." He wasn't about to let her get herself off, no matter how much he wanted to thrust his cock inside of her. She was going to have to wait.

He held her hips so she couldn't do more than sit still, his cock brushing against the folds of her pussy, her skirt discreetly hiding them from Cole's gaze, although he was clearly making an attempt to see through her clothing.

"What else do you see?" Luke encouraged.

He knew what *he* saw. He saw the sexiest man he had ever known. Hardened to perfection. Cole was an exquisite specimen. Luke never expected himself to fall for a man, but fall he had. Head first.

"I see gloriously tanned skin," Sierra said, her voice trembling with anticipation. "I see navy blue eyes that have the ability to see right through me."

Cole moved closer, his jeans now unbuttoned, his boots left behind.

"Take his jeans off," Luke told Sierra. "Slowly."

Reaching around Sierra, Luke gripped Cole's hips, jerking the man closer. Thanks to his abrupt movements, Cole had to put his hands on the back of the couch, leaning over the two of them just to keep from falling, but Luke didn't care. He just wanted to touch him.

Sierra managed to lean around Cole, easing the denim over his lean hips, down his thick, hard thighs until his cock sprang free while Luke glanced up at him then back down between their bodies. Without instruction, Sierra leaned forward, taking Cole's cock into her mouth completely while Luke looked on.

Fuck.

He'd never tire of seeing that. Watching the two of them was one of the hottest things he'd ever had the pleasure of seeing. Being with them, right here, made it even better.

"Damn, baby," Cole ground out the words as Luke looked up at him.

Reaching up, Luke gripped Cole's jaw in one hand roughly and pulled him closer until he could reach his mouth. "I want your fucking mouth on me," Luke growled.

The instant Cole's lips met his, Luke's entire world shifted. There was only this man and the woman sitting between them.

Luke had always been the top in the relationship, always the one in charge, but recently, he sensed a change in Cole. He was more demanding, taking what he wanted when he wanted it. Like now. The way his tongue surged between his lips, Luke almost forgot that he was the one in charge of this little escapade. He was always in charge. Even though he was holding Cole's face firmly to him, Luke knew Cole owned this kiss, and he gave himself over to it. For what seemed like an eternity, Luke had been wanting to hand over the reins, to give Cole complete and explicit control, but there was still something holding him back.

When Cole pulled away, a growl tearing from his chest, Luke knew what Sierra was doing. She was tormenting him the way only she knew how. Gripping her hair and wrapping the black silk around his fist, Luke pulled her head back, holding her still for a moment. He damn sure wasn't ready for this to be over.

"On your knees," Luke demanded, his attention turning back to Cole once more.

Pulling Sierra back against him fully, Luke slid his hands down her sides, over her hips and then down her thighs before he lifted that flirty little skirt up and bared her beautiful pussy to Cole's intense gaze.

The man didn't need further instruction. He easily slipped his legs out of his jeans before lowering himself to his knees between Luke's and Sierra's thighs. Luke could feel Cole's heated breath against his cock, feel the wet heat of Sierra's pussy against his shaft and knew that there was nowhere else he wanted to be.

Ever.

"Aw fuck!" Luke groaned as Cole took his cock in his mouth, using one hand to palm his balls roughly.

Luke couldn't see around Sierra, and maybe that was what he enjoyed most about this little game they played. Having Sierra in his lap, her breasts in his hands, her knees spread wide while Cole stroked him with his rough grip and his wicked tongue, was unlike anything he had ever known. The sensation was exquisite. The warm, wet tongue that laved his dick, paying extra attention to the engorged head had Luke damn near biting his tongue to keep from begging him to finish him off.

The heat disappeared momentarily, and Sierra bucked in his arms, telling Luke that Cole had moved on to pleasure her. She was rocking her ass against his hips where she sat, her upper body pressing against his chest as she tried to get closer to Cole's wicked mouth.

"Tell me what it feels like, Sierra." Luke loved when she gave him a play by play of what they made her feel. It had taken some time before she opened up completely during sex, but Sierra was still blossoming in ways Luke honestly never expected.

Throughout the last year, they'd gone through a lot of things together, including pregnancy, but as each day passed, Luke realized they were still learning so much about one another. With three of them, it was an entirely different world than any of them had ever experienced. They were learning how to handle a permanent, real love between the three of them that wasn't going away. But just like in a traditional relationship, there were plenty of bumps and jolts that threatened to throw them off course, most of them related to insecurity and doubt. It was times like this, when none of those things mattered, that Luke felt the completeness this relationship afforded him.

Cole's warm mouth returned, his tongue darting back and forth over the head of his dick, and Luke growled unexpectedly. "Fuck. Don't ever fucking stop!"

His words apparently spurred Cole on because a callused hand circled his shaft, squeezing with just enough pressure to make Luke cry out. When Sierra leaned forward, using her hand to grip him right alongside Cole, he wasn't sure he was going to last.

Ok, so they had obviously set out to turn the tables on him. With two of them, he knew he wouldn't last, and he wasn't about to come until he was buried to the hilt inside of Sierra.

"Stop," Luke insisted, his breaths choppy, his words barely coherent.

Cole slowed his torturous sucking only slightly before Luke had to shift to keep from coming right in his mouth. "Not yet, damn it," Luke groaned. He knew they'd push him if he let them. He'd been on the receiving end of their combined attention on more than one occasion, and Luke wasn't sure how he ever managed to survive it.

Luke lifted Sierra's shirt up and over her head, and then fumbled with her bra until she was almost entirely naked. The only thing left was the skirt and Luke couldn't take it off of her the way she was sitting now.

"Naked. Both of you," he commanded, trying to catch his breath. "Fast."

Cole reached out and helped Sierra to her feet, and the two of them proceeded to strip one another while Luke had the pleasure of watching. They were beautiful. Both of them.

Sierra, with her long, glossy black hair and tiny, petite body standing beside Cole was a sight. Luke still could not get over how physically perfect the man was. Broad shoulders, muscled chest tapering down to a lean waist, all supported on thick legs.

Once they were as naked as he was, Luke turned, lying back on the couch, his head resting on the cushioned armrest as he gestured for Sierra to join him.

"I can't wait any more. I need to be inside you. Right now."

Sierra nodded as though she understood his urgency. Luke helped her to straddle him, and as he looked up at Cole, their eyes meeting, the breath was sucked right out of him when Sierra impaled herself on his cock in one quick, thrust.

She screamed, and Luke turned back to her. She was so fucking tight. It was damn near painful, but so fucking hot, he wasn't sure he cared at the moment.

"Fuck, baby," he growled the words, unable to move. Somehow he managed to look up at Cole, pleading with him to join them.

Taking his cue, Cole moved around to the end of the couch, reaching into one of the cabinets in the end table before turning back to them. Sierra had personally designed the room, so Luke knew she was aware of where this was going. Within seconds, Cole was kneeling between Luke's thighs on the couch, the heat of his skin brushing against the inside of his knees.

"Are you ready for both of us?" Luke asked Sierra, not sure he could handle her saying no.

"Yes. God, yes." Sierra moaned, staring down at him and that's when Luke noticed her smile. The little minx had obviously been hoping for less foreplay and more action, and she had gotten her wish.

"Fuck." The word escaped Cole's lips in a rush and Luke was now staring back at him. With his cock lodged deep inside of Sierra, he could feel the steely length of Cole's cock as it eased inside of her ass.

Knowing that Luke was all but incapacitated because of the weight now piled on top of him, Cole began thrusting and Luke was grateful. As he rocked Sierra, her body enveloped him, his cock moving in and out of her slowly. Too slowly. *Shit.* Luke needed hard and fast right then. They could worry about the slow, sweet shit later.

"Fuck her." Luke gritted the words through clenched teeth, his eyes locked with Cole's.

When Cole sat up on his knees, shifting Sierra so he had a better angle, Luke took the opportunity to press his mouth to Sierra's. As Cole began pounding inside of her, the sensation so intense, Luke could feel his orgasm building, the tension in his body tightening painfully.

Sierra abruptly pulled back, her mouth breaking contact with his as she dug her fingernails into Luke's shoulders. "Yes!"

Luke didn't even need her to announce it, he could feel the sweet tightening of her pussy around his dick as she came apart between them.

"Come for me, Cole," Luke demanded, staring up at the man, trying to ensure he saw every ounce of emotion that he had in him.

Although they'd managed to overcome a few things, there was still something that seemed to be hanging in the balance between them. Luke figured it was that little piece of himself that he still refused to let go of, even if he was more than a little tempted. He knew they'd get there eventually, but he just wasn't sure when. Until that happened, he made a point to make sure Cole understood exactly how he felt about him. Even if it wasn't verbally.

"Fuck, yes!" Cole groaned, his eyes never leaving Luke's as he exploded inside of Sierra's ass, sending Luke over the edge with him.

Chapter Sixteen

"So, tell me again how this is going to benefit me?" Cole asked Alex as they sat across from one another in the small offices of CISS a week later.

Cole didn't even blink as he waited for Alex to explain his most recent business venture. It seemed a little over the top to him, but what did he know. For the last year, he'd grown into his own in the role of public relations for CISS, the security firm that Alex had built from the ground up. Only now it seemed as though his PR job had been fundamentally ripped away from him when Alex decided he needed him to fill in as the commercial business' lead salesman.

Since Dylan had totally separated himself from CISS and Ashleigh was experiencing difficulty with her pregnancy, Cole hadn't had it in him to tell Alex that he was considering backing out of his role and moving on to other things. He couldn't even commit to Luke, although to his surprise, Luke had asked him to come onboard permanently to help him manage the new club. Specifically handle the in house security team.

Cole knew he was sometimes too loyal, too soft when it came to those he cared about. He tended to let people take advantage of him, and he was beginning to feel the repercussions of having the proverbial bus run over him one too many times.

Although Alex was short one person in the office, he was still working diligently to grow CISS beyond its current operating capacity. Cole was pretty sure it was Alex's way of managing his stress.

"Think about it," Alex explained, a much harder edge to his tone than what Cole was used to as he leaned back in his chair and crossed his arms over his bulky chest.

Cole stared at his boss, honestly trying to see how this was going to benefit them. Any of them. Their business was mainly based in Dallas, Texas, yet for some reason, Alex continued to pursue jobs outside of their city, some of them even hundreds of miles away. Last week, he sent Cole to Houston, but the most recent was in the Austin area and more specifically, the new resort that Travis Walker was building.

"I've tried. Tell me who is going to willingly move down to Austin and manage this for us? Certainly not me, I can tell you that much."

"I didn't expect you to," Alex retorted, sitting up instantly and placing his forearms on the desk in front of him. "I was thinking about sending Jake down there."

"I didn't think Jake was ready for this yet? You're the one who told me that." Cole knew Jake fairly well; the kid had been working for CISS for a while now. He was growing into his own with the company thanks to Dylan bringing him on and giving him a shitload of responsibility. Since Dylan's departure, Cole knew Jake was being pushed to the limit just like he was, but he was surprised to hear Alex was suddenly wanting to give him this much responsibility.

"He's growing into his own," Alex confirmed. "I'm looking to send him and Nate."

Cole took a moment to study Alex. Normally, he would sit back and take whatever decision Alex made with a grain of salt. However, in this case, if Alex did send Jake and Nate to Austin that left no one besides him to fill in, and he was already disgruntled by the fact that he was going on sales calls when Alex was the one who should be making them.

"Why both of them?" Cole had two reasons for his question. One, because he wanted to know why Alex would choose to leave the Dallas office practically empty handed, and two, Cole wasn't sure that sending Dylan's only son some three hundred miles away was going to benefit his current situation any. "Why send both of them to Austin? Do you actually think they can handle it?"

"Only one way to find out." Alex leaned back once again, sounding incredibly nonchalant.

Cole wasn't sure what he thought about that. For as long as he had known Alex, the man put his company first, always taking his time to make sound decisions. This sounded rash, like Alex was almost giving up. As for Nate and Jake being able to handle it, Cole knew Travis Walker, and he knew the way the man reacted to damn near everyone. He wasn't friendly, and Cole wasn't sure Nate or Jake were ready to go head to head with him on a daily basis. Travis wasn't going to settle for second best, no matter what.

"Why those two?"

"They work well together."

"Are you fucking kidding me?" He couldn't help but ask the obvious question. "They're greener than the fucking grass outside your damn window, and you want to send them with a one way ticket to disaster? What the hell is going on, Alex?"

Cole was now standing, having shot up out of his chair completely bewildered by Alex's attitude.

"I don't have time to do it, and I can't just send one of them down there, so I'm sending both of them. You said so yourself, you can't go, so that's my only other choice."

"And where does that leave us? I'm not signing on to handle your sales calls permanently." Cole thrust his hands through his hair, then dry scrubbed his face before turning back to Alex. "This isn't what I want to do."

Alex didn't say a word. He just stared, and Cole felt the man's confusion and above that, he felt the tension. Alex was close to falling apart.

"Are you quitting on me?" Alex asked, pushing to his feet.

Cole sucked in a breath, exhaled slowly and pushed his hands into the pockets of his jeans. He hated to do this, but he was tired of being the one to carry everyone else's load when times got tough. His life wasn't exactly easy, and quite frankly, he was fucking tired of being sent out on the road while Sierra and Luke were getting to spend time with their daughter. Without him. Cole wanted to be home. With Hannah.

"One month," he began. "I'm giving you one month to find a replacement. I'll go to Austin with Nate and Jake, but I'm only staying a week. If at that point they can't handle it, I'm done. I'll come back here and help out until the month is up."

Alex merely nodded his head, and Cole fought the urge to react, to grip Alex's shoulders and shake him until he came to his senses. Instead, he continued to face off with him, his hands flexing at his sides.

"Travis is expecting you. I've explained what we need to get started. He's willing to give Nate and Jake a chance. I'm comfortable with them going. Thanks for helping me out on this one."

Cole didn't hear an ounce of sincerity in Alex's tone and he knew without a doubt, there were problems. It wasn't a secret that Dylan was drinking heavily, refusing anyone's help who attempted to offer, including Alex's and Ashleigh's. The wedding was supposedly still on hold indefinitely, and as Cole stood there, looking back at him, it was clear Alex wasn't handling it well. Not that Cole could blame him. The only problem was, Cole was tired of trying to fix everyone else's problems.

"Travis needs them down there in the next couple of days. He's been a little touchy, and I need him settled down. The four of you can figure it out from there. I'll be out of town myself, at a book signing with Ashleigh in Dallas."

A book signing? What the hell?

Here Alex was, asking Cole to leave Sierra and Luke, and their two month old daughter for a fucking week and Alex was running off to a book signing. How the fuck was that more important?

Reining in his temper was getting harder and harder with each passing second, so Cole turned abruptly, taking with him the information Alex had just shared. This was it. His last trip for Alex.

He hated the travelling, hated leaving Hannah, and he hated that he wasn't getting to spend enough time with Luke and Sierra. He never signed on to travel, and this was getting ridiculous. He'd seen the concern in Sierra's eyes before the last trip he took. He knew they weren't happy with it any more than he was. Not to mention, his own insecurities started rearing their ugly heads lately, and being away from them wasn't going to help.

Chapter Seventeen

Sierra was at home making dinner for herself when Cole walked in the front door. She wasn't big on cooking, but she had been making an effort to eat something more than soup out of a can lately and with Luke at the club until late, she figured Cole might join him, but obviously he had other plans. As soon as he stepped foot in the kitchen she smiled up at him, but the firm set of his jaw and the lack of emotion in his beautiful eyes had the smile falling immediately. He wasn't happy.

"Hi," she greeted hesitantly, continuing to cut up vegetables to toss into the pan, wondering whether she should let him be for a few minutes or if she should push him to talk. Her curiosity won out. "Everything all right?"

"Hey." Cole's deep voice vibrated through her as he leaned in close and kissed her on the neck briefly. Every time he did that she wanted to nuzzle up against him and tell him not to stop.

"How was work?"

Cole didn't immediately answer, and Sierra glanced up after tossing a handful of carrots into the pan, trying to pretend she wasn't worried. Something was wrong, she could feel it, and she could see it in the firm line of his mouth, the wrinkle in his forehead.

She knew asking about work was the fastest way to set him off, but Cole had told her he had to go to a meeting with Alex, which meant only one thing.

"I'd rather not talk about it," Cole answered, moving to the refrigerator and grabbing a beer. "Is Hannah asleep?"

"Yeah, she's been awake for several hours, so I figured I'd let her get a short nap in before I tried to wake her up again."

Cole nodded.

Sierra got the feeling that Cole was beginning to close himself off more than was usual, and her gut told her she shouldn't let that happen. Before Hannah was born, she had to admit, she was a little worried about the relationship between Cole and Luke, specifically as it pertained to Hannah. Knowing that Cole was the father, she worried that Luke would find a way to drive a wedge between them. There'd been a few bumps in the road, but nothing they hadn't managed to handle.

But recently, Cole seemed to be gone more than he was home and when he was home, he chose to spend most of his time with Hannah. It was almost like Cole and Luke had switched personalities. Not that either man was ever fond of opening up and sharing their feelings, but it seemed that as of late, Cole wasn't sharing much of himself with any of them.

Not only was he trying to shut himself down, he was also growing agitated which worried her even more. As Luke began working on smiling more, it was as though Cole was trying to smile less. She knew that Alex played a crucial part in Cole's frustration, sending him out of town often, but Cole never quite explained why.

"If you need to talk, I'm always here." Sierra grabbed the glass of wine she had been sipping on and went to stand closer to where Cole now sat at the breakfast bar.

"Thanks."

The way he responded told her that he wasn't intending to share anything with her now. She had learned a long time ago that with Cole and Luke, she couldn't let them off the hook easy. They didn't open up much, and when they did, it was because she had pried it out of them.

She moved up close to his side, placing a kiss to his big, warm bicep before resting her cheek in the same place. With Cole sitting on the bar stool, Sierra barely came to his chin. Just when she thought he might say something, Hannah's little baby coo came across the baby monitor sitting on the kitchen counter, and Cole abruptly moved from his seat.

"I'll get her while you finish making your dinner," he said and walked out of the room without a backward glance.

Sierra felt the tingle in her nose and the prickle of tears behind her eyelids as she watched him walk away. In just a matter of a few days, Cole had grown incredibly distant. Ever since they had surprised Luke at his office, he hadn't been the same. She had searched her memory, trying desperately to see where things might have gone wrong, but she couldn't seem to find the piece that would put the puzzle together. That day had been explosive, just as it always was when the three of them came together.

Granted, she knew that, for the last week, they hadn't been together except that one time. At least not all of them. She and Luke had managed to steal an hour one morning when Cole was out of town, but since he'd been back, their timing didn't seem to work out. And she knew that unless Cole and Luke were finding time during the day, they weren't getting intimate either because they were off doing their own separate things most of the time.

Sierra made her way back to the stove, stirring the vegetables and tossing in a handful of precooked chicken. Cole's voice came over the monitor as he talked to Hannah. She couldn't help but smile as she always did when she heard either of them talk to Hannah. The way they were with their daughter was the sweetest thing she had ever witnessed. No matter how hard or stubborn the two of them were, when it came to Hannah, their guards came down entirely.

For the next ten minutes, Sierra picked at her food and listened to Cole talk to his daughter. The way he spoke to her brought tears to her eyes several times. Not only what he said, but the way he said it. Cole was one of the most sensitive men she had ever met, although most people never saw that side of him. Because he was so shy, only the people closest to him ever really got to know him. Sierra was truly blessed that he had given her that opportunity.

After cleaning the kitchen and taking a shower, Sierra checked in on Hannah to find that she wasn't in her bed. When she went to the living room, she found Cole laying on the couch watching television with Hannah perched on his chest. Her heart tipped over.

"I'm sorry," he whispered, his beautiful cobalt eyes meeting hers from across the room.

"For what?" she asked as she moved closer.

"For being an ass. It's just been one of those days."

"Want to talk about it?"

~~*~~

Cole eased over on the couch, careful not to wake Hannah, offering Sierra enough room so she could perch beside them. He patted the cushion and waited for her to sit down. With his hand protectively on Hannah's back, he looked up at Sierra.

"Alex wants me to go to Austin."

"What's in Austin?"

"Alluring Indulgence," he told her.

"How does that affect you? I thought it wasn't even built yet."

"It's not. He wants me to go talk to Travis and convince him to let Jake and Nate take over as their security. I think he's expecting them to prove to Travis that they can handle this."

"Why can't he go?"

"He didn't say." Cole hated lying to her, but he also didn't want to share Alex's business. That was one thing about him, he wasn't the gossiping type, and even now, knowing that this was his family, it still felt like a betrayal.

"How long will you be gone?"

"A week." It felt like he'd been gone too much lately. His little girl was growing more and more every day and every second he was away from her he felt like he was missing out on a milestone. He wanted to take her with him, to make Sierra go as well just so he could be with the two of them. He knew better than to want Luke to go along because the man wouldn't do much of anything outside of his club.

Jealous much?

Cole had been feeling a strange envy lately, and he wasn't even sure what he could relate it to. He wanted to think it had to do with the fact that they were all tired from long nights taking care of their little girl, but he was beginning to wonder. Cole wouldn't trade one second with Hannah for anything in the world. He just wondered how she would feel as she got older. About him. About Luke. Would she equally see them as her father? Or would one of them get priority over the other? The thought always managed to depress him.

Letting the gloom bring him down wasn't going to benefit anyone, certainly not him. The more he was pulled away from Hannah, the worse he began to feel.

"Would the two of you go with me?" Cole asked, suddenly wishing he could take the question back when he saw the concern in Sierra's eyes.

"You know I wish we could," Sierra stated, but he wasn't feeling it.

Nodding his head in understanding, Cole glanced down at the perfect angel sleeping on his chest, kissing her downy soft hair and inhaling the sweet baby smell. He wasn't going to push it. Not today.

"Do you know when Luke will be home?" Sierra questioned, standing to move over to the couch on the other side of the room. Cole felt her eyes on him, but he didn't meet her gaze.

"I haven't talked to him today." Cole was under the impression that Luke was working to ensure that Trent and Xander understood who still owned and made the decisions for Club Destiny.

Although the two of them spent more time together as it pertained to the club before Hannah was born, that hadn't been the case lately. Luke was working late nights and Cole was traveling back and forth across the state of Texas it seemed for Alex. Their schedules didn't mesh for them to talk much lately, and when they did, it wasn't usually much more than a few sentences at a time.

"Why don't you go lay down? I've got her and will stay up with her until her next feeding," Cole told Sierra. She wasn't getting enough sleep he knew, and since this was one of those rare times when he wasn't sleeping in a hotel room somewhere, he figured he'd give her a break.

Sierra smiled, but it didn't reach her eyes. Without saying a word, she nodded and disappeared into the bedroom.

Cole remained where he was until Hannah stirred a little while later, probably ready for her dinner. He was starving, but he wasn't in the mood to eat, so he made his way to the kitchen to at least get her settled.

He couldn't seem to get his mind to quiet as he thought about his conversation with Alex earlier that day. He had been telling the truth. He was ready to walk away from CISS because this wasn't what he signed up for. Now that Dylan appeared to be out of the picture, for how long no one seemed to know, Cole wasn't vested enough to want to take on either role.

He wondered whether he was just being overly emotional. There were plenty of reasons, work being one of the main ones. He wasn't getting enough sleep, he wasn't getting to spend enough time with Hannah for his own peace of mind, and besides sleeping in the same bed with Sierra and Luke at night, it seemed as though the three of them were once again drifting apart, just when he thought they'd managed to find their way back to one another.

"You ready for dinner, angel?" he asked Hannah as he reached into the refrigerator and pulled out one of the premade bottles. Sierra hadn't been able to breastfeed because her milk never came in, so they had resorted to formula. He admittedly didn't know much about the differences, but since they didn't have a choice, he opted not to question it, especially after he'd seen the devastation in Sierra's eyes when the doctor told her this was how it would have to be.

Hannah squirmed in his arms as he waited for the water on the stove to heat. Sierra had insisted that they heat the bottles by setting them in boiling water on the stove and checking them repeatedly rather than using the microwave. Again, another one of the baby things he would never have known about without Sierra's guidance.

It didn't take long for the bottle to warm, but by the time it was ready, Hannah had already moved on to a good mad. He smiled down at her, talking quietly as he tried to calm her before giving her what she wanted. Cole marveled at his little girl as he watched her eat with gusto. Just like her dad's, he thought to himself.

He immediately thought about Luke and how close him and Sierra had gotten since Hannah's birth. He knew they hadn't done it purposely, but he couldn't help but feel guilty for some of it. Luke seemed to be reattaching himself to Sierra as though she might slip through his hands. Cole wouldn't say so, but he was pretty sure it was Luke's way of compensating for the fact that he wasn't Hannah's biological father.

When the three of them discussed having children, it hadn't been a simple discussion. Knowing that the three of them couldn't legally solidify their relationship, they had to settle for doing it for love. Because Sierra wanted to know, for the sake of the baby's health, they'd gotten a little creative with their love making, which had surprised the hell out of Cole. When they decided that Cole would be the father, more from Luke's unfounded concerns about his family's health issues, he'd been beside himself with joy. There had been no sense in arguing with Luke even though Logan had confirmed there weren't any health issues that he knew of, so they moved forward as planned. From that point on, until the pregnancy was confirmed, Luke had used condoms with Sierra while Cole had not.

Truthfully, Cole hadn't expected it, but as he lived and breathed, he was grateful for the gift every single day. Although Luke treated Hannah like his very own daughter, Cole wondered whether his own insecurities were pushing him to try and strengthen his relationship with Sierra. Not that the man had anything to worry about.

And it didn't seem to matter because even though Cole was Hannah's biological father, his name on the birth certificate, he still had plenty of his own insecurities. The same ones he was getting damned tired of fighting all the time. There wasn't a single reason either of them should be questioning their relationship, but it seemed they both couldn't quite grasp the concept.

When they were together, during those remarkably few instances when life wasn't pulling one or more of them in a different direction, it could only be described as combustible. The three of them together was like a raging wild fire, and if Cole actually looked at it with rational eyes, their relationship was stronger than ever. Probably most of it could be attributed to the little girl in his arms.

Then again, Cole questioned why Luke wasn't trying to bring himself closer to Cole. Was he doing something wrong? Was he inadvertently pushing Luke away? When it came to sex, the heat was there, so was the intensity in what they were feeling for one another, but it was as though they were both holding themselves back at this point. Sierra always attempted to bring them together, even offering to watch, but Luke was shying away from him more now than before.

Cole knew without a doubt that they were going to collide one of these days. In more ways than one. The emotions that he continued to lock down were going to find their way out, and he would have no choice other than to confront Luke about them.

Whatever happened, he had to remind himself that no matter what, he loved them. All three of them. Every ounce of his heart belonged to them equally, and he knew he'd never be able to live without them.

He only prayed it never came down to that.

Chapter Eighteen

It was late by the time Luke finally made it home. After a rather heated discussion with Trent and Xander, he'd finally decided to call it a night. He left Lucie in charge of the bar and Kane was there to assist. Not because he had to, but because he wanted to be where Lucie was. Those two were going to make it, Luke knew.

When he walked in through the garage entrance, he noticed that all of the lights in the house were off. He'd gotten used to coming home from time to time to Sierra or Cole feeding Hannah in the living room. He glanced over at the monitor on the counter and saw on the video screen that Hannah was sleeping soundly in her bed.

At the moment, he was thinking Hannah had the right idea. Sleep was obviously on his short list of things to do, and he hoped to get to it sooner rather than later. He just wanted to shuck his clothes and fall into bed and not wake for at least eight hours. He'd be lucky to get four, but he wasn't going to complain.

As he moved through the living room, he noticed the light on the back porch was on, so he headed that way to turn it off. That's when he noticed Cole sitting at the patio table drinking a beer and staring out at the pool. He took a minute just to drink in the sight of him.

For some reason, seeing Cole sitting there alone saddened him. He had noticed recently that Cole seemed to be pulling away. For a man with the patience of a saint, Luke didn't understand what might be sending him in that direction. They were all three in this relationship together and as far as Luke was concerned, it was forever.

Granted, he recognized that this wasn't the traditional relationship and considering Sierra was raised by a single mother, Cole had had loving, but not overly doting parents, and Luke had been raised by his grandfather for the most part, none of them truly knew what a real relationship was supposed to be like in the first place. On top of that, they had a daughter together. Initially, Luke thought Hannah was going to bring them all closer together, but for some reason, he felt as though they were all purposely putting a little distance in there somewhere. He knew he was partially responsible on that front as well.

Opening the French doors, Luke walked out onto the patio, and Cole turned his head to look at him. The sadness he had witnessed only seconds before was quickly masked, and Cole attempted a smile, although it fell flat.

"Nice night," Luke said, moving around to perch on the corner of the retaining wall that surrounded the patio.

Cole didn't respond, just nodded his head and then tipped his beer back.

"Want to talk?" Luke asked. The words sounded strange even to his own ears. He hadn't been one to talk much when he met Sierra and Cole, but somewhere along the way, he'd learned how. No, he wasn't the mushy type, and he kept most of his feelings to himself, but he was learning to be more open. At least with the two of them. Or at least he was trying.

"Nothing to talk about," Cole stated firmly.

Damn, the man looked so vulnerable sitting there, his bare feet propped up on another chair, his jeans molded to his impressive thighs and his bare chest and ripped abs on full display. Luke couldn't help but let his eyes wander over the various angles and planes that sculpted the most impressive physique he'd ever seen.

It was true, he might've taken a while to accept what he was feeling, but Luke was finding himself wanting more from Cole as each day passed. Or maybe he was finding he wanted to give more of himself to him.

Hell, who was he kidding? He wanted everything from Cole. They had pledged their love for one another and Luke knew that hadn't changed, but he sometimes worried that their individual fears might possibly push them farther apart. It seemed to be happening already, and they weren't but a year into this relationship.

"How'd it go with Alex?" Luke suspected part of Cole's mood was related to the meeting he had with his boss earlier that day.

"Like usual."

Luke didn't know what that meant. If he had to guess, Cole was about to be off on the road again, and he wasn't sure how he felt about that. Part of him wanted to have a discussion with Alex personally and tell him that this needed to stop because Cole seemed to be away more than he was home these days. The other part of him knew it wasn't his place to interfere with Cole's job.

Instead of questioning him further, Luke turned slightly and faced the pool, hoping Cole would decide he wanted to talk. After several long minutes of silence, he realized it wasn't going to happen.

"I'm gonna turn in," Luke finally said, feeling his exhaustion overtake him suddenly. Sleep was critical if he expected to function tomorrow or any day after that. Who knew what Trent might throw at him then?

Cole nodded again, and Luke chose not to bother him. He didn't hurry inside, hoping Cole would decide to join him. It was clear he wasn't going to do as much, so Luke opted to give him some space.

A few minutes later, Luke was crawling into bed, spooning up against Sierra's warm, pliant body. She murmured something, but didn't wake completely, and Luke didn't want to bother her. The last thing he remembered, before he drifted off, was looking over at Cole's pillow and wondering what was going through his lover's head.

~~*~~

Sierra woke before Luke or Cole the following morning. Before she opened her eyes, she listened to see if she could hear Hannah on the monitor.

All was silent.

Snuggling into Luke's warm body at her back, she reached out to touch Cole, but found his spot on the bed empty. Her eyes flew open, and she noticed he wasn't there. She also noticed that the blankets were still untouched on his side, which meant he never came to bed.

Luke mumbled as she tried to turn over, and when she managed to flip herself over, she noticed his eyes were open. "Where's Cole?" she asked, suddenly worried.

"Don't know," he murmured before closing his eyes again.

"Did he come to bed last night?" she asked, knowing he hadn't, but hoping Luke would wake up enough to tell her something.

"He was sitting outside when I got home."

"Doing what?"

"Hell if I know," he groaned as he rolled over.

Despite her worry, Sierra smiled. One thing about Luke hadn't changed. He was still grumpy in the mornings.

Before she could interrogate him more, Hannah's squeal sounded on the monitor. She sounded happy, and Sierra knew she had a couple of minutes, but she suddenly wanted to see her daughter.

Climbing out of bed, she grabbed her robe and pulled the bedroom door shut behind her as she went to Hannah's room. When she reached the crib, she found Hannah laying on her back, her eyes wide as she stared up at the mobile hanging above her.

"Hey there, pretty girl," Sierra cooed as she reached for a fresh diaper.

Once the morning preliminaries were out of the way, and Hannah was dry and dressed, Sierra cuddled her close to her chest as they made their way through the house. From what she could tell, it was empty. She looked out on the back porch, hoping Cole might still be there – why she had no idea – but he wasn't. When she reached the kitchen, she poked her head out into the garage to see if his truck was there. Nope.

Where did he go? And better yet, *when* did he go?

Knowing that Hannah was going to need her breakfast, Sierra focused on getting the bottle ready before she let her mind drift to where Cole might've disappeared to.

When Hannah was fed and nodding off, Sierra laid her in the small portable crib they had set up in the living room while she went in search of her cell phone. She wanted to text Cole to see where he was and make sure everything was all right. This wasn't like him to disappear, but then again, he'd been acting a little strange the last few days. Or maybe it was longer than that and she hadn't really noticed with everything going on. For some reason, she thought they'd made some progress since Hannah's birth, but again, she felt as though she might not have been paying enough attention.

"Hey, baby," Luke's warm breath heated Sierra's neck, and she sucked in a scream, but couldn't keep from jumping.

"Do you know where Cole is?" she asked without preamble.

"I thought we had this conversation already," he said as he moved to the kitchen and started a pot of coffee. Luke had never been much of a coffee drinker, but Sierra noticed he'd picked up the habit recently. With as little sleep as they seemed to be getting these days, she didn't blame him for trying to get his energy from the same place she liked to get hers.

"I don't consider me asking the question, and you saying, 'don't know' much of a conversation. His truck isn't here, and he never made it to bed last night."

That seemed to catch Luke's attention as his head jerked toward her. He didn't say anything, but he seemed to contemplate what she was telling him. Rather than waiting for him to enlighten her, Sierra continued her search for her cell phone, in the bedroom this time.

When she returned to the kitchen, she heard Luke on the phone.

"Where the hell are you?" Well, at least he was getting right to the point. She couldn't hear Cole's response, but she knew that's who Luke was talking to.

"Austin? What the fuck, Cole?"

There was a long pause and Sierra assumed Cole was talking.

"She didn't tell me that. And neither did you, dammit."

Another pause.

"Why didn't you sleep in bed last night?"

Sierra honestly wished she could hear the answer to that question. It was one she was going to ask Cole personally at the first opportunity. It wasn't ok with her for them to drift apart without talking to one another. Sure, maybe she was just as responsible as they were in making sure they were talking regularly, but with everything going on lately, she would admit she'd probably failed.

With the new club underway and Travis' resort moving forward, they'd spent a lot of time entertaining with Samantha and Logan, as well as the Walkers. If they weren't out together immersed in a crowd of their family and friends, they were generally off doing their own thing. Namely work. And since Hannah was born, their daughter had been everyone's sole focus during whatever free time they found.

Oh God.

Sierra's heart ached at the thought that Cole was drifting away from her. She suddenly remembered his request for her and Hannah to join him on this trip and her heart clenched painfully in her chest at the memory of her telling him she couldn't.

After all they'd been through to get this far, she didn't even want to contemplate what she would do if she lost either of them. Even she had detected the tension ever so slowly intensifying with Cole, but she had expected him to come to her when he was ready. That's the way they worked much of the time. Both Cole and Luke used her to redirect the emotions that they both seemed overcome with. Luke and Cole were very stubborn, particularly hard headed men, and if they didn't have to come out and admit their feelings for one another, they weren't going to do it.

"When will you be back?" Luke's voice pulled her from her thoughts, and she waited.

"Not good enough, Cole. I want to know when the fuck you'll be back. Don't make me call Alex," he growled.

Sierra could only imagine what Cole was thinking at that point. He was a grown man and Luke had no right to try and dictate his life for him, but they both knew that Luke had a hard time not being in control of everything. He wanted things to work the way he expected them to. Unfortunately, with a relationship as complex as theirs, it didn't normally work out that way.

"Fuck."

Sierra turned the corner and entered the kitchen, hoping to calm Luke down before he said something he shouldn't. That's when she noticed that he wasn't on the phone.

"What did he say?"

"He fucking hung up on me." Luke placed his cell phone on the counter, gently laying it down and staring at his fist as though he was about to break the device with his bare hands.

"He's in Austin?" She hadn't expected him to leave without talking to them first, so the thought didn't sit well with her.

"That's what he says."

"You don't believe him?" she asked, wondering why in the world Luke would doubt anything Cole told him. If nothing else, Cole was one of the most honest men she had ever met. He might not talk openly or give his thoughts freely, but when he did talk, he was worth listening to.

"I don't know what to believe right now, Sierra."

Luke sounded angry. More than angry actually. She hadn't heard him like this in months. The cold, detached man she had fallen in love with had changed in the last year, becoming so much more than she ever expected. It was as though his acceptance of the love she and Cole had for him had loosened the rope he kept knotted tightly around his heart.

"Go down there." The words breezed right past her lips before her brain completely formulated the idea, but as soon as she did, she realized it was the only option. Luke needed to go after Cole. She had a feeling that the stress that lingered over their relationship had more to do with the two of them together and how Hannah fit into the equation than with the three of them as a whole. She didn't want to think about what that might mean for her, but right now, she wasn't important. Cole was.

"What?"

"You heard me. Go down to Austin. He said he'd be there for a week. I'm sure you can come up with an excuse to check in with Travis and you know Kane can handle the bar in your absence. This can't wait until he gets back, Luke."

Luke glanced from her then to the living room. She knew he was thinking about Hannah.

"I'll have my mother come stay with us for a few days while you're gone," she told him quickly, not wanting him to come up with any excuses. She knew he wasn't willing to leave her alone for one minute unless he absolutely had to. "I'd go with you, but Hannah has a checkup scheduled this week, and she can't miss it."

To Sierra's surprise, Luke didn't argue. He stared at her, and she wondered what he was thinking. The expression on his face was unreadable.

This was the only solution. The two of them could spend a few days alone and maybe, just maybe, they would be able to work this out. If not, Sierra feared that the wonderful life as she knew it was about to crumble at her feet.

As far as she was concerned, that wasn't an option.

Never would it be an option.

Chapter Nineteen

Cole dropped his cell phone into the cup holder and stared out the window of his truck. His stomach churned around what felt like a boulder sitting right in his gut. Oh, and his palms were sweating, probably because he'd been clenching and unclenching them while listening to Luke.

He hated how he felt right at that moment. Hated that he was wondering whether Luke and Sierra would be better off without him. He would still have Hannah, but they'd probably only allow him to see her on weekends, and that was something he didn't even want to think about.

His eyes misted, and he fought the urge to let loose. The emotions were intense, yet for some reason, Cole didn't know what his problem was. If he thought about it, he was bringing this all on himself. But there was no denying the anxiety or the vulnerability he felt these days. He felt as though someone had finally tugged on the frayed string that had originally been holding him together and all of a sudden he was unraveling.

Shit.

He wasn't the one who was supposed to have postpartum depression, damn it.

He didn't know what provoked him to hang up on Luke, but he just couldn't talk to the man, or listen to his disappointment or demands. It was clear he wasn't happy with him for up and leaving without even saying goodbye, but when he had gone to his bedroom the night before, something about seeing Luke and Sierra curled up together made him feel like the third wheel all of a sudden.

Was it so fucking wrong that he wanted a little more from the two of them? Looking back, he knew he had been the third from the beginning, and taking the chance on this relationship was something he didn't regret, but he couldn't help but feel there was something more. Something he wasn't getting.

He loved Sierra. Loved her to the point of distraction. He wanted to hold her every second of every day. He loved seeing her sleepy, sexy face every morning when he woke up. And his heart tumbled over itself when he saw her holding Hannah.

Then there was Luke. The man held a part of him that Cole would never be able to explain even to himself. He had been in love with Luke for years, yet he had kept it to himself because Luke hadn't been ready to accept the fact that he wanted something more than he was admitting to.

Cole feared that he longed for something more from Luke for the simple fact that he wasn't getting it now. With Sierra, he didn't question how she felt about him, although they had some difficulty in making this a threesome in the relative sense. It was almost as though they were separate couples. Luke still held himself back a little and Cole felt it. He didn't like it, but he felt it nonetheless.

Grabbing his phone and the small bag he had packed, Cole decided he might as well go into the hotel. The reservations were made, and he just needed to check in. Then maybe he could sleep for a while. He wouldn't see Jake or Nate until tomorrow because he hadn't told anyone he was heading down early.

Maybe he could go by and see Travis and check out what they'd done on the resort thus far. He knew it was coming along quickly. Travis Walker wasn't a man to procrastinate, and he was staying on top of the contractors, ensuring they were doing things the way he wanted. Even though Travis was the type of man who seemed to have everything under control, Cole was glad he didn't work for him. He was pretty sure he wouldn't be able to contain his temper quite as well as he usually did. Which even he would admit was less and less these days.

Once inside, he checked in, trying to be polite to the pleasant young woman who seemed to be starved for attention. He wasn't in the mood to talk, but somehow, with a smile, he managed to get through the ten minutes it took for her to handle the process. As he made his way up to his room on the third floor so he wouldn't have the interruption of anyone being above him – a gesture made by the lonely woman at the front desk – he couldn't get away from his thoughts.

He felt like a dick for hanging up on Luke, but the man's threats had finally pushed him past his limits. It was one thing for Luke to be angry that he disappeared without a word, a decision he still questioned but realized it was too late to change the outcome now. It was something entirely different for Luke to threaten to call Alex. He couldn't help but feel like a recalcitrant child when Luke acted like that and Cole was as far from being a child as anyone possibly could be.

Once inside the less than spectacular hotel room, Cole placed his bag on the floor by the bed and then collapsed on the king sized bed that filled up most of the room. Staring up at the ceiling, he thought back to what had gotten him to this place.

During the drive down, he'd accepted the fact that he overreacted by disappearing in the middle of the night. He'd been upset, he wouldn't deny it. At least not to himself.

The fact that Sierra and Luke were both so immersed in themselves had him feeling a little lonely. Not that he'd made the situation any better by leaving, but he knew if he didn't walk out the door, he'd only miss his daughter that much more and hearing that Sierra didn't want to come with him and bring the baby had been a knife wound to his heart that still throbbed.

He understood. At least he tried to.

They didn't need to be traipsing across the state with a two month old baby, but Cole hadn't had a choice in coming to Austin. He might've told Alex that he was done, but he couldn't leave the man hanging. It wasn't in his nature. He would handle this last assignment and then he'd figure out what to do next.

He knew what he wanted to do. Now he just had to wonder whether the offer was still on the table.

~~*~~

Luke hated the drive from Dallas to Austin. He hated the traffic, hated the long expanse of two lane highway that felt endless at times.

As he pulled into the hotel parking lot three hours later in the small town of Coyote Ridge, he let out a brief sigh of relief. Cole's truck was there which meant at least he wouldn't have to go looking for him. He was too fucking tired to chase the man down.

Grabbing his phone, he sent Cole a text, asking what his room number was. He didn't expect to get an answer quite so quickly, and he was surprised that Cole didn't question him when he sent the text back. Without responding, Luke walked into the hotel and headed right for the elevator, not bothering to make eye contact with the woman sitting at the desk.

Once he made it to the third floor, he glanced up and down the long corridor, trying to figure out which end Cole's room was on. Finally noticing the sign with the numbers, Luke went to the left. Before knocking, he took a deep breath, acknowledging the fact that his temper wasn't going to fix this situation. No matter what happened next, he knew he couldn't blow up at Cole the way he was known to.

No matter what Cole's reason for leaving, Luke fully intended to figure out what was going on with him. Sierra might've made the suggestion for him to come down to Austin to find Cole, but Luke had been thinking about it already. Before he walked out the door that morning, he and Sierra had a long conversation, one that involved him telling her this wasn't a temporary thing for him, and he wasn't about to allow Cole to walk away. Luke was pretty sure Sierra needed that assurance and it pained him to realize that they still hadn't managed to cement their relationship to the point that the three of them weren't still wondering what might happen.

Luke was tired of the *what might be's*. He wanted a fucking guarantee. He wanted to know that Cole loved him as much as he loved Cole. He wanted to know this was forever. Now he just had to figure out how they were going to seal this deal once and for all.

Lifting his hand, Luke stared at the ugly almond door before rapping his knuckles firmly. He thought he heard movement on the other side of the door, but he began to question himself as long seconds passed. Just when he was about to knock again, the door opened. He had to take a step inside to keep it from slamming in his face as Cole immediately turned and walked the other direction.

Remembering he had to handle this with at least a little bit of patience, Luke swallowed hard and moved inside the room, shutting and locking the door behind him.

The tension radiating from Cole was nearly enough to keep Luke a safe distance away. The only problem with that would be that Luke didn't want to be a safe distance away. He wanted to be right up in Cole's face, forcing him to understand how he felt. God only knew it was time. Based on what he understood from Sierra that morning, they both still had some insecurities, although she'd learned to listen to her heart, knowing that, in the end, it would all work out the way it was supposed to.

God he loved that woman. He had vowed right then and there as they sat side by side on his couch that he would make sure she knew just how much. Each and every day.

"Why'd you come? Don't you have a club to run?" Cole's words were laced with venom, and it didn't take a rocket scientist to realize what part of his problem was.

"You're more important to me than my club," Luke told him, keeping his voice low and steady.

"Am I?"

Luke wanted to retaliate, to snap at Cole the way he was snapping at him, but he couldn't bring himself to do it. He knew what he'd put Cole through for the longest time. He didn't need to be told that he wasn't the easiest man to get close to. He knew that about himself. Except when it came to Cole and Sierra, but even that hadn't been an easy point to get to for him. Only now, Luke wanted them to be as close as he could get them.

"Yes, you are," he responded, taking a few steps closer to where Cole was now staring out the window at the little bowl of water that the hotel proclaimed to be a pool.

When he was standing less than an inch away, he reached around Cole and closed the curtains on the window, the blackout panels sending the room into darkness, with the exception of the pale yellow glow from a lamp on the desk.

His body suddenly realized that the two of them were alone. They were alone, and there wasn't anything that could interrupt them. This was an opportunity they'd never had before, and it was his chance to show Cole exactly what he meant to him.

They would hash out their differences verbally, but Luke knew that before it was over, he would have Cole naked beneath him.

Chapter Twenty

Cole didn't react when Luke closed the curtains, obscuring his ability to escape the reason he was here. Little did Luke know, but the fact that he came after him meant more than any words they might say between them in the next few minutes.

As much as he wanted to tell Luke to leave him alone, Cole didn't want to be alone. He wanted to handle this like men, to discuss whatever the issues were between them, even if he had only conjured them up in his head. There were things he needed to say, things Luke needed to hear. And he knew there were things Luke had to say as well. He just wasn't sure the man was going to be able to say them.

Cole dropped his head, staring down at the floor as he tried to figure out what the best way to handle Luke was going to be. His own anger was set on rapid boil, but that's because he'd let all of his emotions fester for far too long, and it was time he finally got some things off of his chest. He just didn't know how to start.

When Luke's hands gripped his shoulders, Cole tensed. He was prepared to stand his ground, not willing to give in to his desire until they'd reached some sort of understanding because for the two of them, it was so easy to give in, so easy to let all of the issues, all of the concerns get brushed away because they'd become so apt at resolving their emotional disputes with sex.

To his surprise, Luke didn't try to move him, he merely kneaded his shoulders firmly, moving to stand even closer until the warmth of Luke's large frame was at his back. Another breath escaped him as he tried to let the magic of Luke's fingers ease the strain from his muscles.

"I told you why I came, now I want to know why you ran," Luke whispered, his breath warm against Cole's ear.

Cole instinctively shrugged his shoulders, signifying he didn't have an answer. He immediately felt Luke's grip tighten briefly before releasing, letting him know without words that he wasn't satisfied with that answer.

"I know this has nothing to do with Hannah or Sierra, so I can only assume it's between you and me. Am I right?"

Cole pulled away, managing to ease from between Luke's body and the wall in front of him before pacing to the other side of the room.

"I'm not sure it is about you, Luke. Maybe it's about me," Cole said, not looking directly at him, but feeling the other man's eyes tracking him.

"What does that mean?"

"It means that you and Sierra aren't the only two in this relationship, but maybe I'm wondering why that is." Before Cole could begin his next sentence, he found himself slammed up against the wall, Luke's hard, ungiving form restraining him, his hand flat against his throat, his thumb and forefinger cupping his jaw, forcing him to look at him. Luke wasn't hurting him, but Cole instantly went on the defensive, fighting back the urge to retaliate.

"Don't say it." Luke's voice broke, although he tried to hide the emotion.

Cole felt the answering emotion well up inside of him, and he immediately had to blink several times to keep the tears at bay. He felt so lost, so confused, but as he looked into Luke's bright eyes, he wondered if he had imagined it all.

"You're in this because we love you. And yes, before you say otherwise, I do love you," Luke said, his voice still gruff. "I don't want you wondering why."

"How can I not?" Cole questioned him. "I feel like the fucking third wheel, dammit."

Luke let him go, stepping back and staring at him as though he'd just spouted a third eyeball. "What the fuck? What have we ever done to make you feel like that?"

Cole watched Luke's face, his incredulity clearly reflected on his stern, yet concerned face. "Let's see," Cole barked. "Could it be that neither one of you can make time for me? It's like I'm a second thought, something else always seems to be more important. Did you ever notice how you will drop everything when Sierra wants to see you? You don't do it for me, Luke. Something always gets in the way, whether it's the club or Trent or now Xander. It's as though the rest of the world can't survive without you, but I'm supposed to sit back and wait until everyone else is through with you to get my turn."

"I –" Luke's mouth abruptly closed.

"You what? You don't find some way to keep yourself busy, unable to give me your undivided attention unless you're ready? Well, I hate to break it to you, but that's exactly what happens. I'm the third wheel in this, Luke. I'm sick and fucking tired of coming last. I'm tired of being the fall guy, coming to everyone else's rescue all the damn time and still waiting for someone to rescue me." The last word damn near escaped on a sob as a lump formed in Cole's throat. He hadn't meant to say quite so much, but it was exactly how he felt.

Cole waited patiently for Luke's denial, for him to come up with an example which would make him realize this was all a figment of his imagination. A minute passed. Another. Luke didn't say a word, he just stared at Cole, his lips a hard line, his dark brows slanted downward as though he were lost in thought.

"I was hoping I'd imagined it all. I wanted to be the selfish asshole who was looking for more than he was getting, but I'm not, am I, Luke? I'm no one's priority."

"Bullshit," Luke barked, the word choppy and broken as he took one step closer. Then another. "You're *my* priority. Always my priority."

"Yeah?" Cole didn't back down as Luke slowly moved forward. He could see the emotion finally taking Luke the same as it had him the more he thought about it. "You've got a funny way of showing it."

"Ever wonder how *I* feel?" Luke asked, and Cole couldn't hide his own surprise.

"Did it ever cross your mind that I'm the one everyone seems to come to when they have a problem? I'm the one everyone expects to take charge and make things right. Did it?"

Cole couldn't answer. Luke was right. Most people did go to him when they needed something. As much as he tried to handle things on the home front when Sierra needed something, or Hannah, Cole knew that wasn't the case with most people. Luke was the one who had to make the final decision on the club, taking the weight of it with him and dealing directly with the aftermath ever since.

Luke's gaze locked with his and he waited.

"Have you ever thought that, at some point, I want to give up control? That I'd prefer to have someone else take care of me for a change?"

Cole wasn't sure what Luke was getting at. He heard the words, but he didn't understand. It wasn't like Cole could step in and handle the club. Luke wouldn't allow it. It wasn't like…

Cole's breath caught in his chest.

"That's right," Luke said as he moved closer, obviously noticing the second Cole understood what he was saying.

When their bodies aligned once again, Cole didn't try to move, he didn't put up his defenses either. He stood his ground, but allowed Luke to get as close as he wanted. Aside from their chests touching, nothing else on their bodies did.

"You don't know how many times I've thought about it, Cole. Thought about handing all control over to you. And I'm not just referring to the club, although you're the only person in the world I would trust to handle it. I'm tired of handling it all. Tired of making the decisions, being in control. I want someone to lean on. I want to lean on you." Luke's voice trailed off before he penetrated Cole with his eyes once more. "I want to let you take what you want from me. Except that's not what you want, is it? You need me to be in control, just like everyone else does, but you need it differently."

"That's where you're wrong," Cole whispered.

"Am I?" Luke leaned in closer, his mouth just a breath away. "Is it my imagination that you love to feel the connection between us when I'm inside you? Did I just dream up that you need me to force you because it's your opportunity to leave the decision making to someone else? To know that you don't have to figure out how to fix something?"

Cole couldn't answer because Luke was right. Everything he said was the absolute truth. Except there was more, more than Luke was willing to admit.

"We've come to a stalemate," Luke stated, not moving away. "From what it sounds like, we're both looking for something that we aren't getting. And this time, it's between the two of us, only we haven't owned up to it."

The pain that lanced through Cole's chest at the thought of what Luke was saying nearly brought him to his knees. He did need more, but he needed more from Luke. He needed to feel like he wasn't second fiddle, needed Sierra to trust him as much as she trusted Luke to handle the difficult things. Most importantly, he needed this man to let him in, let him take care of him for once.

"Running doesn't solve that problem, Cole."

He wasn't about to disagree. "Where does that leave us?" Cole asked through the painful lump in his throat, the one threatening to choke him.

~~*~~

"It leaves us here to figure this out," Luke said, his heart pounding painfully against his ribs. "I want more, Cole. But I don't want anyone else. You and Sierra are all I need. I've always known that. Maybe I don't know how to express it." Taking one step back, Luke put some distance between them before he did what he wanted and slammed his mouth down on Cole's and got lost in what his body had to offer rather than talking about this.

Talking wasn't his thing. Neither was it Cole's and look where it had gotten them.

"Do you know how hard it was for me the day Hannah was born?" he asked, turning away so Cole couldn't see the emotion he couldn't seem to get a grip on. He wasn't going to cry.

"I thought about it," Cole admitted.

"She's your daughter, Cole. You and Sierra created that child, and I love her with every single fiber in my body just like she were mine. That doesn't make it so. That doesn't mean she can't be taken away from me if the three of us don't…" He couldn't finish the statement. Luke didn't even want to consider life without Sierra and Cole in it.

This wasn't temporary, it wasn't part time, and it wasn't just because. This was a forever love. One Luke wasn't willing to walk away from. This was just a small hill they had to get over, heaven knew there'd be more, but they had to make it over this one. Luke didn't expect this to be easy, but he expected it to last.

When the silence began to get to him, Luke turned to face Cole, noticing the man was just staring at him.

"I love you, Cole." He had to swallow before he continued. "I'll never stop loving you. You and I both know it's not easy for me, but you stuck it out with me once. Don't give up on me now," Luke begged, his tone reflecting every insecurity he'd ever felt, his eyes blurry as he tried to hold in what he feared would eventually overwhelm him.

The next thing he knew, Cole's mouth was pressed firmly against his, his arms wrapped around him, his brawny hands holding him in place as he explored the kiss. Luke let himself get lost in Cole, just like he always did. Although they may both be challenged when it came to expressing themselves with words, it wasn't the case when they gave in to the desire that still pulled them together.

Cole pulled away, lightly brushing his firm lips against his and Luke didn't want to move, didn't want to let go of what they both needed right then and there.

"I love you," Cole whispered and Luke answered with a growl, quickly lifting Cole's shirt up and over his head, tossing it to the cheap motel carpet.

"I want you naked," Luke demanded, moving back slightly, more so than he even wanted to so they could get rid of the clothes that were hindering their ability to feel one another.

Within seconds, probably a personal best for both of them, they were naked and on the bed, Luke coming down on top of Cole. They were a tangle of arms and legs and mouths, neither of them able to get close enough, but still trying desperately as they devoured one another.

"I need to be inside of you," Luke said when he broke the kiss, lifting up so he could stare down at Cole. He saw the sudden flash in his eyes, something akin to sadness and Luke realized exactly what Cole was looking for.

Maybe he'd been wrong. Maybe Cole wasn't always looking for Luke to be the one in control. "Right now, I need this," Luke whispered, pressing his lips against Cole's gently. "I know what you need, and I fully intend to give it to you, but right now, I need this." Luke realized he was probably being selfish, but he couldn't explain his need to feel Cole surrounding him completely.

Cole nodded his head in agreement, pulling Luke's mouth back down to his and the kiss that ensued started out slow, but it quickly morphed into an inferno that threatened to incinerate them both. When Luke broke the kiss again, Cole smiled that sexy, knowing grin.

"In my bag."

Luke managed to lean over the edge of the bed and retrieve the lubricant from Cole's bag, not willing to ask why he brought it with him. He could only hope that Cole had the forethought to consider that this might happen. Luke hoped that was the case. He hoped that Cole trusted him enough to know that he would come after him.

Right now was about healing their hearts. When they got home, Luke would work on showing Cole just how much he trusted *him*.

~~*~~

Cole held onto Luke for dear life.

Looking up at him, seeing the intensity in his handsome face as he slowly inched his way deeper inside his body was one of the most incredible feelings he'd ever known.

There were times when they needed something else, something rough, something equivalent to sky diving from thirty thousand feet. But right now, this was what they both needed. Although the need was there, the ferocity in Luke's gaze mirrored what was burning deep in Cole's chest. Slower, gentler.

"Fuck," Cole groaned as Luke slowly continued to slide deeper, not retreating until he was lodged all the way inside of him, their eyes locked on one another.

"You feel so good," Luke growled. "So fucking good. I don't want to stop."

When Luke started talking, Cole feared he wouldn't be able to last. It wasn't very often that Luke expressed himself in this way. Usually, it was with his body, but hearing the rumble of his chest as he tried to control himself sent a surge of power through Cole. He did this to Luke. Him. What was happening right here, right now, between them, this was all about what they felt for one another.

Luke's hands slid up the backs of Cole's thighs, lifting his legs, pushing them closer to his body as he began to pull out before returning with short, shallow thrusts that had Cole nearly begging for more. Somehow, he managed to keep his mouth shut, did his best not to beg for that something more that would take the edge off. They would get there, and for now, he just needed to feel.

Tossing his head back, Cole closed his eyes as Luke practically bent him in half, directing his cock at an angle that damn near had him jumping off the bed. "Oh, fuck." The words were ripped from his chest as the pleasure intensified on every upstroke. "Luke."

"Tell me," Luke whispered, causing Cole to open his eyes and peer up at the man who was now leaning over him. "Tell me exactly what it feels like when I'm buried deep inside of you."

"So fucking good." Cole tensed again as Luke purposely slid in slower, changing the angle again. "Fuck! You keep doing that, and I'm gonna come."

"I want you to come." Luke started pumping his hips faster, holding his body braced on the back of Cole's thighs, his hands pinning his legs down on each side of his chest. "I want to see you stroke your cock and come for me."

Cole began stroking slowly, but he found he began to mirror Luke's pace. When Luke thrust harder, Cole's hand tightened around his dick painfully. "Fuck me," Cole begged. "I want to feel you come inside me."

There was a turbulent flash of emotion that Cole witnessed in Luke's eyes, seconds before he began pounding into him harder and harder, no longer adjusting the angle because the lust had taken over and they were in a race to the finish line, neither of them holding back.

"Fucking come for me," Cole practically barked the order at Luke, holding off his own release as he waited impatiently.

"Yes. God, yes!" Luke's voice echoed through the small room as his body stilled, his release spilling inside of Cole as he let himself go, his own orgasm ripping through him, stealing the breath from his body, followed by the last remnants of his heart that he might've been holding back.

Chapter Twenty One

The second Cole walked into the house, he made the decision that he wasn't going to travel ever again. Without stopping, he immediately made his way to Hannah's room where he found her fast asleep.

"Sorry, she just laid down for her nap," Sierra whispered sweetly as she moved up close to his side. "I would've kept her awake if I knew you would be here so soon." Cole pulled Sierra up beside him, leaning down so he could inhale her flowery scent, pressing his lips against the top of her head. God, he missed her.

Not wanting to wake Hannah, Cole laced his fingers with Sierra's and led her out of the room and back to the living room.

For the entire five days he'd been gone, Cole had thought about both of his girls almost every minute. Even though Luke had stayed for one day with him, trying to convince him that he needed to talk to Travis – which he knew to be a lie, but loved the man even more for it – Cole still wanted nothing more than to be home with the three of them. As much as it pained him to stay the entire week and to watch Luke drive away, Cole needed time to himself. Time to think.

Now that he was home, he knew they probably needed to have a talk.

"Is Luke still at the club?"

"Yes. He said he's leaving right at five."

Cole nodded, trying to hold back the smile that the information caused. Although Cole and Luke had succumbed to healing their wounds by divulging in one another repeatedly during the time they were alone together in Austin, they'd managed to do some talking as well. Needless to say, they had both agreed that some changes were in order, and there was no need to put them off.

Cole led Sierra out onto the back patio, grabbing the baby monitor on his way so they could listen for Hannah while they were outside. He never let go of her hand until he was situated in one of the chairs, pulling her down on his lap where she snuggled against him easily.

"I missed you," Sierra whispered.

"I missed you too, baby." Cole brushed Sierra's hair back, tucking it behind her ear as he glanced down at her where she rested her head against his shoulder.

"Luke said the two of you managed to talk some things out." Sierra didn't pose it as a question, but Cole sensed she was looking for some sort of affirmation that they were, in fact, good once again.

"I'm sorry I walked out the way I did," Cole said first, intending to get into the details, but needing her to know that he realized he'd been wrong. "I should've talked to you and Luke first."

Sierra lifted her head, giving Cole a front row view into ice blue eyes that saw so much more than he ever expected her to. "I didn't mean to hurt you."

"No," Cole slid his hand into her hair, gently pulling her close until their cheeks were pressed against one another. "Baby, you didn't hurt me. I hurt myself."

Sierra forced him to release her, obviously wanting to look him in the eye.

For the last week, Cole thought nonstop about what he could've done differently, and he wasn't sure he could've done anything, aside from not running away when he should've stayed and fought for what he wanted. The selfish part of him told him that he needed for Luke to come after him the way that he did, needed to know that what he felt for him wasn't one sided. That was the difference between Luke and Sierra, she might be busy, she might be just as distracted as Luke, but he didn't have any doubts as to how she felt about him. Why that was, he still didn't understand.

"You aren't the only one who did some thinking while you were gone."

Cole watched as Sierra fidgeted with the two rings on her left hand, watching as she turned them repeatedly over and over on her finger, as though she were searching for the right words to say. He didn't say a word, unsure where she was going and scared he was about to find out.

"A lot has happened between the three of us in the last year. We not only found one another, but we fell in love, moved in together and most importantly decided to have a baby together. That's a lot for such a short period of time."

Cole wasn't sure he agreed. At his age, he was ready to settle down, had been for a while, but hadn't found what he was looking for until Sierra and Luke. Now that he had the family he never thought possible, he wasn't willing to let anything come between them. Not even his own insecurities. At least not anymore.

"I've questioned our circumstances, just like I know you and Luke have. The fact that we can't get married… and I'm not talking about a piece of paper that the state blesses us with. That's not what marriage is to me."

"Who says we can't?" Cole asked suddenly. They had a reception to announce to their family and friends the status of their relationship more so because Luke wanted to shout it from the rooftops when he finally accepted what was in his heart for so long. "It won't be legal, but there isn't anything to say that we can't have a ceremony."

A small smile tipped Sierra's lips and her eyes sparkled. "You'd do that for me?"

"Baby, I'd do anything for you." Cole cupped her face with his hands, loving how soft her skin was, how big his hands were in comparison to her. "I want you to know that. To trust me. To know that no matter what, the most important things in the world to me are you, Hannah and Luke."

"I do trust you, but that goes both ways," Sierra whispered, sounding as though she were hesitant to call him on his insecurities.

"I know that." Cole glanced past her, not seeing anything in the distance aside from his own thoughtful reflection of the things he'd been dealing with over the last few days. He knew where she was going with this, and he agreed.

"Cole, we've had so much change in our lives over the last year. Always something more to do, something else to worry about tomorrow. Life's going to be that way. We're going to be busy. We're blessed to have what we have. Family. Friends. The club. Each other. It's not going to be a smooth road, but we need to talk it out. If you need more attention, which I think all three of us feel that we do, ask for it."

Cole knew that was easier said than done. He'd had this same conversation with himself on more than one occasion. He'd put the blame on Sierra and Luke because they were so involved with their jobs while Cole was disgruntled with his. That wasn't their fault. He hadn't even shared what he and Alex had talked about.

The tips of Sierra's soft fingers touched his chin, turning his face gently to look into her eyes. "I don't want to hear about what's happening with you from my best friend."

Cole's brow furrowed as he tried to understand what she was getting at.

"Ashleigh told me that you gave Alex your notice."

That.

No, he hadn't shared that information with Sierra. There were several reasons, the least of which was that he didn't want her to worry. Cole knew money wasn't something they had to worry about, but that didn't mean he didn't want to be a contributing member of their family. He'd had his doubts, worried that he had been impulsive in his decision to leave CISS. He still wasn't sure whether it was the right decision or not, but now that he was home, he fully intended to work on that.

"I think it was the right decision," Sierra added, causing Cole to tilt his head in question.

"You do?" He hadn't imagined getting Sierra's support on his decision. He had no reason to believe otherwise, but for some reason, he felt as though he'd let her down without talking to her first. He already knew how Luke felt, they'd had a brief discussion about him coming to work with him, not *for him* Luke had clarified. Cole had yet to discuss anything further with Luke, but he hoped to soon.

"I do. You weren't happy. I'm not sure even you realize how much you try to carry everyone else's burden. Even when it isn't yours to carry. Remember Lucie? You walked around for years carrying her secret with you because you cared about her. I'm glad things worked out for her, but she shouldn't have put you in that position. We don't tend to think about it because of who you are."

Sierra pulled his face a little closer, keeping her eyes locked on his before she continued, "You're the man who saves the world. Not the man who merely tries. You're the man who comes through for everyone, even at your own expense. Well, I'm the woman who loves you, and I'm not willing to sit back any longer and let anyone take advantage of you. Including yourself."

Cole's heart struck up a heavy beat, his chest constricting. He knew he'd become a sounding board for his friends, knew he was often the guy who stepped up to the plate when no one else did. It wasn't something he could stop doing though.

"Don't get me wrong," Sierra said, lightly brushing her lips against his. "You're the most loyal, most honorable man I know. I would never want you to change that. I just want you to be put first more often."

It was as though she had a portal into his thoughts. She understood him. Probably more than he understood himself.

Cole couldn't resist kissing Sierra right then, tipping her head with his hands and allowing his tongue to slide past her smooth, sexy lips. He could get lost in her. Day, night. It didn't matter. Whenever he had the opportunity to put his mouth to hers, the entire world could fall apart around him, and he wouldn't care.

"We don't do this nearly enough," Sierra whispered against his lips.

"No, I would have to agree, you don't," Luke's gruff voice sounded from behind him and Cole didn't try to look, he just smiled.

"Hey," Sierra smiled up at him.

"No, don't let me interrupt," Luke insisted with a smile in his voice, pulling out one of the chairs from the patio table and moving it around so that he had a clearer view of the two of them. "I think it's been far too long since I got to watch."

Cole felt the slight shiver that ran through Sierra. The smile tipping her lips was bright enough to rival the sun any day. When she turned her attention back to Cole, he pulled her face closer, letting his lips press to hers again, his body immediately responding to Luke's presence and the soft, pliant woman sitting in his lap.

"Do you care to direct as well?" Sierra asked as she peered over at him, her lips still brushing against Cole's.

Cole was a little surprised at how excited Sierra was getting. It was still fully daylight outside, and although the entire yard was discreetly hidden from prying eyes by various trees and plants outlining it, they didn't generally engage in these types of activities outside in broad daylight.

"Don't mind if I do," Luke answered, crossing one ankle over the opposite knee as he regarded them both silently for a moment. "Let's start by removing his shirt. That'll provide some serious incentive."

Cole grinned, looking up at Sierra as she sat up straighter, then shifted so she was straddling his legs on the chair. He had to move to allow her more room because the metal armrests were almost in her way. When her cool fingers slid beneath the waistband of his jeans, and underneath his shirt, he sucked in a deep breath. She took her time lifting his shirt, trailing her fingers up along his chest as she went.

Cole wasn't a vain man, but he admittedly worked hard for the body that he had. He didn't cheat on his diet, and he routinely worked out. He'd done it for most of his life, although lately, he'd done it more for these two. The way they looked at him, their eyes devouring him when he went without a shirt, or when he was naked, was more inspiration than he'd ever had before.

Like now. Although he kept his eyes trained on Sierra's face, he could see in his peripheral vision how Luke was watching him just as intently.

"So beautiful," Sierra whispered. "I love to kiss you right here." Her lips pressed against his right pec, directly above his nipple and the muscle beneath instantly hardened. "And here," she said as she left a wet, hot trail down to his nipple with her tongue. He didn't try to hold back the growl that her ministrations pulled from deep in his chest. When she used her teeth to tease his nipple until it hardened in her mouth, he instinctively grabbed the back of her head and held her closer, not wanting her to stop.

"It wouldn't be fair not to give the other one the same attention," Sierra mouthed the words as she moved her lips across his chest.

At this rate, Cole wasn't sure he was going to be able to hold out for whatever Luke had in mind.

But he sure as hell intended to try.

Chapter Twenty Two

Coming home to witness a scene like this one was the way Luke wanted to come home every single day. From inside the house, he had noticed that Sierra and Cole were outside, snuggled together as they talked. He'd given them a few minutes, choosing to check on Hannah although he knew they had the monitor because he'd seen it sitting on the table. Being as quiet as he could be, he returned to the back door, unable to resist joining them when he saw them kissing. God, watching them was hotter than hell.

And now, as he sat across from them, seeing Sierra tease Cole's broad, hairless chest, he wasn't able to hide the erection now straining behind his zipper.

Truthfully, he was a little surprised that Sierra was opting to do this in broad daylight, but he wasn't going to bring it up because he sure as hell didn't want her to stop. He was pretty sure Cole felt the same way.

"Now it's your turn, baby," Luke told Sierra when she sat up to face Cole once again. "But I want Cole to keep his hands to himself."

Sierra grinned as she slipped her shirt up and over her head, not hesitating as she did. The evening air was comfortable, maybe a little on the cool side, but Luke didn't think her nipples were puckering because of the air temperature. After removing her sheer, lacey bra, she paused, seemingly waiting for him to tell her what to do next.

"From where I sit, it looks like Cole's ready to feast on your pretty breasts. But remember, he can't touch you."

Luke had to rub his hand over the length of his denim covered cock when Sierra leaned forward, lifting the beautiful pink tipped mound and pressing it against Cole's mouth. Luke's eyes met Cole's momentarily before his lover began to lick and suck until Sierra was moaning, holding Cole's head to her breast as she ground her chest against him, her other hand squeezing and pinching her other nipple. They didn't need his instruction for a few minutes as she continued to alternate, her hand squeezing and teasing one breast while Cole devoured the other.

"I think one of you, maybe both, are overdressed," Luke growled as he continued to stroke himself through his jeans. In a minute, he was going to have to free himself from the constricting denim or he wasn't going to be able to stand the pain. They got him so damn hard, and he was doing nothing more than watching.

Sierra slipped off of Cole's lap, quickly sliding her own jeans and panties down over her hips before ridding Cole of his. Luke watched in awe at how excited she appeared to be. Truth be told, they hadn't been all that spontaneous lately, usually opting to sneak in a little time while they were in bed, but with Hannah, they rarely had opportunities like this and Luke knew they needed to grab them up whenever they could.

"Now sit on his lap, but face me," Luke demanded as he pushed up from his chair. He didn't bother removing his own clothes because this wasn't about him. This was about the two of them right now.

When Sierra situated herself on Cole's lap, taking the initiative to stroke Cole's beautiful hard cock against the lips of her pussy, Luke was the one growling. He lowered himself to his knees, watching for a moment before he used his fingers to open the soft, swollen folds, exposing her clit so that she could tease herself more.

"Damn that's fucking hot," Luke groaned. He had to admit, this was one of his favorite positions, but usually he was the one with Sierra in his lap. He loved the raspy warmth of Cole's mouth on his cock and the way Sierra squirmed in his arms while he pleasured her as well. Now it was Luke's turn to return the favor, and he was tired of waiting.

"Link your hands with his," Luke demanded and waited not too patiently while Sierra slowly released Cole's cock from her grip before letting Cole twine his fingers with hers. "Keep them at your side. I don't want to see either of you moving."

Luke noticed the way Sierra tried to grind against Cole's cock, but in their position, she wasn't going to be able to do anything without Luke's help. Keeping his fingers on the lips of her sex, he held her open as he lowered his head, using his tongue to gently flick over her clit while brushing his cheek against Cole's smooth, satiny length, the stubble on his jaw scraping lightly against him. Both of them tried to get closer to him, but Luke moved just out of their reach.

Using one hand, Luke cupped Cole's balls while continuing to graze Sierra's clit with his tongue slowly, making sure he wouldn't send her over any time in the near future.

To Luke, teasing them was one of the most fascinating aspects of their foreplay, but watching Sierra fly apart was even more thrilling, only he wasn't ready for that just yet.

He turned his attention to Cole, sliding his mouth over the smooth, swollen head of Cole's cock, sucking hard while he used his thumb to press circles against Sierra's clit, his other hand roughly kneading Cole's balls. Both of them groaned, but when Sierra tried to move her arms, Cole managed to hold her back and Luke smiled to himself. The man didn't mind sexual torture of any kind, but one of these days, Luke was going to push him to his limits.

Not today though. He knew they didn't have all the time necessary to do everything he wanted to do to them, so he focused on Cole, taking him fully into his mouth, slowly at first then moving more intensely up and down his shaft until the muscles in Cole's forearms were standing out in stark relief, his release close.

Stopping abruptly, Luke felt the tension in his own body as his need intensified, but he managed to ignore it. "I want to watch you ride his cock. I want to watch as he slides deep inside your pretty wet pussy."

Dropping back until his ass rested on the back of his heels, Luke remained on the ground at their feet, his eyes focused on Sierra's glistening pussy as she hurried to do as she was instructed. Luke knew it had nothing to do with anything he expected. Her urgency was due to the fact she was going to fly apart at the seams any moment, and he wanted to see it firsthand.

Using the arms of the chair as a brace, Sierra slowly slid down on Cole's iron hard shaft, her body taking him in inch by delectable inch until she was fully seated with him inside of her. She began to move, slowly at first and then faster as Luke used his thumb once more over her clit, his other hand sliding just beneath Cole's balls, teasing that sensitive spot that always had Cole groaning with frustration. Like now.

"That's it, baby. Fuck him hard and fast."

Luke couldn't see Cole because he was hidden behind Sierra's petite body, but he could see the muscles in his legs as they tightened, hear his growls as he tried to hold on until Sierra was right there with him. It didn't take long before Sierra's moans intensified and she cried out, her body stilling until Cole lifted her hips and thrust up inside of her once, twice before he too was groaning his release.

Luke was hard enough to pound railroad ties into cement with his dick, but he knew his satisfaction would have to wait. If, for no other reason than he was holding out.

For just a little while longer anyway.

~~*~~

Every muscle in Sierra's body was relaxed, and she wondered whether she was going to be able to walk into the house on her own two legs.

She hadn't expected that. Although, she absolutely was not disappointed. It had been far too long since they'd done something quite so spontaneous. For most of her pregnancy, Luke and Cole had both been too cautious with her. Then there was the restrictive time after Hannah was born when she had to settle on watching, or those downright intriguing times when they managed to send her into hyperspace with only their mouths. But now there weren't any excuses.

Quite frankly, she was looking forward to more times like this. Not only the sex part, but the conversation she and Cole had had prior to. For the first time in a long time, she felt as though he was actually trying to open himself up on an emotional level that she hadn't expected.

Luke lifted her tired, well sated body from Cole's lap and carried her inside before depositing her in the shower. At first she expected him to join her, but he didn't. For a few minutes, she was a little disappointed, but when Cole came walking in, he more than made up for it with his presence.

"Come here," he whispered, his voice a little gravelly. "I'm not done with you just yet."

A zing of heat raced through her, her muscles clenching deliciously as she thought about what that meant. She might've just had him minutes before, but she was more than ready again. That's what times like those did to her. Just being outside knowing that someone could be watching was a turn on in itself. Not that they were watching, but the fact that they could be, somehow heightened the pleasure.

Cole cupped her face in his big hands, and Sierra had to go up on her toes to meet his mouth, absorbing his hunger with her tongue as he kissed her without an ounce of the gentleness that she usually expected from him. She liked this side of Cole. The dominant side, the aggressiveness that he rarely let free. He was so much like Luke; however, she was almost positive she was the only one of them that would admit it. His needs were just as fierce, and he had desires that hadn't been sated yet. She knew it. He knew it. And she was certain Luke knew it.

"God, you taste so fucking good," he groaned into her mouth. "I need to be inside of you again."

Sierra nodded her head, wrapping her arms around his neck as he lifted her easily, his hands gripping her bottom as he pressed her against the tiled wall, his cock sliding deep inside of her in one thrust, forcing a moan from her lips.

"Just like that," she encouraged. "Slow and deep. Cole. Oh, God, Cole."

Sierra had no idea why she was rambling, but she couldn't help herself. She was entirely lost to this man. After everything she'd been through that week, worrying that her seemingly perfect world was coming apart, she was more than willing to give him anything to make him stay. Not that she believed sex was what he needed most of all, but she had vowed that she was going to stop taking so many things for granted and focus on what was important. There was nothing more valuable to her than her two men and their sweet little girl. Nothing.

"Look at me," Cole said roughly, lifting his mouth from her neck as he stared back at her with eyes nearly black, outlined with a small ring of midnight blue.

Sierra gave him her full attention, body, mind and soul right then and there. As he continued to ease deeper before slowly retreating from her body, she tightened her muscles the way he always enjoyed.

"Sierra…" Her name was but a tortured whisper on his lips, and Sierra had to fight back the tears. This wasn't about sex. This was emotional, and she felt it in every molecule of her being.

"I love you," she answered him although he hadn't asked a question. "I love you with everything that I am. I promise you, from this moment on, I'll never let you walk away again."

"I don't want to walk away. I *won't* walk away. I swear to you, Sierra. I'll never walk away again."

Sierra saw in his eyes what she heard in his voice. Cole had needed them, even if he wasn't much for asking for what he needed, she should've known. He was going through a rough time, and she'd allowed their lives to get too off course to notice. It wouldn't happen again.

"Come for me, Cole," she mouthed the words against his lips as the water poured down over them. "Come inside me, baby."

Cole's body hardened even more as he began thrusting faster, deeper until she couldn't hold back her impending release any longer. "Come with me, Cole. Oh, God!"

Sierra's body let go at the same time Cole did, his release meeting hers at the exact moment her heart latched onto his... Tighter this time.

Chapter Twenty Three

One month later…

Cole was just a couple of miles from the site of the new club when his cell phone rang. He figured it was Luke, trying to determine how much longer it would be before he arrived. The man was impatient like that.

Grabbing his phone from the cup holder, Cole hit the green talk button, answering with a smile.

"I'm driving as fast as I can."

The deep, sexy laugh that echoed through the truck's speakers made Cole smile.

"Change of plans," Luke said in a deep, gruff voice.

"Hell. Do you know how far this place is out of the way? I'm less than five minutes away," Cole answered, not taking his foot off the gas. He'd have to go just a little farther before he'd be able to turn around.

"You're still going the right direction," Luke said, rambling off another address before disconnecting the call.

Pulling off to the side of the road so that he didn't risk having an accident, Cole entered the new destination into the GPS on his phone and waited until the directions were displayed. He was a little confused, but it wasn't like he could question Luke. As soon as he recognized which way he needed to go, Cole put the truck in Drive and took off down the two lane highway once more. He watched as the club passed on his right and paid attention to the signs because according to the automated voice, he was going to exit in less than two miles.

Five minutes later, Cole was pulling into a gigantic circle drive in front of a monstrous white stone house. Figuring this must be Xander's house, Cole parked behind Sierra's Escalade and Luke's truck before climbing out.

He was immediately drawn to the house, admiring the wide front steps, the pristine lawn and garden as he made his way up to the front door. Before he had a chance to knock, the oversized solid wood door opened and there in front of him was Luke, cradling Hannah in one arm, his hand placed protectively against the back of her head as she rested her cheek against his shoulder. Cole walked inside, pressing a kiss on Hannah's head as he passed before taking in the rest of the house.

He waited for Luke to say something, but he was left to follow behind him without a word. When they stepped into the open, airy kitchen, Cole was more than ready to question him as to why they were there.

He noticed Sierra was sitting outside, staring out at the beautiful landscape, the colossal stone swimming pool that matched the house, equipped with a waterfall and slide. Unlike their house, Cole noticed there wasn't a house anywhere in the near vicinity.

"What's going on?" he asked Sierra when he joined her. He felt Luke standing behind him, heard him cooing to Hannah as the baby gurgled sweetly.

"What do you think?" Sierra asked, her smile brightening as she stood up to greet him. She walked right up to him, and Cole instinctively pulled her into his arms, letting her wrap her arms around his waist as she pushed up on her toes to kiss him on the mouth.

"About what?"

"The house?"

Cole was confused. He'd never been one to praise someone else's home openly, but for some reason, he expected that Sierra was looking for something. "It's nice."

"Nice? That's all?"

Cole laughed, looking down at her then behind him at Luke. "What's going on?"

"This was her idea," Luke replied, tilting his head toward Sierra as he grinned.

"I want to buy this house," she told him as she took a step back, holding both of his hands in hers.

Her statement had him pausing, waiting to see what she would say next.

"Come on, let me show you around," she said, sounding like an excited child who had just been released to run wild on the toy aisle at a department store.

Cole let Sierra lead him through the house, listened while she explained details about each room. He realized the house was even bigger on the inside than he expected. Six bedrooms, seven bathrooms, two living areas, a huge den. The master bedroom was probably three times the size of the one they had now. The list of rooms went on and on, and Sierra never stopped talking until she was showing him the garage, big enough to hold six cars and then some.

"So, what do you think?" she asked when she was finished with her impromptu tour.

"I'm not sure what I'm supposed to say here," he admitted with a grin.

"It's for sale." She laughed, smacking him gently in the middle of the chest. Leaning up on her toes, she pulled his head down gently and whispered in his ear, "I want us to buy this house. Our house. For the four of us."

"But we have a house," he told her, watching as Luke came to stand beside them.

"But we don't have *this* house," she said sweetly.

"She's not going to be satisfied until you say yes," Luke told him, his own smile mirroring Sierra's.

"What's wrong with our house?" Cole asked, trying to pry more information out of Sierra. It was clear she was up to something, and he didn't want to admit that he liked where this was going. The house was spacious enough to grow with them, much bigger than Luke's. It offered them the privacy he knew they all wanted, and it was close to the new club that Luke had finally decided to purchase and had closed on just a week before.

Sierra pretended to pout as she grabbed his hand firmly and pulled him back inside. She led him back through the kitchen, through the dining room and into the den. Once they were in front of the couch, she gently pushed him and Cole sank down on soft, buttery leather at her insistence. To his surprise, Sierra straddled his lap, staring right into his eyes as she did.

"I want this to be our house. Look at it, Cole. I mean really look at it. This isn't your house, it isn't Luke's house. It isn't my house. This is our house. The place where I want us to live, to raise our children, to spend the rest of our lives."

Cole tried to hide the emotion building in his chest. He knew what she was getting at. Since the day they met, they'd been feeling their way through this relationship. They had moved in with Luke, but the house always felt like it still belonged to him. This wouldn't belong to any one of them specifically, it would belong to all three of them. Together.

"It's not like I'm going to tell you no," he answered her, hoping his voice sounded firmer than it felt.

For the last few weeks, they'd been making adjustments to their schedules, ensuring they had time for one another. Luke had gracefully handed off the nightclub to Kane, asking the man to step up and take over for him, relieving him of his other duties because of the overall changes Luke was making to the structure of Club Destiny. Since Luke owned the building where the nightclub resided, he had come up with a plan, with Cole's help, to redesign and incorporate the original fetish club square footage, once it moved.

At Luke's request, Cole had accepted a permanent position within the club. Owner. They renegotiated the contracts when Logan opted to sell his shares of the club, but only to Luke and Cole, which meant they once again held the majority of the shares. Just the way Luke wanted it.

"You might not tell me no, but I want us to do this because it's what we all want. Can you picture it?"

Sierra's crystal blue eyes shone brightly with a light that could only come from her excitement. Cole placed his hands on each side of her waist, gripping her firmly. "Baby, I understand what you're getting at, and I'm fully onboard with the idea. I'd love to buy this house, make it a home for the four of us."

Luke approached, easing down on the couch beside them with Hannah still looking around intently.

"I'll be more comfortable having the girls close to the club. I wasn't keen on the idea of driving as it was," Luke added.

Cole knew that had been Luke's biggest hang up about the location of the new club and he'd voiced his concern repeatedly. Cole completely understood, and he liked the idea as well.

Sierra leaned in close, pressing her mouth against Cole's ear, her warm breath sending chills down his spine. "It gives us more privacy," she whispered. "I like the idea of being naked under the stars with the two of you right out there in the pool."

Cole liked the idea of Sierra naked anywhere.

Sliding his hands down to her hips, he pulled her closer, grinding his quickly rising erection against the soft spot between her thighs. "Baby, keep talking like that, and we're going to christen this place before we ever close on the deal."

"Are you saying yes?" Sierra asked, pulling back and smiling from ear to ear.

"If it's what you want," Cole said, glancing between her and Luke, "I don't need any more convincing."

Sierra squealed, but then slammed her mouth against his and Cole's entire body ignited. He pulled her flush against him, driving his tongue into her mouth, hearing Luke chuckle as he rose to his feet. A moment later, breathless and horny as hell, Cole heard Luke on his cell phone.

"We're ready to make an offer. Let me know when you want to meet."

~~*~~

Luke disappeared into the kitchen, listening to the realtor on the other end of the phone as he stared down at his daughter, her eyes bright and a small smile tipping her lips. It seemed as though she knew what had just happened and she was fully in agreement.

"We're out at the house now. I'm willing to pay the full asking price, no stipulations. Write up the contract and bring it by, but let the sellers know I want this to move quickly."

Luke was more than ready to move on. When Sierra brought up the idea of buying a house closer to the new club, he couldn't have been happier. Since he wasn't interested in turning their entire lives upside down all on his own, he hadn't mentioned the idea. As soon as she brought it up, he had called a realtor he'd been referred to by Xander, and they got to work. Keeping Cole in the dark wasn't his original intention, but he had wanted it to be a surprise.

For the last few weeks, things had started to fall into place for all of them. With Cole officially walking away from CISS, he had pushed to get him to join him in the new club venture. Luke still felt that he was too damn old to be starting over, but with Cole by his side, he felt as though they could do anything.

"What do you think, baby girl?" Luke asked Hannah, lifting her so he could see her pretty blue eyes. Another smile curled at the edges of Hannah's little lips, and Luke knew she was onboard with the direction their lives were headed, even if she didn't realize it yet. "Yeah? That's what I was thinking too."

A few minutes later, Sierra and Cole joined them in the kitchen, while Luke waited for the realtor to call him back with a place to meet to sign the papers.

"Come here, angel," Sierra said to Hannah when she approached, reaching up to take their daughter.

Luke kissed Hannah quickly before handing her over to her mother and turning to Cole. He motioned him out through the back with a nod of his head and the two of them headed outside onto the patio.

"What do you think?" Luke asked when they were alone. He admired the yard, the pool, the adjoining hot tub, and the immaculately kept lawn.

"It's nice," Cole stated coolly. "Was it her idea? Or yours?"

"Hers." Luke hadn't expected it when Sierra came to him with the idea, but it didn't take long for him to see where she was coming from. The fact that they all four lived in his house, still furnished with his things, definitely made the space feel less like theirs than it should feel.

"What do you think?" Cole asked.

"I think it's certainly time. It seems like the right thing to do. We'll give her carte blanche to design it however she chooses, and we'll finally have a home that suits our needs."

Cole nodded, but Luke couldn't get a read on his thoughts.

"Is there a problem?"

"No."

"Now why don't I believe you?" Luke could tell something was on Cole's mind, but he had no idea what it was.

He stared back at him for a long time, not giving him any space until he spoke up a minute or two later.

"I don't want the two of you thinking that you have to do this for me. I –"

Luke moved closer, putting his hand on Cole's arm, feeling the subtle shift as tension coursed just beneath the surface. "You what?"

"I'm not running again. I just don't want everyone to think they have to walk on eggshells or change everything because of me."

Luke moved even closer, leaving only a breath of space between them. "We're not, Cole. We all want to be happy, and this was Sierra's idea to bring us on an even keel. With a house that belongs to the three of us, we've helped to erase some of what's left of that line that still separates us."

Cole met his gaze, a spark of heat echoing deep in the midnight blue reflecting back at him. Luke felt an answering heat building deep inside. He knew what Cole was thinking.

There was still another line that they had yet to attempt to erase, but they were getting closer. It was inevitable, and Luke wouldn't say as much now, but he was more than ready.

Part Three

Chapter Twenty Four

Two months later…

"How are you feeling?" Sierra asked Ashleigh as they sat at a small table in the back of the little café they'd started visiting at least once a month for lunch.

"Better," Ashleigh answered with a smile. "It's been a rough four months."

Sierra could only imagine how tough things had been on Ashleigh. She only recently learned that her friend was pregnant, and although she'd been a little hurt that Ashleigh hadn't trusted her with the news during a time when she knew she could've used a friend, Sierra understood.

According to Ashleigh, it had been a rocky first few months, but her doctor had assured her that the pregnancy was progressing nicely, and she was finally able to enjoy a little more time out of bed. Having been restricted to very little activity due to some initial concerns, Sierra hadn't seen much of her until recently.

"How's Alex?" Sierra worried that Alex harbored some hard feelings toward Cole for leaving CISS, but she hadn't been able to get anyone to confirm her fears.

"He's doing much better these days." Ashleigh's smile lit up her face. "Really, Sierra. He's happy for the three of you. He realizes how much he put on Cole there for a while, and he still feels guilty about it."

"What about Dylan?" Sierra knew from talking to Ashleigh that Dylan wasn't doing well.

Based on what she'd overheard from Luke and Cole, Dylan was suffering from depression, and they speculated that it was brought on by the anniversary of his wife's death as well as both of his children being out of the house. It sounded to Sierra like Dylan was having a hard time dealing with being alone. From what she could tell, he decided the best way to deal with his emotional state was by numbing himself with alcohol.

"He's actually doing a little better." Ashleigh glanced away as though she were trying to rein in her emotions.

"What is it?"

Ashleigh paused for a second, and Sierra saw her swallow hard.

"Alex was originally trying to send Nate to Austin. He wanted him and Jake to manage Alluring Indulgence's security division down there. Ever since Nate informed Alex that he wasn't looking to go, Dylan seemed to come around."

"Did Alex come up with this idea before or after Dylan stopped working at CISS?"

"Before. I think that's part of what triggered his depression. He's not ready for either of his kids to leave him. I think he feels abandoned."

Sierra could understand. He had up and moved, selling the ranch where he and Meghan had raised their kids just to be closer to Stacey when she started college. For Nate to possibly move three hundred miles away probably was a little difficult to cope with.

"Is he working again?"

Ashleigh leaned back in her chair, placing a protective hand over her baby bump and smiled. "Depends on what you mean by working?"

The smile told Sierra there must be a story behind it. "Is he back at CISS?"

"He is. For now. He's trying, I have to give him a little credit. Ever since the fight –"

Sierra put her hand up, interrupting her friend. "What fight?"

Another smile. "Well, let's just say Alex is a little hot headed when he gets worried. Not that I think it was the best approach, but he and Dylan apparently went rounds."

"Like physically?"

"Yep."

"Were they hurt?"

"Nothing that needed stitches or an emergency room, no. You'd think the two of them could settle their differences like grown men, but they went about it like little boys fighting over the only toy on the playground."

"Oh." Sierra had no idea what to say to that. From the laughter bubbling out of her friend, it seemed that it wasn't serious. At least she hoped not.

"Alex was worried about the pregnancy," Ashleigh explained, her smile disappearing. "First of all, we didn't plan it, and then when I started having problems, we didn't tell anyone. We were so worried. I was worried about the baby, I was worried about Dylan. And then of course Alex was getting a little out of control. He didn't mean any harm, but I don't think he knew how to deal with what he was feeling."

"So they duked it out?"

"Yes. When Cole told him he was leaving the company, he was at a loss. He'd piled so much on Cole in an attempt to try and cover for Dylan, hoping he'd come back to work. When it didn't seem like that was going to work out the way he intended *and* Cole decided to walk, Alex went to talk to Dylan. Needless to say, Alex gave him a piece of his mind."

Sierra tried to picture what it would look like for Dylan and Alex to go toe to toe. The image in her head made her smile although she had no idea why.

"And now?"

"Dylan is back at work. He's made some stipulations, and they are looking for another person – or two – to come in and pick up some of the extra work. Jake and Nate won't be going to Austin, but I overheard Alex on the phone with Gage Matthews. You may know him as Chance Reed."

"The undercover cop?"

"That would be the one. I don't know what they plan to do at the moment, but he's supposed to be meeting with Alex in the next couple of weeks.

"Alex and Dylan decided to promote Jake, and he'll be handling a lot more responsibilities as well. Dylan insists that Nate finish college, so he doesn't want him too involved and taking away from his school work."

Sierra thought about everything Ashleigh had just told her, and she realized how far out of the loop she had been. They hadn't talked much since Hannah was born, and Sierra wondered which of them was more to blame for that. They'd become so close that it sort of surprised her that she put such distance between the two of them. Enough that she didn't even know her best friend was pregnant.

"Enough about them. I want to know how things are with you. How's the new house?" Ashleigh asked, sipping her water.

"It's amazing. Cole and Luke let me decorate it before we moved in. I didn't do any of the work, but they let me pick out anything and everything I wanted. I think I managed to incorporate all three of our styles. Oh, my gosh! I want you to see it."

"Alex and I are hoping to come out there in a couple of weeks. I'm trying to take it easy, and if he knew I was out and about today, he'd probably have a coronary."

"He doesn't know you're out?"

"Oh, he knows I have been. He just doesn't like it, so I don't usually tell him until after the fact."

Sierra knew that feeling all too well, although she felt as though Cole's and Luke's overprotective nature during her pregnancy hadn't had substantial reasons behind it.

"Well, as soon as you're up to it, I want you to come to the house. If you're not, then Hannah and I will stop by and keep you company."

The waitress chose that moment to bring their food and Sierra was glad for the reprieve. She could see the concern still written on Ashleigh's face, and she was worried for her friend.

Half an hour later, after the two of them had stuffed themselves on chicken fingers, French fries and cream gravy - Sierra's one true weakness - the conversation had somehow turned back toward Dylan.

"Is Dylan still seeing Sarah?"

Ashleigh looked down at the table before she spoke. "No. Last I heard, he broke things off with her. If you heard her tell it, they weren't serious, but I've talked to her twice since then and I can tell you that she cares about him."

"Have you talked to him about it?"

"No," Ashleigh said, shaking her head back and forth. "I would never get myself involved in my brother's love life. If you ask me, he's a fool for letting her go."

"Do you think they'll work things out?"

"Not if Dylan has anything to say about it. From the brief conversation I had with him, he feels guilty for moving on. We've all told him that's what Meghan would want, but I don't think he can come to terms with it. The surprising thing is Sarah is just as familiar with loss as Dylan is, but for some reason, he sees his situation as entirely different."

Sierra wanted to ask for details, but she didn't want to seem like she was digging for dirt. She didn't know Sarah that well, having met her only once or twice at a couple of parties. From what she saw, she and Dylan appeared to get along rather well, but it never did seem like an intimate relationship from the outside looking in.

"Sarah's husband died," Ashleigh blurted.

Sierra didn't ask, but she gave her friend her full attention.

"Oddly enough, her husband took his own life."

Sierra's heart stopped beating for a brief second. Despite not knowing the man, she was suddenly overwhelmed with sadness.

"I think Sarah's scared too," Ashleigh continued. "I don't blame her. It had to be hard to lose him. And then to have to go through with Dylan the same sort of thing she went through with her husband…" Ashleigh let the words trail off.

Sierra sipped her tea, trying to swallow the lump that suddenly obstructed her throat. She didn't want to cry, but for some reason, thinking about what could happen to Dylan if he didn't get help was more overwhelming than she expected.

She only hoped and prayed that whatever was going on with him, he'd find the strength he needed to move forward. Before it was too late.

Chapter Twenty Five

"Where's Sierra?" Luke asked when he walked in the front door.

"Lunch with Ashleigh," Cole said, reminding Luke of the conversation they'd had just that morning.

"Right."

"Everything all right?" Cole stood from his place on the couch and made his way to the kitchen. He had been emailing one of the contractor's they hired to do some work on the new club.

They were adding a second floor with a similar setup to the original club. They all agreed to tear down the interior bathrooms and rebuild with an open concept main floor. The second floor would wrap around the exterior only and allow a visual of everything that was going on below from the wrap around hallway.

"Couldn't be better," Luke growled and Cole knew something was up.

"Did you meet with Trent this morning?"

"How'd you guess?"

Cole smiled. He still wasn't sure how Trent managed to push Luke's buttons, but he found it rather amusing. In recent weeks, Luke had admitted openly that he'd much rather work with Xander than Trent. Cole figured that was because Xander was closer to their age and he had a feeling that Trent's outgoing personality became annoying at times.

When Luke stood in front of the refrigerator, Cole chose that moment to move up behind him, pressing intimately against his back. "I know a way to get your mind off of him," Cole said gruffly against Luke's ear, loving the way his body tensed in response.

"Think so?" Luke didn't turn around as he continued to pretend to search the refrigerator, although Cole noticed that he clearly wasn't looking for anything specific anymore.

"I know so."

Although the three of them were attempting to christen every room in the house, one by one, they hadn't made it to the kitchen yet.

"Then I only have one question," Luke growled, closing the refrigerator door, but not turning around.

"What's that?"

"Who's in charge this time?"

Cole's entire body reacted to the question. He knew Luke wasn't giving him complete control. At least not yet. They had begun to do things a little differently lately, and the best part about it, they both seemed to want the same thing. They were taking their time though. Cole knew it wasn't easy for Luke to give up his hard earned control, but he was enjoying the hell out of pushing him to the breaking point.

"Turn around," Cole demanded, answering the question by his simple command.

Luke slowly turned to face him and the desperate desire swirling in his eyes was unmistakable.

"Hannah just laid down for her nap, so I've got plenty of time," Cole told him.

"That right?" There was a noticeable tremor in Luke's voice, and Cole recognized it to be the same lust now coursing through his veins.

"Naked. Now." Cole didn't give him a chance to argue, he merely turned to walk away, finishing his statement over his shoulder as he headed out of the room. "As much as I'd love to do this right here, I've got a better idea. When you're ready, meet me upstairs."

This house was different from Luke's, however, he and Luke had commandeered one of the guest bedrooms for themselves. Well, more like for the three of them when they wanted to go all out, but they found that they used it more than Sierra lately. Lately she seemed content to observe, or so she said. Cole didn't buy her story because every time she came to watch, she ended up getting herself off with her own hand, but he didn't argue with her.

Cole made his way to the room they used to play in. They installed a lock when they moved in, although they didn't use it regularly. Sierra liked the idea of being able to lock it for when they had company, and of course when Hannah got older. No reason to advertise what they had going on in there.

During the move, they managed to depart with some of the items Luke had acquired from the club. They didn't feel as though they'd get much use out of it because BDSM undoubtedly wasn't their thing, although they had invested in a four poster bed for the room that worked perfectly for what Cole had in mind.

As he was getting things in order, Luke walked in. Cole had to smile. He was still fully dressed, but his jeans were unbuttoned, and he was stroking his impressive length slowly.

"You're not naked."

"I figured I'd let you do the honors," Luke stated, still seeming to think he was going to be the one in charge.

Oh, how wrong he was.

Cole did like the idea of helping Luke get naked though. He had no intention of giving up control to Luke this time, but he knew that getting Luke right where he wanted him wasn't going to be a sudden thing. The more they worked toward it, the more Cole could tell Luke was obviously open to the idea. Today, since they were alone for a little while, Cole fully intended to show Luke what the future had in store for him.

After making his way across the room to Luke, Cole relieved him of his clothes without preamble and then did the same with his own. When they were both naked, Cole took a minute to study him blatantly. The man was perfection. Tall, lean, sexy as fucking hell. He knew Luke had started working out more ever since they began interacting with Xander and Trent on a daily basis. Xander Boone was intimidating, to say the least. At six-foot-six-inches, two hundred and seventy five pounds, the man was a fucking mountain. Even Cole found himself putting in a little extra time at the gym from time to time, although neither of them would admit it was because of their own egos.

"What now?" Luke asked, his voice raw and gruff as he stared back at Cole.

Cole wanted to tell him to get on the bed, but he opted to kiss him first. Moving in close, Cole laced his fingers in Luke's silky dark hair and pulled until their mouths aligned. The slow, sinuous thrust of tongues continued as Cole took what he wanted. Driving his tongue in deep, he mimicked what it would be like when he finally took exactly what he wanted from Luke, although he knew that today wouldn't be that day.

When Luke's hands came up, his fingers digging into his scalp, pulling him roughly against him, Cole let loose with all the passion he held in check each and every day. It didn't seem to matter how long the three of them had been together, Cole found he wanted both of them with the same intensity he'd felt from the very beginning. Possibly even more so.

When the kiss halted because they needed air, Cole used his fist full of Luke's hair to tilt his head back slightly. Keeping his tone low and insistent, he instructed Luke to get on the bed.

The answering growl that tore from Luke's chest had Cole's dick harder than before, which was saying a lot considering what his brain had been conjuring up for their little rendezvous. His body was primed and ready for this.

Taking one step back, he easily released his grip on Luke's hair, their eyes never breaking contact. It was a battle of wills and Cole would be damned if he was going to lose. Not this time. Several long seconds ticked by before Luke turned and made his way over to the bed, his tall, mouthwatering form moving gracefully and with ease. Without question, Luke situated himself in the middle of the bed before lying back against the pillows. Cole eyed the feast laid out right there before him.

With his cock jutting up from his body, his legs spread, and his arms folded behind his head, Luke McCoy damn near managed to steal his breath. The man was hotter than the fucking sun.

Swallowing hard, Cole reminded himself that he wasn't in a hurry. Based on his calculations, they had about an hour and that was plenty of time for what he wanted to do next. As Luke looked on, he retrieved the items he needed from the bedside table and turned to face him. Handing Luke a long piece of black silk, he instructed him to blindfold himself.

Luke's eyebrow cocked briefly at the same time a small smile tilted his lips, but he did as Cole instructed, tying the fabric behind his eyes, effectively blocking him from seeing what was happening. That's when Cole grabbed the other items he needed. He wasn't about to show Luke because the man would find a way to turn the tables, and Cole wasn't about to let that happen.

"Stroke your cock," Cole instructed as he moved around to the bottom of the bed. "Do you like being blindfolded?"

Cole held out through the silence, waiting patiently for Luke to answer. He knew that his boldness had caught both Luke's and Sierra's attention lately, but Cole was tired of sitting back, waiting for what he wanted.

As much as he understood the dynamic between him and Luke and the reason that it worked so well, he knew there was more that they needed from one another. The only way he knew to make that happen was to open himself up some. Maybe not the easiest way to handle the situation, but as far as Cole was concerned, it seemed to be working.

~~*~~

Luke's cock was hard as granite.

That fact wasn't what surprised him, but being blindfolded – willingly – was.

In all of his life, Luke never imagined he'd be giving in so easily to anyone. Except this was Cole and when it came to this man, he knew he'd go to the lengths of the earth just to make him happy.

Considering they spent months, hell, probably years, dancing around what would turn out to be one of the greatest loves of Luke's life, he shouldn't have been shocked at any of the emotions Cole managed to draw out of him. Least of all his willingness to succumb to what Cole clearly wanted from him. He still wasn't sure how he never noticed the true alpha nature that Cole harbored deep down.

Remembering that Cole had asked him a question, Luke answered. "I don't mind it," he said without enthusiasm.

"You don't mind it? Or you like it?"

Luke fought the urge to smile. He couldn't see Cole at all, but he could sense his eyes on him. "What do you think?"

"I don't want to assume. Tell me." Cole's tone was laced with demand, and Luke felt a surge of defiance down deep. He wondered if that's what Cole felt when he gave in to him.

"I like it," Luke ground out. "I'd like to feel your fucking mouth on my cock more though."

Cole's raspy chuckle sent another surge of adrenaline pumping through him, and Luke had to squeeze the base of his cock to keep from giving in too soon.

The bed shifted, and Luke prayed like hell Cole was about to wrap his incredible mouth around his dick. When he felt movement up near his side, he knew he wasn't going to get what he wanted, and he growled in frustration. What came next damn near made him come in his own fucking hand.

Cole's firm grip slid into his hair. A sharp bolt of pain rippled through his scalp as Cole turned his face in the direction that he felt movement, and the smooth tip of Cole's cock brushed lightly against his lips.

"I want to feel your lips on my cock first," Cole told him.

Luke wanted to defy him, wanted to pull away, but he didn't. Considering he wasn't tied to the bed, he was free to move in any way he wanted, he could've easily taken control of the situation, but he kept one hand flat on the bed, the other firmly gripping his own cock.

He let his tongue dart out over the engorged head that rubbed lightly against his lips and reveled in Cole's answering groan.

"You don't know how long I've waited for this," Cole told him as Luke began using the flat side of his tongue along the swollen vein running down the underside of Cole's cock. "I've wanted to fuck your mouth and watch you take me as deep as you can."

Luke didn't say a word and other than using his mouth, he didn't move. He gripped the comforter that he was laying on with both hands, forgetting all about his throbbing cock as he focused on giving Cole exactly what he wanted. When Cole shifted, Luke was forced to move his hands up toward the top of the bed. It was then that he found himself practically pinned to the mattress with Cole's muscled thigh against his right side, his right calf against his other side so that he was practically straddling his head.

"Suck me," Cole demanded as he pushed slowly inside of his mouth and Luke opened, allowing him in deeper as he stroked with his tongue, letting Cole use him the way he'd used Cole so many times before. As much as he wanted to deny that he didn't enjoy it, being at Cole's mercy was almost liberating. He didn't have to worry about commanding the situation, or someone looking to him for direction.

"Fuck that feels so good." Cole pressed deeper, and Luke turned his head slightly to better the angle, allowing the swollen head to brush against the back of his throat briefly before Cole pulled out again. Long minutes passed as Cole continued to fuck his mouth, somehow maintaining control much longer than Luke would've been able to.

"Do you want me to come down your throat?" Cole asked as he pulled out slowly, then began sliding back in.

Luke used his teeth lightly against the vein along the underside and Cole groaned again. When he pulled back out, Luke answered him, "Take what you want from me."

Luke wanted so much more than he was willing to ask for at the moment, and he knew that was more due to fear than anything else. Instead of telling Cole to fuck him, he let him use his mouth until his hand tightened in his hair once again and Cole was fucking past his lips ruthlessly.

"I'm gonna come. Fuck!" Cole's breaths were uneven, and Luke could feel his body vibrating at his side as he continued to fuck his mouth. He sucked harder, wanting to push Cole over, giving in to the same hunger that was building inside of him.

"Fuck yes!"

Cole's cock stilled, swelling even more before Luke's mouth was filled and he was swallowing desperately, trying to suck him dry.

Cole didn't move for what seemed like a long time, but Luke didn't try to force him either. He remained as still as possible, making sure Cole understood that he wasn't going to put up a fight. Now that Cole had taken the edge off, he wanted to see what would come next.

Chapter Twenty Six

Cole was still trying to catch his breath and get his head to stop spinning by the time he managed to make it to his feet beside the bed. That was the first time that had ever happened, and he knew he'd never forget the way it felt to fuck Luke's mouth while he gave in to him, relinquishing that control that seemed impenetrable at times.

Moving around to the other side of the bed, Cole grabbed two of the scarves they used frequently to secure Sierra to the bed and made quick work of tying Luke's arms to the headboard. He watched Luke's face, enjoying the tense lines as he fought to hold himself back. He'd much rather use handcuffs, but he knew better than to make Luke feel as though he couldn't get free if he absolutely wanted to. He was willing to push the man only so far this first time.

When he had him as secure as he could get him, leaving his legs free for now, he crawled up on the bed, his cock beginning to harden once more at the sight of Luke sprawled out before him.

"Spread your legs wide," Cole instructed him, half expecting Luke to refuse. When his long, thick legs moved outward, Cole's breath lodged in his chest. The amount of trust Luke exuded with that movement alone was more than Cole expected. Now he just needed a little verbal reassurance. "Do you trust me?"

"Implicitly." Luke's answer was immediate and honest, making Cole smile.

Leaning forward, he brushed his lips over the head of Luke's cock, watching it bob in response. He refused to touch him with this hands just yet, wanted to tease his lover as long as he possibly could. He knew he couldn't hold out for too long because Hannah would be waking soon, and Cole refused to walk away without giving Luke what he so desperately needed.

After a few minutes of torment with only his mouth, Cole began stroking Luke's rigid cock with one hand. He nearly jumped when he felt a soft, cool hand on his back. Turning slightly, he smiled at Sierra as she moved closer, being as quiet as possible. As though she understood what his plan was, she handed him the tube of lubrication that was lying on the edge of the mattress before climbing on beside him. Cole moved when she did so as not to give her presence away.

He released Luke's cock, his eyes roaming down his beautiful body as he popped the top on the lubrication, noticing how Luke's thighs tightened at the same time his breathing increased. Surprisingly, Luke didn't ask any questions.

When he had his fingers coated, he leaned down, wrapping his lips around Luke's thick cock once more, sucking him deep several times as Sierra slid her hand down his spine, making him tremble from just her touch. This time, when he pulled away, he cupped Luke's balls with the hand free of lubricant, squeezing gently at the same time Sierra leaned forward and sucked him deep in her mouth.

"Holy fucking shit," Luke groaned, his body bucking up off the bed.

"Lift your knees," Cole demanded and Luke's legs instantly bent, his feet planted firmly on the bed as he continued to thrust in Sierra's mouth.

Cole didn't hesitate before sliding one lubricated finger into Luke's virgin ass slowly, doing his best not to hurt him. Luke's moans intensified, and Cole considered it his acceptance, so he began fucking him slowly, squeezing his balls as he did. Watching Sierra suck Luke was enough to make his own cock hard once more, but he knew there wasn't anything he could do at this point. He wasn't going to push Luke.

Slipping the second finger inside Luke, Cole began fucking him with slow, shallow strokes repeatedly until Luke was pushing against his hand, groaning in earnest.

"Fuck!" Luke's body bucked up off the bed. "Make me come, Cole. Goddammit, make me fucking come!"

Taking Luke's demand as permission, Cole began fucking him harder, his fingers going deeper, angling to intensify the pleasure as he leaned down and sucked Luke's balls into his mouth. He didn't let up as Sierra wrapped one hand around the base of Luke's cock as best she could, stroking him in a rhythm that matched Cole's fingers burying deep inside Luke's ass.

"Fuck!" Luke ground out the word, his body tensing, his ass gripping Cole's fingers as his balls tightened and he came with a barely restrained roar.

It was only a few minutes before they heard the sweet sound of Hannah cooing from the monitor sitting on the nightstand, and Sierra quickly dismissed herself, leaving Cole to untie Luke. He released one of Luke's hands before disappearing into the adjoining bathroom, quickly washing the lube from his hands before returning to find Luke still lying on the bed in the same position he left him, though he was no longer restrained or blindfolded.

He wasn't sure if he should say anything, but he moved closer to the bed.

"Come here," Luke demanded, his tone firm.

Cole was a little nervous, wondering whether Luke was going to deny exactly what just happened. When he didn't say another word, simply reached over and grabbed Cole's arm until he was tumbling down onto the bed, he was shocked. Luke quickly flipped them until he was on top of Cole, his lips coming down against his in a kiss that reflected the same desire that he knew still lurked just beneath the surface.

Neither of them were in any shape to go again, – at least not right away – but Cole knew that the next time this happened, there weren't going to be any hard limits between them.

Luke broke the kiss, his fingers laced tightly in Cole's hair, his arms beside his head. Their eyes locked on one another – midnight blue versus stormy green.

"Thank you."

Cole couldn't hide his shock at Luke's words. He wasn't sure what he was thanking him for.

"Next time…" Luke's words trailed off, but Cole didn't tear his eyes away. He wanted to know what Luke was going to say.

"What? Tell me."

Luke didn't say a word for long seconds, his eyes never straying. "I trust you," Luke whispered the words, but Cole heard so much more than just those three syllables. Luke might not say it out loud, but he was acknowledging more than Cole ever expected him to.

~~*~~

By the time the day dwindled to night, Luke was still riding a high from what had happened earlier in the day with Cole. He had thought of little else and he wondered if he ever would. In fact, he'd been so taken aback, he opted not to go back to the club although he was supposed to meet Xander. The man would just have to wait because quite frankly, Luke needed a little time. He didn't want to be alone, but he wasn't interested in doing anything other than lounging around the house with Sierra and Cole.

Now that Hannah was down for the night, Luke and Sierra were sitting outside under the stars while Cole cleaned up from dinner.

"You ok?" Sierra asked as she moved to sit on his lap.

"Never better," Luke said, realizing he'd been saying that a lot lately, but for the first time in as long as he could remember, he actually meant it.

Sierra smiled at him as she snuggled up against him. "That's the first time I've ever believed you when you said that."

Luke grinned, sipping his beer while holding Sierra against his chest.

"It's true."

"Does it have anything to do with what happened earlier?"

"Yeah," he admitted honestly, not looking to elaborate on the subject, even if this was Sierra and he knew she'd be curious.

The three of them had evolved in different ways since they met, more so since they decided to give this relationship a go permanently, but Luke hadn't exactly expected to go down the path he was venturing down now. And not just his path with Cole. Although he liked to insist, even to himself, that he was always going to be the one in charge, he liked the fact that he could hand over the reins from time to time. Knowing that he could trust Cole and Sierra with his life only made it that much easier.

"I'm happy," Sierra said when the silence descended for a little too long.

Luke didn't need to ask her why. He could tell. For the last month or so, they'd made some significant changes in their lives, and so far, they'd drastically improved their relationship. Not that Luke wanted to get into the habit of making changes just for the sake of trying to fix issues, but in this case, it was long past time.

The new house, the new club, it all seemed to fit into their lives. Much more so than watching Sierra and Cole try to form their lives around his. Luke preferred things the way they were now.

"Did you have lunch with Ashleigh today?" Luke asked absently.

"I did. She's doing better. The doctor is letting her out of bed, although I'm not sure Alex knows she's actually doing it."

Luke chuckled, taking another long pull on his beer. He remembered how he and Cole were when Sierra was pregnant. Even at the time he knew they were probably taking things a little overboard, but no one could've told him that at the time. It was a male thing. He and Cole wanted to protect her, even from herself. It might not make sense, but it's the way it was.

"Did she mention Dylan?"

"Yeah, she did. I don't know if he's doing better or if she just wants him to be doing better."

"Kane said he hasn't seen him in the bar as frequently as he was there for a while."

"She said Dylan and Alex got into a fight. A physical fight."

Luke laughed, the image of the two of them going at it flashing through his mind's eye. "Wish I could've seen that one."

Sierra smacked him playfully on the chest, and Luke laughed again. "What was that for?"

"You're a typical male."

Well, he could've told her that. He didn't say as much though.

Cole chose that time to walk outside, carrying two beers. He handed one over to Luke before taking a seat on a chair opposite them.

"What's up?" Luke asked Cole, noticing he had a concerned look on his face.

"Nada," Cole answered solemnly, staring out at the water.

Sierra obviously took his nonchalance to mean something because she sat up and faced him squarely. "What's wrong?"

"I just got off the phone with my mother," he said, not looking at either of them.

"And?"

"She and Jackson want to come visit."

Luke grinned to himself, trying to hide his smile behind the lip of his beer bottle. Victoria and Jackson had taken quite an interest in Hannah, but Luke fully expected them to because Victoria was her paternal grandmother. In fact, they'd taken quite fondly to Sierra as well, even before the pregnancy so, needless to say, when they learned that they were going to be grandparents, they were quite excited. For some reason, Cole was somewhat uncomfortable by their visits.

"That's wonderful," Sierra said, getting up and moving over to sit on Cole's lap. "Do you have a problem with that?"

"Not necessarily, but you might."

"Why would I have a problem with it?" Sierra was watching Cole intently, and Luke was waiting for what Cole could've possibly come up with for his reason.

"They want to keep Hannah overnight," Cole stated. "Something about wanting to give us a night alone."

Sierra smiled which actually surprised Luke. She had only let Veronica watch Hannah overnight one time, and that was the week they had moved in to the new house. Luke thought they were going to have to tranquilize her to keep her from freaking out. She'd made it through the night, but not until she called her mother at least five times. Veronica had secretly texted Luke, asking that he intervene. That or take her phone away.

"I think that's great. Are they staying with my mother when they come down?"

Cole's head jerked toward her like she'd actually slapped him and he stared at her like she'd lost her mind.

"You're ok with it?"

Luke fought the urge to laugh. He really did find this amusing.

"And you're not?" Sierra asked. She glanced over her shoulder at Luke, and he simply smiled back at her. "What about you?"

"I don't have a problem with it," Luke told them. "You know Veronica's going to make sure Hannah is just fine if that's what you're worried about."

Cole laughed, a sound that was hovering on hysterical. "I don't know what the hell has gotten into you two, but shit, please do me a favor and warn me when you're going to transform into completely different people."

Sierra laughed, throwing her arms around Cole. "And just think, that'll give us an entire night to ourselves."

"Baby, I suggest you abstain from any sort of sexual activity until that time because I can tell you, no one will be sleeping that night." Luke tipped his beer up as he said the words and laughed when they both just stared back at him.

Oh yeah, he couldn't wait.

Chapter Twenty Seven

"Sierra?" Xander's rugged, deep voice echoed across the enormous warehouse and had her stopping what she was doing and turning to face him. From the sound of it, he didn't expect her to be there today.

"Hey," she greeted him, turning back to put the last finishing touch on one of the flower arrangements she'd just put together in the main reception area.

At her suggestion, Luke and Cole decided to go with her idea of enclosing a section of the front of the warehouse to greet guests as well as set up at least two meeting rooms for potential members to meet. With nearly fifteen hundred square feet, Sierra felt they almost went a little overboard, but the outcome was better than she expected. At the very least, the area offered a little more privacy than allowing the main doors to open right into the club, and considering the changes they made, Sierra thought that was a crucial addition.

"Have you seen Luke?" Xander asked as he stood just a few feet away.

"He's giving Logan and Sam a tour of the place," she said with a smile.

It still amazed her how the group managed to utilize the one hundred thousand square foot warehouse effectively and turn it into an immaculate new club that was receiving more than one hundred applications per day.

"Thanks," Xander stated before turning and heading out of the reception space. Before he made it to the exit, he stopped. "Hey, Sierra."

"Yeah?" She turned to face him again.

"The place looks amazing."

His compliment made her smile. It was the first time he'd told her as much. Sierra had grown quite fond of Xander Boone over the last few months. For such an intimidating man, he was one of the sweetest she'd ever met.

"Thanks," she replied, grinning as he once again turned and exited into the newly designed club space.

Sierra had put a significant amount of work into the place, hiring various consultants to help her with the new design, ensuring their overall objective was met. Her biggest concern was that she was going to make the place appear too commercial considering what they had to work with at the beginning. The overall structure of the building was one of the most unique she'd ever seen and now that they were nearly finished, she was more than a little proud of their final product.

There had been several meetings initially with Luke, Cole, Trent and Xander to discuss and outline how they could incorporate what each of them was looking for. What they ended up with was so much more than she expected. Considering the amount of money they put into the place, Sierra shouldn't have been all that surprised.

"Hey, baby."

Cole's rich, sexy voice caught her attention and had Sierra turning to face him.

"Hi," she replied, walking across the spacious lobby area to greet him appropriately.

"Want to do one more walk through?" Cole asked as he held her close, placing a kiss to her forehead as he pulled her against his body.

"That would be perfect," she answered. Sierra was more than a little nervous about the soft opening scheduled for tomorrow night, although no one else seemed to be.

Cole took her hand, and they followed the same path Xander had taken a few minutes before, leaving the lobby and going into the club area.

The space opened up perfectly, an exquisite design of glass and steel that spread out before them, and Sierra stopped to take it all in. It was still hard to believe that this used to be one insignificant space that boasted more concrete than anything. Now, thanks to her insistence, there wasn't anything left of the drab, well-worn brown slab. It was sufficiently hidden by plush carpet, rich, dark hardwood, and expensive, yet understated tile flooring.

Cole stopped just inside the space, glancing from floor to ceiling as she stood beside him doing the same. The main floor had been remodeled completely, and despite Luke's initial intention to keep the restrooms that had been centered right in the middle of the warehouse, Sierra had suggested that they redesign them and move them to a more appropriate location. She insisted that this wasn't going to be a meat market. If they were looking for a much more upscale clientele, then they were going to have to work for it.

Now, directly in the center of the warehouse, on the main floor, there were four glass enclosed rooms that butted up against one another. From where she and Cole stood, Sierra could see straight through to the opposite end of the club, which she certainly liked. The restrooms had been moved to the opposite end of the building, no longer the focus of the space.

On each end of the glass enclosures, two bars stood opulent and proud, backlit with red LED lights that reflected off of the blue tinged glass. When the overhead lights were turned off, which they would be during operating hours, the bars would practically light up the entire area.

In order to keep the openness, a second floor had been added, although they kept a similar design to the other club, incorporating twelve hundred square feet of rooms, some private, some enclosed in glass and visible to anyone who wanted a front row view. From where Sierra stood looking up, she saw mostly steel beams and catwalks and a very sexy wrought iron railing that outlined the second floor. The upstairs rooms outlined the perimeter of the building and accessible from the narrow hallway, which meant that, from the first floor, there was a brief glimpse of each room through the railing, but guests would be mostly hidden from view. Some of the rooms had glass fronts, which would offer occupants the ability to be seen from the outside if that was, in fact, their choice. Others had solid doors that afforded them a measure of privacy.

Cole led her past the first bar, the large glass rooms that could be reserved for the most adventurous types who wanted to be the center of attention, the second bar and then stopped in front of the dance floor. Sierra was a little amused by the fact that Trent insisted on a dance floor. It was nice, she had to admit, and she couldn't wait to see what sort of dances went on there. Trent was currently in the process of trying to persuade Luke to let him hire some dancers of his own. He'd even had a couple of catwalk stages designed and installed for that very possibility. Sierra was pretty sure Luke would cave eventually, but for now he seemed to enjoy making Trent beg.

After checking the few details she had left on her list of the first floor action items, Sierra moved to the stairs with Cole directly behind her. At the top of the back stairs, they turned to the right, entering a code that would allow them access to the main offices.

The area was soundproofed with the most expensive material, but Sierra still doubted it would filter out all of the noise. Because she had a couple of items she needed to follow up on, she stopped by Trent's office first. He wasn't in, so she stepped in, checking to ensure that the blinds had been installed and that the broken tile in the en suite bathroom shower had been fixed. When those items were checked off, she followed Cole to the next office, which belonged to Xander.

"Come in," the rusty baritone called from behind the closed door when she knocked softly.

Sierra opened the door slowly and stepped inside.

"Cole," Xander greeted him quickly, then turned his attention back to his computer screen.

"Just wanted to make sure they were able to get your requests taken care of," Sierra stated, glancing around quickly. She was well aware of the fact that Xander Boone had some rather intense kinks and his office had been outfitted to accommodate those, which she found rather amusing.

"Sure did," he answered with a sly grin, not looking up from his computer monitor.

"Perfect," Sierra said shyly and then backed out of the room with Cole behind her. She heard him chuckle, and she couldn't hide the smile as she shut the door.

"What are you laughing at?" she asked, turning to face him.

"You."

"And why do I amuse you?"

"You're just so damned cute." Leaning down, he kissed her on the nose before she turned away.

"Cute? I'm cute," she mumbled beneath her breath as she moved on to Luke's office.

Out of respect, not knowing whether he was inside talking to Logan and Sam or not, she waited for him to answer. When there wasn't a reply, she opened the door and stepped inside.

All four men's offices were exactly the same size, and they all lined the far back wall of the warehouse, sandwiched between the exterior wall and a wall of windows that overlooked the entire space. From each office, they had a unique view of everything that was going on below them, as well as several of the rooms. Their windows were mirrored so no one else could see in, even if the lights were on, but they could see out.

Luke's blinds were open, and as Sierra stepped inside, she noticed Logan and Sam heading back down the front stairs to the main floor with Luke a few feet in front of them. Wanting to have a minute or two to talk to Sam, Sierra made quick work of checking the last few items on Luke's list and then moved quickly to Cole's office through the adjoining door. The other offices did not connect to one another, but Luke had insisted that they have adjoining doors, although either or both could be locked from each office.

"Were they able to fix the issue in the bathroom?" Sierra asked as she checked to see that the carpet had been fixed per her request.

"Not sure. Maybe you should check?" Cole said gruffly, and Sierra glanced back at him over her shoulder.

"You're a devious man, Cole Ackerley." Laughing, she headed to the opulent bathroom that looked exactly the same in each of the offices to see that the shower door was now in place. Before she could turn around fully, Sierra found herself pressed against the tiled wall with Cole's solid chest sandwiching her from the front.

"One of these days, we're going to christen this office," he growled, his lips coming down to hers softly.

"Promise?" she asked breathlessly, wrapping one leg around the back of his in an attempt to pull him closer.

"Absolutely."

The kiss deepened, her nerve endings danced merrily and she suddenly wished they had a few spare minutes.

Cole pulled away, smiling down at her. "I know, I know. You're supposed to be refraining for the time being."

Sierra laughed. Yes, if Luke had his way, she would not be having sex until later that night. The night she'd been looking forward to since Cole had told her that his mother was coming for a visit. Hannah would be spending the night at her mother's, and Victoria would be there to happily coo and cuddle with her granddaughter.

As much as she hated to be away from Hannah, and she knew Luke and Cole felt the same way, she was looking forward to having this night with them. Sort of like an opportunity to tie up some of the loose ends they'd all been feeling were present in their relationship.

In fact, that meant she had one errand to run before tonight.

"Come on," she said, grabbing Cole's hand and leading him back into his office and then out into the hallway. "I need to check two of the rooms, and then I'm good."

They finished with the impromptu walk through and then headed back to the main reception area where she found Sam waiting for her.

"Can you do me a favor?" she asked in a conspiratorial tone after Cole left her to go back and talk to Luke. Sierra had a plan for the following night when the club opened, and with Sam's help, she just might be able to pull this off.

Chapter Twenty Eight

Luke was the first one home after having spent the better part of the afternoon with Xander going over the last few details before the soft opening of the club tomorrow night. They were ready. More than ready, actually.

Because of the changes they'd made, some of them significant, some not, Luke knew his new club was a fitting tribute to the old club that they were officially letting go of. At least the fetish piece of it.

Before he did anything else, he called and ordered dinner to be delivered, grateful for the services that would deliver practically anything from any restaurant right to the front door. Since he knew tonight wasn't the sort of night that should be celebrated with pizza and beer – well, without the pizza anyway – he knew he had to come up with something.

A few minutes after he hung up the phone, Sierra walked in, a smile spread across her face.

"What are you grinning about?"

"No reason," she laughed as she walked into his arms, wrapping hers around his waist as she looked up at him. "Have I told you how much I love you lately?"

"No, in fact, I don't think you have," he joked, pressing his lips to the top of her head.

"Well, then, I guess you'll have to wait a little longer until I tell you again." Sierra stepped away from him, and Luke smacked her on the ass as she turned.

"What's in the bag?"

"None of your business," she answered slyly as she moved just out of his reach and disappeared into the other room. "Don't you dare come into the bedroom until I tell you that it's ok," she hollered as she headed toward the master bedroom at the back of the house.

Grabbing a beer out of the refrigerator, Luke hoped it would help to calm his nerves. Or maybe just curb his excitement. He had been waiting for tonight for what seemed like forever, although it had only been a week since Cole mentioned his mother was coming into town. It had given him plenty of time to work himself up about the prospect of what would happen. Giving up total control, or even the prospect of it, was much more difficult than he expected that it would be.

Twenty minutes later there was a knock at the front door, and Luke went to answer, knowing it was the food and wondering where Cole was. He should've been there by now. Signing the receipt and adding a generous tip, Luke took the paper bags and went to work in the kitchen, getting everything set up.

By the time he was finished, Cole was strolling in the door with a grin on his face.

"What's with everyone smiling today?" Luke asked, trying to add some of his usual irritation to his voice, but failing miserably. Although he was nervous, he wasn't sure anything was going to spoil this night for the three of them.

"I know you didn't cook this," Cole said as he headed right for the fridge, grabbing a beer and then turning to face him. "Where's Sierra?"

"In the bedroom. She threatened bodily harm if either of us go in there. Ok, maybe not you, but she told me to stay out and if I can't see her naked, *you* can't see her naked." Luke put the last plate on the kitchen table and pulled out a bottle of wine for Sierra.

"Don't you dare come in here!" Sierra yelled from the master bedroom and Cole turned to look at Luke, both of them grinning from ear to ear. This ought to be good.

"We won't come in, but you have to come out here and eat first. Then we'll play," Cole yelled back.

Long minutes later, Sierra joined them in the kitchen, looking exactly the same as she had when she went in half an hour ago. Luke had no clue what she was doing, but he had to admit that he was a little disappointed that she wasn't naked when she joined them. Not that they would have made it through dinner if she was, but he still liked the image the thought planted in his brain.

"What are you doing in there?" Cole asked when the three of them were seated.

Luke didn't hesitate before starting to eat. He figured the sooner he started, the sooner he'd finish which meant Sierra would be naked that much faster.

"Wouldn't you like to know," Sierra said with a wickedly sexy smile.

"I really would," Cole answered with a laugh, although Luke had to give him credit, he was trying to keep a straight face.

"Soon enough," Sierra turned her attention to her food, but Luke could tell they weren't going to make it far. She was pushing her steak around on her plate more than she was eating, and he wanted to pull him right into his lap and devour her whole. Screw dinner, she was more than enough for him.

Granted, he had forced her to restrain from sex for the last week, but he knew she wasn't the only one who was suffering because his dick was already getting antsy. As much as he wanted to, Luke didn't think he was going to be the stoic one tonight.

Fifteen minutes later, Cole was ready to jump Sierra right there at the kitchen table. Just the way she was acting, seemingly nervous and a tad bit coy made him want her more than normal, which was saying a lot. Figuring he was going to have to make the first move because Luke looked as though he were trying to outlast them both, probably on purpose, Cole pushed his plate away.

"Ok, baby, when do we get our surprise?" Cole asked, turning his attention to Sierra as he sat back in his chair, taking a long pull on his beer.

"I need ten more minutes," she said, giddy as a kid on Christmas morning.

"Ten minutes, that's all you get," Luke said gruffly, leaning back with one arm resting on the table, the other slung behind the chair back. Cole admired Luke for a minute, noticing how incredibly sexy he looked when he wasn't as stressed. In the last few weeks, even with all of the changes they'd made, some rather significant such as the club, he seemed more at ease.

"What the hell is she doing in there?" Luke asked with his usual grumble in his voice.

Ok, so much for him being less stressed.

"Hell if I know. I'm pretty sure she's making us wait on purpose."

"More than likely," Luke smiled, probably thinking he looked cool and collected, but Cole could see the tension in his jaw. He began subtly stroking his dick through his jeans. Even seeing that much was driving Cole out of his mind, so he forced himself to his feet and started for the living room.

"Want to go find out?" Cole asked, stopping in the doorway and pacing back into the kitchen. He had no idea where he was going. It wasn't like he wanted to ruin Sierra's surprise, but in his experience, Luke wasn't going to last much longer. Patience was not one of his strong points.

"I can think of something that would help to take the edge off," Luke informed him gruffly, and Cole remained right where he was, facing Luke and doing his best not to glance down to ogle the way Luke continued to rub himself.

"Are you asking or telling?"

Luke's sexy smirk made Cole's dick stir. He waited, wanting to hear which direction this was going to go. As far as Cole was concerned, Luke was going to give in tonight. He was just either going to do this the easy way or the hard way. Cole didn't care which it was. He was prepared to give and take tonight, whatever it took.

"Come here," Luke insisted, not an ounce of request in his tone.

Cole didn't move a muscle. He crossed his arms over his chest and stared back at Luke, waiting patiently for whatever the man could come up with next. He made sure there wasn't any emotion showing on his face, but inside, his blood was quickly coming to a full boil, his lust sparking like a downed electrical wire.

When Luke stood to his full height, Cole spread his legs, ensuring he could maintain his defensive stance once Luke pressed against him, which he knew was going to happen any minute now.

Just as he predicted, Luke was standing a breath away, his intense hazel eyes churning with the same heat coursing through every muscle, every fiber, every molecule within Cole.

For a solid week, Cole had dreamed about this night. He'd come up with a million scenarios on how it would play out and not for a second did he doubt that Luke was going to exert his dominance initially. Cole didn't have a problem with it.

Luke's eyes darted from his eyes down to his lips, and Cole fought the urge to move forward. He wanted to taste him, to inhale the hunger that he knew was brewing deep in Luke's chest, pushing him to want things he'd probably never thought he'd want.

Tonight he would want them.

Cole would make sure of it.

"I want to see your lips wrapped around my cock," Luke grumbled, his voice husky with need. "Remember how you fucked my mouth? Driving your cock deep in my throat?"

Cole remembered, and his cock went instantly hard at the reminder. Again, he didn't say a word, just kept his eyes fixed on Luke's.

"I've thought of little else since that day," Luke continued. "Only I was fucking your mouth, hard and fast while you sucked me dry."

Cole fought the urge to lick his lips.

"Put your hands down at your sides," Luke instructed.

Cole let his arms slowly slide down by his sides. He fought the urge to take control of the situation. He was certain that he could quickly turn the tables, and Luke would be the one taking instructions. The sparkle in Luke's eyes was evidence of how easy it would be, but Cole wanted to make this last.

"Unbutton my jeans."

Slowly, Cole reached for the waistband of Luke's jeans, quickly pulling the small disc free and then dropping his arms back to his sides.

"Do you know how fucking hot you make me?" Luke asked, and Cole was momentarily thrown off course. He expected another command, not a question.

"I think about you all the time. Think about what it feels like when I slide my cock deep in your ass, fucking you while you're buried deep in Sierra's sweet pussy. It makes my cock fucking hard."

While he talked, Cole noticed that Luke was unzipping his own jeans, pulling his cock free. With more restraint than he thought possible, he kept his eyes locked with Luke's, refusing to look down and watch. Damn it, he wanted to watch. He wanted to see Luke stroke his massive erection, wanted to see the small bead of moisture that would form on the tip. Hell, he wanted to do just as Luke described and take his cock deep in his throat, letting him fuck his mouth until he lost control.

"I sit in my office and think about what you look like on your knees, my dick buried in your mouth." Luke brushed his thumb over Cole's bottom lip, pushing the very tip in past his teeth and Cole lost the battle with himself. Sucking Luke's thumb hard, he pulled it fully into his mouth until Luke hissed.

"But you know what I think about most?"

Cole had no idea, but if Luke kept this verbal foreplay up much longer, he was going to rip his clothes from his body and fuck him with or without permission.

Luke leaned in close, pulling his thumb from Cole's mouth. "I think about what it'll feel like when you fuck me. I want to feel you inside of me, Cole. I want you to fuck me until I can't take it anymore and then I want you to come in my ass."

Cole's entire body began vibrating with the need that took over.

"Is that what you want? Do you want me to give up control to you? Do you want to top me, Cole?"

He didn't need to contemplate the answer to Luke's question. There was only one, and he couldn't hold back the word. "Yes."

The next thing Cole knew, Luke was kissing him, his tongue thrusting forcefully into his mouth as their arms reached around the other, hands sliding into hair, pulling each other closer as though they would run if there wasn't something there to hold them together. Pressing his denim covered cock against Luke's thick erection, Cole suddenly wished he was naked.

Wished they both were.

The sound of the bedroom door opening, then closing again had both of them pausing, although neither of them let go. If Cole knew anything, he knew Sierra enjoyed watching them. Without looking at her, he knew she was probably biting her plump lower lip, hope that they would continue blooming inside of her.

As much as Cole wanted to continue this, the night was young, and they had all the time in the world. Tonight would be about stamina and distance, not speed.

"Starting without me?" Sierra asked as she slid up alongside them, her arms wrapping around them both.

"Just warming up," Luke growled, releasing Cole's hair from his grip as he turned to pull Sierra up against them.

"I have another way to warm you up," Sierra added. When her hand slid into his hair, Cole turned his head to face her, witnessing the wanton woman being unleashed.

"Now you're talking," he told her, leaning down and pressing his lips to hers. "Lead the way."

"Come with me," she motioned with her hands and they followed instinctively. Shit, she wasn't going to have to tell them twice.

Cole fell into step behind her as she made her way to the back porch and his dick continued its incessant throbbing. They hadn't yet christened this patio, or the pool for that matter, and he suddenly had the desire to do exactly that. He didn't give a damn how cold the water was.

Sierra moved around to the hot tub, and Cole realized she must've planned ahead because the jets were on and there was steam coming up from the water.

"Strip," Sierra demanded, causing Cole's body to harden, his hands to fist at his sides to keep from grabbing her. Since when did she garner control?

"Is that an order?" Luke asked, bemused.

"Yes." She sounded fairly confident, and Cole wasn't about to question her further. He made quick work of removing his shirt, but he didn't do any more. If she was going for the control position, he was going to make her work for it.

"What are you waiting for?" Sierra asked, appearing confused.

"While we're getting naked, what are you gonna be doing?" Cole inquired.

"Hmmm, what would you like me to be doing?" she asked sweetly, glancing back and forth between the two of them. Cole watched as she raked her eyes up and down both of them, one after the other.

"Gettin' naked," Luke growled.

"You want me naked too?"

So she was going to play the innocent act tonight, was she?

Cole took the decision out of her hands when he moved closer, easing between her spread thighs as she sat on the half wall that surrounded the hot tub and pool. He could see Luke in his peripheral vision, and he realized the man wasn't going to waste time. He was now totally naked and moving into the hot tub.

Their eyes met as Luke came to stand behind Sierra with the bubbling water up to his thighs, his cock standing tall and proud, making Cole's mouth water. He wanted to taste him.

"Naked," Luke demanded, sounding significantly more dominant than Sierra had, and Cole took a step back, toeing off his shoes and then his jeans, leaving him just as naked with his cock jutting up from his body eagerly anticipating one of them. Or both of them. On a normal day, he might just push his luck. Today wasn't normal. And he was pretty damned certain his cock couldn't get much harder.

Cole resumed his position between Sierra's thighs and his breath lodged in his chest when she brushed her soft hands over the swollen head of his dick lightly, as though she were doing it absently. The gleam in her ice blue eyes said otherwise.

From behind, Luke lifted her t-shirt and tossed it on the pool deck alongside the rest of their clothes. Clad in her bra and a pair of leggings, Sierra was sexy as fucking hell, but Cole wanted to see the rest of her.

He didn't have to work too hard because Luke effortlessly unhooked her bra, pulling the straps down her arms and then tossing it to the side as well, freeing her breasts to the crisp evening air. He wasn't sure whether it was the breeze or lust that made her dusky pink nipples pucker, nor did he care.

"Pretty," Cole mumbled as he leaned down and sucked a pebbled tip into his mouth without preamble. If she was going to tease him with her fingers, he was going to offer his own form of payback.

"Cole." His name came from her lips in a breathless moan, and Cole smiled to himself. He laved one nipple, then moved to the other before Luke was repositioning her so that she was lying back in his arms, her upper half being supported by Luke while her hair was immersed in the water.

She didn't question them, although Cole knew the position was rather awkward. Her trust in them was humbling. Moving slowly, Cole helped her out of her leggings and her panties before he slipped into the hot tub, lifting her until her entire body was in the tub. Sierra was laying in the water, her body supported by both of them, her eyes closed while her generous breasts hovered just above water level offering a stimulating visual treat.

When Luke leaned forward to take one soft, pebbled nipple into his mouth, Cole did the same and Sierra gasped, her fingers slowly twining in his hair, holding him close to her chest as they both feasted on her. Gentle wasn't in his current repertoire of skills because he was so fucking hard, he could barely think straight. He sucked and nipped at the puckered tip, making Sierra moan as he slid his hand down between her thighs, his finger caressing the smooth, hairless lips of her pussy. God, he loved that she kept herself bare down there.

Sierra bucked her hips, trying to force his fingers inside of her and Cole smiled against her skin.

"In a hurry?" Luke asked, releasing her breast from his mouth with a pop.

"Yes, damn you," she groaned.

"I'm thinking you've earned a little teasing after what you put us through since you got home," Luke offered, his hand laying flat against her belly while Cole continued to finger her clit. "And you should know better than to try and rush me," Luke scolded her gently. "It only makes me want to draw it out more."

"Ugghh!" Sierra tried to pull away, but Cole took the weight of her body in his arms while Luke lowered himself to one of the lounging seats. Using the buoyancy of the water, they turned Sierra so that her head was beside Cole's face, her shoulders pushing against his clavicle as Luke lifted her legs and placed them over his shoulders, her heels resting on the ledge around the hot tub.

"I want to hear you scream when you come, Sierra." Luke didn't wait for a response as he lowered his mouth to Sierra's pussy while Cole looked on.

Her body hovered just on top of the water, Luke's face buried between her soft, supple thighs as he feasted on her slowly, intently. As she squirmed, using her leverage against the edge behind Luke to thrust her hips to meet every thrust of his tongue, Cole held her upper body, wrapping his arms around her.

"Luke!" One syllable turned into several as Sierra drew out his name.

Wanting to push her past the point of no return, Cole brushed his lips against her ear, then nipping the lobe firmly and whispered loud enough for her to hear him over the hot tub jets. "It's so fucking hot to watch the way you writhe when Luke's eating your pussy."

Another moan from Sierra, only this time, she turned her head closer to Cole's, and he couldn't resist adjusting the angle so that he could kiss her. She devoured his mouth as he ate at her lips, trying, yet failing to reach the pinnacle as Luke continued to lap at the sweetness between her thighs.

"Oh, God!" Sierra screamed, breaking the kiss and Cole noticed Luke had added his fingers to the mix as he continued to use his tongue to torture her, his gaze traveling up her body and resting on Cole's eyes. Had they been anywhere else, Cole would've joined Luke, lapping Sierra's pussy right along with him. He found that she loved the hell out of it when they ate her at the same time.

Sierra began to moan in earnest and Cole knew she was close, he just didn't know whether Luke was going to let her take the edge off yet or not.

"That's it, baby," Cole encouraged her. "Fuck his fingers. Come for us, Sierra." Cole helped her along by wrapping his arms around her and pinching and tweaking her nipples as Luke watched on. "So fucking pretty," he crooned in her ear and she cried out. "Make her come, Luke. I want to watch her come in your mouth."

Apparently his words did it because Sierra's scream rent the night air as her body stilled, her smooth, graceful muscles tensing and flexing. God she was so fucking pretty when her orgasm consumed her. So damn pretty, he wanted to watch Luke do it again.

So Cole suggested as much.

~~*~~

An hour later, Luke's balls were damn near ready to explode. Not only was he sporting an erection that could easily rival a steel pipe, he was so damn ready to come he could barely see straight. After he and Cole managed to get Sierra off several times, she insisted on ruthlessly teasing them, but never letting them come which wouldn't have bothered him so much, except it was beginning to get a little painful.

"I'm going to take a shower," Sierra told them when they walked in the back door.

"A shower?" *Was she fucking kidding?* Was she torturing him on purpose?

"Yes. Want to join me?" she asked coyly, her sexy little ass swaying back and forth as she walked toward the master bedroom. Completely and deliciously naked.

"Fuck yes," he growled, glancing over at Cole who was already in motion. Apparently Cole wasn't much for waiting either.

The shower was large enough to afford them plenty of space and Luke found himself crushed between Sierra's softness and Cole's hardness, the difference between their skin textures driving him insane. He no longer had to wonder what Sierra had come to the bedroom to do because the second he walked through the door, he felt as though he'd been transported to another realm.

Candles in various shapes and sizes lined every available surface, their tips glowing and dancing, bouncing off of the mirrors and dousing the room in a soft, mellow glow. Music streamed from who knew where, a sexy, jazzy tune that didn't help Luke's heightened state in the least.

It was painfully clear that Sierra was more intent on the buildup than she was to getting to the finish line and Luke fought to keep himself from begging them to move this along. The smell of jasmine and vanilla spiced the air as Sierra poured a handful of body wash into her hands before slowly gliding her fingers over his chest while Cole stood behind him, his arms weaving around his lower body, his rough, wet hands stroking his cock slowly.

Within minutes, Luke was ready to beg them to finish him off, which they obviously had no intention of doing. The torturous way they played him, using hands and lips and teeth had put him on edge, damn near to the point of pain. It was both exquisite and downright agonizing.

By the time they were finished with the most sensual shower he'd ever experienced, Luke wasn't sure he was going to make it much longer without taking matters into his own hands. Literally.

Not only had they teased him with their hands, they'd tortured him as they did the same to one another, forcing Luke to watch as Cole washed his own body, taking extra care to stroke his soapy cock longer than Luke knew was necessary. It was almost like the two of them were working together to drive him insane.

Cocking his head to the side, Luke studied them for a second. Was that what they were doing? Were they ganging up on him?

"Hold up," he barked, stopping Sierra in her tracks as she leisurely dried herself off.

Her little eyebrow darted up, and Luke knew the answer before he even asked the question. They were holding back. They were getting him all worked up and holding back on him, probably because they thought he was going to freak out. Or worse. Run.

Cole stood to his full height, his deliciously tanned skin glistening from the remaining water droplets, staring at him as though he were about to burst into song and no one would know what to do with him.

Enough was enough.

Gripping his cock firmly, Luke began stroking himself as he stared at Cole. "Come here."

Cole hesitated a fraction of a second before taking slow, measured steps toward him until he was standing within inches.

"On your fucking knees," Luke growled, glaring at Cole. That aggression that he'd suppressed for so long was rearing its ugly head, and by God, Cole was going to be his outlet. He'd refrained from this for far too long and ever since the day Cole had tied him to the bed, he'd been dreaming about what would happen when they both unleashed their pent up tension. There were going to be fireworks unlike anything they'd ever known.

The only muscle in Cole's body that moved was the one in his jaw that flexed as he stood absolutely still. He was just as worked up, yet he'd been holding back.

Luke took a step forward, closing the gap as Sierra moved around to stand behind him. "Remember what I told you earlier?"

Cole looked like a statue, the only thing giving him away was the way his eyebrows cocked as though he were trying to think about which part Luke was referring to.

"I asked you if you wanted to top me," Luke reminded him. "Is that still the case?"

"More than anything," Cole said with an answering growl.

Luke leaned in close, reveling in the feel of Sierra's soft, smooth hands flowing over the muscles in his back. "Then. Fucking. Do. It."

As though a switch had been flipped, Cole's hand snaked out, sliding into Luke's hair, and he pulled his head down hard. Their mouths crashed together, and Cole never loosened his grip, but Luke fought the urge to grab him. He would prove to them both that he could hand over the control he held close to his chest at all times. Maybe not to just anyone, but Luke would willingly give them exactly what they wanted. If they wanted to own his pleasure, then he would give them the opportunity.

Ragged breaths filled the air as the kiss consumed them both, Cole's body rigid and ungiving as he owned Luke's every desire from that moment onward.

When Cole pulled away, their eyes met once more, turbulent desire reflecting back from the midnight blue orbs. Luke bit his tongue, doing his level best not to demand what his body was so desperately in need of.

"On your fucking knees," Cole growled low and intent and a spark of lust the likes of which Luke had never known speared him. Cole's firm grip in his hair held tight as he used the unleashed power in his arms to force Luke down to his knees.

Sierra's sharp inhale had Cole glancing over at her, but Luke didn't turn. He couldn't. He was fucking mesmerized by the demand in Cole's voice, the need in his grip. Never would he have thought he'd give in to this. Hell, he never expected to want it, but he wanted to hand over the reins for a little while. As long as Cole wanted to take them, he'd willingly let go.

"On the bed," Cole instructed Sierra as he stood stone still with Luke now kneeling in front of him.

Luke felt rather than saw Sierra as she stepped away slowly, climbing up on the oversized bed.

"I want to watch you play with your pretty little pussy while Luke sucks my dick," Cole added, and another sharp pang of intense desire raced through Luke's veins.

Damn, where the hell has *this* Cole been? This was an entirely different side of a man he thought he knew so well. A side he could quickly get used to.

Cole's fist tightened in his hair and another bolt of pleasure/pain ricocheted through him, making his dick harder than steel and begging for attention.

"I want to see your lips wrapped around my cock. I'm gonna watch you suck my dick, but I'm not gonna come in your mouth."

Luke tried to nod, unsure when he'd fully relinquished control, but it was gone. All of it. He was as submissive as he'd ever been and eager to please this man. His lover.

The smooth head of Cole's cock brushed against his lips and Luke opened instinctively, his eyes locked with Cole's as he slid his tongue over the satiny tip. A bead of moisture clung to the tip and Luke lapped it up before reaching for Cole's shaft with one hand.

"No hands," Cole barked. "I want your mouth. Only your mouth."

Luke barely restrained the growl that rumbled in his chest. Cole owned him, every part of him, and he suddenly wanted everything he could give him. Memories of the time Cole had tied him up assaulted him and Luke suddenly wanted to be on the bed, flat on his back with Cole's impressive body pressing him into the mattress. He wanted to witness his strength, to feel the delicious weight of his body, to look into his eyes as the man took him to places he'd never imagined he'd go.

Dropping his hand, Luke used his lips, teeth and tongue to pleasure Cole as they settled for an intimate stare off.

"I love watching my dick slide in and out of your lips. The heat of your mouth consuming me," Cole mumbled.

He broke eye contact with him to look up at Sierra, and although Luke couldn't see her, he could imagine what she looked like. Her long, black hair spread out around her as she propped herself on a pillow, her fingers teasing her clit. Watching her bring herself pleasure was one of the hottest things Luke had ever witnessed and he was disappointed he couldn't see her now.

Cole's thrusts increased as he held Luke's head immobile, driving his cock deeper until Luke felt the flared head at the back of his throat. He fought the urge to gag, not wanting to disappoint Cole because at that moment, he knew that his pleasure was going to be found in Cole getting his. This side of the coin was much different from what Luke was used to, but with Cole at the helm, he felt as though this was exactly where he was supposed to be.

"Fuck." Cole jerked his head, ramming his cock deep but slowing. "Keep that up, and I won't last."

Luke wanted him to come, but he was torn between wanting to send his lover over the edge now and waiting until he could feel him buried inside of him. Surprisingly, he wanted the latter much more than he expected. He'd dreamed about it lately, waking up with his dick in his hands and a hard on that he knew would never be sated until Cole took exactly what he wanted.

The feeling was surreal and goddammit, Luke was fucking tired of waiting, but he knew he couldn't pick and choose what he could control. His patience was wearing thin after what Sierra had put him through earlier and since he and Cole had talked in the living room, he'd been ready for this.

Cole stopped thrusting, holding Luke's head still but tilting it so their eyes met once again.

"It looks like our woman needs some attention."

Luke nodded, unsure what he was even trying to relay, but he was more than willing.

When Cole let go of his hair, Luke stood to his feet, and he turned to face Sierra. His cock pulsed when he noticed what she was doing. A purple vibrator in her hand, she was teasing her clit as she stared over at the two of them, her bottom lip between her teeth. She was hanging by a thread and Luke was more than ready to make her come again.

"My turn to watch," Cole stated firmly. "Eat her pussy while she sucks you."

Luke could easily get onboard with that. Anything to get him closer to Sierra was in all of their best interest. He only hoped he could keep from coming when her talented mouth took hold of him.

They were undoubtedly testing his limits tonight. Luke just prayed he could outlast them. He'd always managed before, but then again, he'd never had them gang up on him like this.

Fuck. He hated tests.

Chapter Twenty Nine

Once they were situated on the bed, their bodies seemingly twisting and contorting until the perfect position was reached so that oral pleasure was the optimal goal, Sierra was vibrating with need. Sixty nine was one of her favorite sexual positions.

Watching her men and the way they found pleasure in one another was so damn hot, she was surprised she hadn't come ten times already. She knew her patience was being tested tonight. If anything, Cole was unquestionably the most patient out of the three of them and tonight he was clearly in control. Something she fully intended to reenact on multiple occasions in the future.

The man was intoxicatingly sexy, but when his true alpha side dominated, he was a force to be reckoned with and her body reacted to his authority in cataclysmic proportions.

Luke hovered above her, his thick cock begging for her attention, and she wasted no time, wrapping both hands around the base and feeding him into her mouth as she tried to keep it slow. With his mouth doing wicked things between her thighs, it took a tremendous amount of effort to focus on bringing him the utmost pleasure. She didn't want to make Luke come yet, but in this position, he had more control than she did. He pumped his hips, driving his cock into her mouth as she angled her head to take all of him, moaning as she did.

Cole found the items she'd bought specifically for this encounter, wanting nothing more than to please Luke in every way possible. From beneath Luke's massive body, Sierra could see Cole clearly, their eyes speaking all of the words neither of them could say. As much as she tried to convince herself this was about them, it was just as much for her.

Seeing her men together, knowing that they'd finally overcome the last hurdle that would bring them as close as physically possible was something she'd only dreamt about. Since the day she met Luke, he'd been running from this side of himself. It took long enough for him to accept the fact that he actually loved Cole, even though he tried to convince himself it was just lust. No way in hell did two people look at one another the way they did if it was just lust.

Sierra released Luke's cock from her mouth, sliding her tongue down his shaft then over his balls, laving them with her tongue before taking one, then the other into her mouth. The way Luke moaned against her sensitive flesh had her bucking beneath him, trying to grind her clit against the perfect friction of his tongue. He was holding back, keeping her perched on the razor sharp edge as her body burned for that little push that would ignite the steady flame into a wild inferno. He wasn't going to give it to her though. She knew him too well. Knew that her teasing in the hot tub had earned her some payback and Luke's punishment was always of the most exquisite nature.

When Cole reappeared in her line of sight, she saw that he'd taken the toy and the lube from their packaging. He was breathing hard as he watched them, and his need was intensifying. She wasn't sure how much longer they'd last. Hell, she didn't want them to.

Easing herself down, Sierra slipped her arms behind Luke's thighs as she leaned up, using her tongue to explore the sensitive area just beneath Luke's heavy sac, the same place that she'd teased Cole on numerous occasions, usually resulting with her being fucked into oblivion.

A startled groan came from the opposite end of the bed at the same time Luke's body stilled, his muscles rigid.

"Does it feel good?" Cole asked Luke. "Do you like having Sierra's tongue tease you?"

"Fuck." That was Luke's only response as she continued moving closer, her tongue reaming his ass as his body remained incredibly still.

Cole leaned in, joining her and Luke's growl filled the room. The two of them teased and tormented Luke until his body was bucking back against them. It was a good thing his muscles locked or Sierra would've worried he'd crush her. She didn't let up, driving her tongue inside of him when Cole took a step back, flipping open the cap on the lubrication and coating the medium sized rubber dildo that she'd purchased exclusively for him. For this.

She knew taking Cole's generous cock wasn't an easy thing, but so worth it. They'd had a brief discussion about it one afternoon when Luke was still at work, and Sierra had made the suggestion. That had been an afternoon that would be burned into her memory forever. It was clear to her that Cole didn't want to hurt him, although he was desperate for the need to be inside of their lover.

Once Cole had the fake cock prepared, Sierra returned her attention to Luke's balls, licking and sucking as she began stroking his cock. When Luke's mouth returned to her pussy, she nearly flew up off the bed, not having expected it and moaning as he plowed her pussy with his skilled tongue until she was riding the edge once more.

"I've got to prepare you to take me," Cole explained to Luke as he began teasing his anus with the toy, barely pushing the end against Luke's virgin ass.

"Fuck," Luke growled as the dildo inched in slowly.

Sierra turned her head to watch, reaching her other hand out and stroking Cole at the same pace she was stroking Luke. She smiled when both men began to growl and moan, their lust burning like a forest fire that just ignited an acre of dry brush.

"Luke!" Sierra screamed his name when he penetrated her with two fingers at the same time Cole pushed the dildo in farther, slowly fucking Luke.

"I want to feel you," Luke bit out. "I don't need the damn toy, I fucking need *you*. Right now."

Trying to fight her own orgasm, Sierra managed to twist completely beneath Luke until their mouths were aligned and she was kissing him, pulling him farther up on the bed to give Cole room to join them. She could see the tension in the lines on Cole's handsome face. He was hanging on by the skin of his teeth and quite frankly, so was she.

"I want you inside me," Sierra whispered to Luke as she ran her hands up over his shoulders, then into his hair. "I want to feel you when Cole takes you."

In a blur of movement, Luke shifted and rammed his cock inside of her, damn near sending her plummeting into ecstasy before she was ready. Oh, hell, who was she kidding? She was more than ready, but she wanted them to come together. She needed this as much as they did.

"Cole." Sierra glanced over Luke's shoulder, pulling him down until their chests rubbed. "Please. Now."

~~*~~

Cole knew the second his dick slid inside of Luke that he was going to go off like a rocket. Somehow he was holding on, but the heated grip of his lover's body was more than he could take. In his attempt to prepare Luke, he'd damn near come just from watching as Luke's ass took the toy and he began bucking and thrusting, begging for more. Cole was ready for Luke to beg.

With his cock lodged to the hilt inside of Luke, and Luke inside of Sierra, he leaned forward until he could brush his lips over Luke's back.

"I need this. I need you," Cole whispered, speaking to both of them. He wanted them to acknowledge that he was right there with them.

Sierra's hands came up to slide down his cheek, and Cole leaned into her touch, closing his eyes as he began to move slowly, Luke's body so damn hot. When Luke's hand shifted over the top of his pressing down into the mattress, his fingers twining with his, Cole almost lost the last vestiges of control he was barely hanging onto.

Luke's head turned to the side and their eyes met.

"I love you," Luke whispered. "I need you." There was a world of emotion in his answering words, and Cole slowly began to push in, retreating partway, then back in. Over and over, he took Luke gently, his balls tightening close to his body as he fought the urge to slam into him, to let the pleasure take over.

"Cole," Luke groaned. "Make me come. Please make me come."

Cole couldn't resist Luke's request. Releasing Luke's hand, Cole lifted his upper body until he was balanced on his knees, his cock tunneling slowly in and out of Luke because he couldn't stop himself. The sweet heat of Luke's body and the tight fit had that sudden surge of energy building at the base of his spine.

Gripping Luke's hips, he adjusted Luke until his lower body was hovering just above Sierra. When he began thrusting harder, his fingers digging into the firm muscle at his sides, Cole felt the impact of Luke's thrusts inside of Sierra. When her moans filled the bedroom they shared, it only spurred him on until he was fucking Luke harder, faster.

"Come for me," Cole ground out. "I need you to come for me, baby." Cole was speaking to them both, and as though they were under his control, Luke's muscles tightened, his ass damn near choking his dick as he growled.

"Coming. Fuck yes!" Luke bellowed at the same time Sierra wrapped her arms around his neck, pulling him against her as she met Cole's stare. She mouthed her I love you and Cole lost it, coming hard and fast inside of Luke, his cock jerking repeatedly until he was spent, hardly able to hold himself up.

Half expecting awkwardness, Cole retreated from Luke's body before heading to the bathroom to get a warm wash cloth. When he returned, Luke was lying on his back, his arm across his eyes and he felt part of his heart crack. He'd seen this reaction before, and it scared the hell out of Cole.

Using the washcloth, he cleaned Sierra first, then climbed on the bed alongside Luke. Luke grabbed him, pulling him on top, his mouth slamming against his as Luke delved inside with his eager tongue, Cole returning the kiss as he slid his hands into Luke's hair, holding him close. The emotions were churning, and he prayed that the bridge they just crossed was the right one.

Luke's lips eased off of his and he pulled Cole's head until their foreheads touched.

"I love you," Luke whispered. "I've loved you longer than I was ever willing to admit."

There was a crack in Luke's voice and Cole's breath lodged in his chest. Sierra moved in beside them, her hand running over Cole's back, a tear slipping from her eye and running down her cheek.

Cole couldn't get the words out, knowing the instant he tried to say them, his own sob would tear free. For the first time in his entire life, he felt as though he fit. Better yet, now he didn't feel as though he only fit in one place. He didn't want to be the piece that only fit one way, he wanted to bend with them, and now that he wasn't only the middle piece, he felt as though that last connection was complete.

"Next time, I want you to look me in the eyes when you make love to me," Luke said.

Cole's heart grinned, and it traveled all the way to his mouth. So there would be a next time.

He wasn't sure life could ever get better than this.

Chapter Thirty

Sierra wouldn't lie, she was nervous as hell.

Tonight was the soft opening of their club and even after all the work they'd put into it, she still prayed there weren't any substantial hiccups that would ruin what she hoped was the biggest night of their lives.

With the changes that Luke and Cole made, with Xander and Trent offering their input, she knew this place was going to be even bigger and better than Club Destiny. Although she'd only toured the fetish club once during operating hours, and she had enjoyed it, she knew they'd evolved significantly since Luke and Logan designed that club.

Stepping into the living room, Sierra caught sight of Luke and Cole standing on the back porch, both sipping beer as they stared out over the pool. She stopped in her tracks, taking a minute to admire them both. Her men were otherworldly attractive when they were dressed casually, but wearing tuxedos... Just wow.

Both men were tall, Luke a few inches taller than Cole, with long, lean bodies that were prone to make heads turn. She smiled to herself at the thought. They were hers and tonight, she intended to make sure everyone knew it too.

Aside from their public announcement of their relationship, the three of them didn't flaunt their very untraditional lifestyle. Tonight she had the opportunity because of the venue and she fully intended to take advantage of it. After persuading Sam to help her, Sierra had managed to put a surprise in place that even Luke and Cole didn't know about. Not an easy feat, mind you.

A low, seductive whistle caught Sierra's attention, and she looked up to see that Luke had made his way inside while she was still staring at Cole through the large windows overlooking the acreage behind their house that seemed to flow for miles.

"Woman, I'm not sure I can let you out of the house in that," Luke said warningly.

Sierra did a little spin in front of Luke and then took his outstretched hand when she turned to face him again. "You like it?"

"Stunning," he whispered. "Then again, you're always stunning."

Sierra absolutely loved the dress she had found. It was a turquoise silk sheath with a cowl neckline, delicate beaded straps and a sweep train that flowed beautifully behind her when she walked. The color set off her eyes, and she'd known it was perfect for this event as soon as she slipped it on the very first time. Admittedly, Sierra didn't dress up much these days, so she'd been looking forward to this night for some time now.

"Gorgeous." Cole's voice drifted her way when he moved into the house, shutting and locking the back door as he did, his eyes never leaving her.

"Thank you. I was thinking the same about the two of you."

Her men could rock a tux like no other man in the world.

"Are you ready?" Luke asked, still holding her hand.

"As I'll ever be."

Sierra smiled at the two of them, another sudden surge of gargantuan butterflies taking off in her tummy. She prayed she could make it through this night.

Luckily she'd had the forethought to wear waterproof mascara.

Less than twenty minutes later, they were pulling up to the club in Sierra's Escalade with Cole at the wheel. The vehicle came to a stop near the front doors, and Luke exited then opened her door and helped her out. The valet retrieved the keys from Cole and then he joined them. Standing between them, Sierra slipped one arm through one of each of theirs and then smiled up at them.

Showtime.

The club was already open, and as they walked toward the door, Sierra stopped to stare up at the sign that lit up the darkened sky against the mirrored glass, backlit by the white fiber optic lights. Beautiful. And the new name incorporated everything in one single word.

Sierra allowed Cole and Luke to lead her inside where they were greeted by two unusually large, extremely dangerous looking security officers who were employed, along with others, permanently with the club. Because there was no anonymity to go along with this club, they had to ensure the safety of their guests and members. They didn't anticipate anything; however Luke wanted to be cautious. He said he wasn't interested in putting his family at risk; therefore, he felt better with them there. She wasn't going to disagree.

"Good evening," Trent greeted them as they approached the main doors that would lead from the reception area to the club area.

"Trent." Luke shook hands with Trent followed by Cole, but neither man let go of her arm, so Sierra settled for smiling up at him.

The intensity of Trent's gray eyes sent a shiver down Sierra's spine. It was no wonder the man was a sex symbol on the big screen, and being this close to him, she felt his physical presence down to her toes. She was still a little surprised by the fact that he was still unattached, although she had a feeling his involvement with the club might just change all of that. Then again, what did she know?

"You looked beautiful, Sierra," Trent complimented her as their eyes met. Yes, he was in on her little secret. And even though she had no idea whether she could trust him or not, he'd never given her a reason not to, and she'd needed all the help she could get for what she was pulling off.

"Thank you," she said shyly, feeling the way both Luke and Cole seemed to move in closer to her, as though they were ensuring Trent knew exactly whom she belonged to.

As if anyone ever questioned it.

"Enjoy your night," Luke stated firmly as he continued toward the door, opening it and stepping back so that Sierra and Cole could enter before him.

Once inside, Sierra's senses went on instant overload. What she'd seen yesterday during the bright light of the day looked so much more intimate at night. The entire space was blacked out from any outside light thanks to the electronic shutters that closed down over each of the windows. The lights were dimmed in the ceiling, but most of the entire space was lit red thanks to the lights that adorned each of the bars.

Right in the center were the oversized glass rooms, already occupied, although tonight the scenes were scripted to cater to the various guests that had been invited. Sierra noticed Mistress Serena in one of the rooms, and she remembered the scene she'd witnessed months ago at the club when Luke and Cole had taken the Walker brothers on a tour. Sierra found it fascinating how very normal Serena seemed in the daytime, although she still carried that air of dominance in everything she did. Quite frankly, Sierra liked the woman and there might be a small part of her that wished she could command her men as easily as Mistress Serena commanded everyone she came into contact with.

A waiter approached them, carrying a tray with several wine glasses perched on top. He held the tray out, and Sierra took one, but not surprisingly, both of her men passed. She'd learned early on in their relationship that Luke and Cole were not wine drinkers. Thankfully, they didn't feel the need to pretend with her.

Luke leaned down close to her ear so that she could hear him over the music that echoed through the open space. "I need to take care of a couple of things."

Sierra nodded her understanding before placing a kiss on his lips. Luke then leaned over to Cole, presumably whispering the same thing, and Sierra watched them closely. They may never be the kind to engage in public displays of affection on a routine basis, but if anyone were to watch them closely, they'd see that Luke and Cole portrayed their love for one another every time they made eye contact. The sight made her tummy flip excitedly. Still, to this very day, Sierra was easily turned on by watching these two men together. She was pretty sure she'd never get enough.

Sam came walking up at the same time Luke started walking away. The two of them stopped, shared a quick hug before continuing on their paths. When Sam approached, Cole leaned down and kissed Sierra on the neck and whispered that he'd see her in a bit. With a nod and a kiss, she sent him on his way and turned her attention to Sam.

"What do you think?" Sierra asked as the two of them stood side by side, wine glasses in hand and admired their surroundings.

"I think it's phenomenal. There is a classy feel to this place that I love. Although it's a playground for the wickedly taboo, it feels... normal."

Sierra laughed.

Normal.

She wasn't sure she even knew what normal was anymore. Considering the Domme currently wielding a whip while a naked man knelt at her feet inside a glass box stood just a few feet from her, Sierra was thinking they'd somehow come up with a new definition of normal.

"Have you seen Xander?" Sam asked, and Sierra turned to face her friend.

"Not yet, no. Is he here yet?"

"Supposed to be. He might be talking to Logan though."

Sierra noticed how Sam didn't make eye contact as she spoke which told her one thing. Her interest in Xander might very well be more than just platonic in nature.

It was clear, based on the conversations the two of them had shared that Sam and Logan were still interested in finding another third; however, they weren't at all interested in having another person filter in and out of their lives. It'd started with Luke, Sierra knew, and then Tag. Both men had gone on to find permanent relationships, which wasn't all that surprising; however, Sierra knew it had to be difficult on Sam. She wasn't a promiscuous woman and her heart got involved a little each time, meaning when both of those men had moved on, she'd lost a little part of herself.

Sierra couldn't even imagine what that must feel like. She knew intimately what it felt like to be with two men, what it meant to be in an untraditional relationship that had some significant sexual stigmas assigned to it, and she absolutely couldn't fathom one of her men walking away and ever being replaced. Although, in that regard, she and Sam were different. Sam and Logan were immensely happy just the two of them, which Sierra respected. They simply liked to add a little spice to their lives.

Glancing back around at the club, Sierra realized this was just the place to allow that to happen.

Now, if she could muster up the nerve to do what she'd come to do tonight, she'd feel like she fit in just fine.

Chapter Thirty One

"Where'd McKenna run off to?" Cole asked his stepbrother when he approached him at the bar a short while later.

"Dancing," he answered, turning to face the overcrowded dance floor behind them.

Cole chuckled as he searched the floor for Tag's fiancé. "Don't dance, huh?"

"Not the kind of dancing she's talking about," Tag said honestly.

Cole watched as the pretty red head in the brilliant emerald green dress moved gracefully around the dance floor with Trent. He found it odd that Tag was even letting another man touch her. Although, Cole would probably do the same. He was equipped with two left feet and dancing was clearly not in his stockpile of skills.

Cole took the beer the bartender handed him and turned to face the crowded place. They'd had a better turn out than he expected. Although only about one-third of the people in attendance were actual members, he had a feeling that would probably be changing fairly quickly.

The atmosphere was significantly different from the fetish club, and he found that he liked this one better. There was a different air to the people in the much more elegant setting. First of all, there were more couples than he was used to. More importantly, there were a large number of ménage relationships in attendance. Since Cole knew that Luke specifically wanted to target that demographic, he wasn't surprised. Not that he had an issue with his relationship or the fact that most people looked at them strangely when they went out in public, but Cole liked the opportunity to be around like minded individuals.

They weren't just a ménage club. They'd managed to keep a lot of the fetish elements, along with the BDSM aspect that drew a significant amount of interest, or so it seemed. Simply put, they were a sex club, incorporating a vast number of preferences and desires.

Xander's intimidating form caught Cole's eye from across the room. Turning to see who he was talking to, Cole noticed the woman on his arm. She wasn't substantially tall, probably close to a foot shorter than Xander. The black flowing gown she wore accentuated her generous curves and Cole appreciated the fact that she wasn't one of the model thin women whom a man of Xander's size would likely break in two. There were many times that Cole feared he and Luke would hurt Sierra, being as small as she was, but this woman looked like she could easily handle a man like Xander. He found it interesting because he'd never seen Xander with a woman, but these two looked fairly intimate.

His attention turned to the most beautiful woman in the room. He watched as Sierra gracefully moved toward the area that had been sectioned off for the night to be used for a few people to address the attendees. Standing behind the podium was Logan, holding a microphone which meant they were about to introduce the owners.

"See you in a few," Cole told Tag, turning to head in Sierra's direction. He wasn't the type of man who enjoyed being the center of attention, and he'd tried numerous times to talk Sierra out of this meet and greet introduction, but as with most things, she'd won that argument.

There was a tap on the microphone, followed by a squeal that got most people's attention although it didn't seem to be the intention. Choosing to stand off to the side, Cole watched as Logan handed the microphone to Sierra. He'd half expected Trent to do the honors of introducing the club, but during a brief conversation the day before, everyone felt as though the club would get more attention without the famous actor standing in front of the room.

"Where've you been?" Cole asked Luke as they waited for the crowd to gather around and quiet.

"Just talking to a few people."

Before Cole asked for specifics, Trent commanded the attention of the crowd by his mere presence.

"Thank you for coming tonight," Sierra greeted the group. "I'd like to take a minute to introduce myself and my wonderful husbands."

Cole's breath lodged in his chest. Did she just refer to the two of them as her husbands? His heart did that strange swelling thing, and for a second he thought he was going to pass out.

"I guess that's our cue," Luke said, taking Cole's hand and pulling him toward the front of the group of at least one hundred people gathered around.

"My name is Sierra, and many of you have already met my husbands – Luke McCoy and Cole Ackerley. If you haven't, well, then I'm not exactly sure how you got in here tonight."

The group laughed at Sierra's joke. Cole went to stand on one side of Sierra while Luke stood proudly on the other. He couldn't help but wonder how this turn of events had come about. If he remembered correctly, he'd insisted he not be brought forward to have to address anyone. If someone needed to speak publicly, Cole was more than happy to hand the mic over to the famous actor who seemed to enjoy being in the spotlight.

"First of all, I'd like to welcome you all. I hope you've had a chance to look around, you know, if that's your thing."

Another round of laughter.

"In any case, if you haven't, I urge you to. My husbands have put a lot of themselves into this place, and I'm so very proud of what they've accomplished. Many of you might not realize it, but this club is like a second child to us. A lot of blood, sweat, and yes, tears have gone into this place.

"Tonight is all about giving you a glimpse into what it is like to live our lifestyle and the various other lifestyles you might not be familiar with. The three of us have spent the better part of the last year learning to live openly in a ménage and quite frankly, not one of us was quite equipped for what that meant when we went into this."

Cole listened intently, suddenly confused as to the description of their relationship. They didn't make a habit of sharing the most intimate aspects of their lives and quite frankly, he'd have been just fine with a brief name introduction.

"We knew that we loved one another. Knew that we were devoted to one another. We even knew that we wanted to have children together, but as you can imagine, it hasn't been a smooth road the entire time.

"This is one of the reasons we opted to add some variety to our club that, if you were a member of Club Destiny, you wouldn't have seen. It isn't just the ménage lifestyle that people don't understand; however, it is one that the three of us are intimately familiar with.

"Which brings me to the reason that I am standing up here before you tonight, introducing you to my husbands."

Cole glanced down at Sierra again at her reference. His heart was beating wildly in his chest.

"I've had the honor of meeting several of you who are much more familiar with what we go through on a daily basis, and it was during these conversations that I've learned a lot about options."

Cole stared down at her confused, his expression mirroring Luke's almost perfectly. He had no idea where Sierra was going with this. By now he expected their introductions to be complete and for them to be standing back watching someone else in the spotlight.

"As you can tell by the complete look of shock on their faces, neither one of them has a clue where I'm going with this. Since I know all of you are probably ready to get on with the evening, I'm going to ask for your attention for just a few more minutes."

Cole glanced up at Luke, their eyes meeting over Sierra's head. What the hell was she talking about?

Sierra turned, putting her back to the crowd as she faced both of them at the same time.

"I know that the two of you weren't expecting this, but I need you both to listen to me for just a minute," Sierra said seriously, and Cole's heart pounded even harder than before. If she wasn't careful, she was going to make him have a panic attack right here in front of all these people.

~~*~~

Luke stood as still as he could in front of all of his guests who were giving the three of them their undivided attention. It was eerie, to say the least.

Sierra's smile was bright, and the sheen of tears in her eyes put him on edge. One thing he couldn't handle was when Sierra cried. His heart broke each and every time it happened and now, standing before her, completely unaware of what she was doing, he felt as though he was about to have a heart attack.

Thankfully, she handed the microphone off to Sam, who handed her something in return, but Luke could only make out that one of the items was a sheet of paper. Great. Maybe she'd prepared a speech.

"It's not a secret that I'm not the dominant one in this relationship," Sierra said with a huge smile. "In fact, I've always willingly handed the control over to one or both of you, and I happen to prefer it that way. However, I needed to make a stand, and this was the only way that I could come up with."

Luke watched her, feeling the eyes of the group behind her boring into him.

"I need you to let me get through this before either of you say anything at all."

Luke nodded, as did Cole, but neither of them said a word. Luke wasn't sure he'd be able to find his voice if he had to.

Sucking in a deep breath, Sierra took the piece of paper and unfolded it, glancing down as she did.

"Back when the three of us made this official," Sierra motioned the three of them with her hand, "the two of you gave me rings which I proudly wear each and every day."

At the mention of her rings, Luke glanced down at her finger, expecting to see the two bands they'd given her, but they weren't there. His heart skipped a beat, and he wondered whether they'd be making use of those defibrillators they'd had installed.

"I won't lie, I've always dreamed about having a wedding, wearing a white gown and walking down the aisle. However, all of those little dreams of mine seemed so insignificant when I met the two of you and fell in love with not one but both of you at the same time. I decided I could easily live without that tradition because it didn't mean anything if I couldn't have both of you.

"However, one thing I'm not willing to sacrifice in this relationship is the comfort and reassurance that the little piece of paper that so many people take for granted can bring to a relationship. Having that paper might not be necessary when it comes to explaining my love for both of you, but it is something that would help us not to feel so temporary."

Luke swallowed hard as he watched a single tear streak down Sierra's face as she glanced back and forth between them. He no longer felt the stares of the people behind her because somewhere along the way, he'd tuned out everything except this woman and the man standing beside him.

"In the last couple of months, the three of us have finally come to terms with our own insecurities, and honestly, I wasn't surprised to find that each one of us felt exactly the same way. This isn't temporary. It never has been. I know we're feeling our way through this, but one thing I'm not willing to do is to let either of you think that we won't get through the ups and downs. Together."

Glancing down at the piece of paper and then back up at them, Sierra smiled. It was the most beautiful smile he'd ever seen.

"I've learned from some very open and honest people, who have been so kind as to share their experiences with me, that we aren't the only ones who have wanted something more… how should I say this? Permanent?

"Hold this," Sierra handed him the piece of paper, "but don't read it."

Luke grinned. He was just about to do exactly that. Watching her, he noticed that she had a small black velvet box in her hand that had been hidden behind the paper. She slowly opened the lid and reached inside before looking back up at them both.

"I'm not willing to marry just one of you because I wouldn't be able to choose and quite frankly, I don't want to. I want to marry both of you. I don't need the State of Texas to give me permission to do this in order for me to make it official. When you read the paper – not yet, when I tell you to," Sierra inserted the last part as Luke was just about to look down at the paper.

The crowd behind her laughed.

"I want this to be binding because no matter what, my heart belongs to both of you and it always will. I know that the two of you feel the same about me, as well as one another," Sierra said as she swallowed hard. Luke wanted to reach out and pull her into his arms. He fought the urge.

Sierra reached out and took Luke's hand, sliding something over his left ring finger and then doing the same to Cole before she looked back up at them, more tears filling her beautiful blue eyes.

"What you're holding might not be a marriage license honored by our great state, but it is a legal contract. It's real. Paper or not, I need you both to understand that you belong to me. Today, tomorrow, forever." Glancing down at the rings and then back up at them, Sierra continued, "I had them engraved."

Sierra pulled her ring from her finger and held it up for them to see. Luke noticed that she did have the original rings they had given her, only now they were soldered together to form one.

"All three of them say the same thing," she said, her voice breaking. "Everlasting Devotion."

As though her last words opened the dam, Sierra's tears began flowing steadily, and Luke was unable to stop himself from reaching for her at the same time Cole did.

Applause broke out behind them as the three of them stood motionless in front of a sea of people witnessing this moment right alongside them.

~~*~~

"I have a question," Cole said when they took a step back from one another after she managed to silence her sobs somewhat.

Startled, she looked at Cole as he stared down at her, a serious expression on his handsome face.

"Did my mischievous brother help you to get this taken care of?"

Sierra noticed Luke glance her way, but she didn't take her eyes off of Cole. She settled for a sheepish little smile, one that she hoped would soften the lines on his face.

When she'd talked to Tag, he had been more than happy to help her get the legal documents necessary to make the changes and he'd actually been happy for them. Tag had told her that although they'd had a reception of sorts, he felt as though they'd possibly missed a step. Sierra took that to mean that Cole had obviously talked to his stepbrother at some point, which only reaffirmed her reason for wanting to do this.

In their attempt to ensure their friends and family were at ease with their decision, they'd managed to deny themselves one thing. Granted, they didn't need a piece of paper, or even rings, but they did need the openness that they'd been missing all along.

It was clear that what she felt for them, they felt for her, but they hadn't confirmed as much in words. Now, they had the opportunity to go beyond words, making it as legal as they possibly could to show that they were in this together.

"So, what do you think was going through Tag's mind when I asked him to help *me*?" Cole asked, reaching beneath his tuxedo jacket and pulling a piece of paper from his back pocket and holding it out for her to take.

Sierra cocked an eyebrow as she took the paper from his outstretched hand, feeling the presence of so many eyes still on her, probably all waiting for this to be over with. She unfolded it slowly, then started at the top. Cole had essentially had the same contract drawn up as she had, only there was one addition. Out of all of the legal mumbo jumbo listed, the one thing that stood out clearly was the request for a name change from Hannah Gabriella Ackerley to Hannah Gabriella McCoy-Ackerley.

With tears in her eyes and a sob escaping, she handed the paper to Luke and moved into Cole's arms, her eyes never leaving Luke's face.

She knew the instant he read that part because his eyes got wide and she was almost positive she saw a sheen of moisture, but he quickly masked it and grabbed her arm, pulling her against him at the same time he pulled Cole in close. Sierra wished she could be as strong as they were, but she couldn't control the sob that tore from her chest. Never had she believed she would be so lucky as to share this unconditional love.

And the fact that these two men had enough love in their hearts to share with her *and* each other only made it that much more significant.

Chapter Thirty Two

Luke was finally beginning to feel his limbs once more. There for a little while, he thought he was having a heart attack. As if Sierra's impromptu little ceremony hadn't sent his heart soaring into another realm, Cole had to follow it up with his request to change Hannah's name. From the second he saw the words, he'd pulled Sierra and Cole into his arms to keep from breaking down in front of so many people.

Hannah was going to have his name. Although she shared part of his name – Gabriel – as her middle name, this was beyond what he ever anticipated. In his heart, she was just as much his daughter as Cole's, but now…

"I love you," he whispered to both people standing within the circle of his arms. Looking up, Luke forced the lump in his throat down as he pressed his lips to Cole's. When he pulled away, he cupped Sierra's face in his hands and kissed her, tasting her tears and feeling her love as it bubbled there for everyone in the room to see.

He knew without a doubt that the three of them had been working toward the same thing all along, and maybe they needed this formality to ease some of their insecurities, but in Luke's heart, he knew where he belonged.

Another round of applause broke out around them, and thankfully Trent's voice came across the speakers as he took the microphone and began his little spiel about the club.

"Well, I guess it's no secret as to why we named the club what we did," Trent told the crowd.

Luke glanced up instinctively at the single word etched in script on the glass mirror behind one of the bars. Maybe there had been a reason that he'd come up with that name, and he hadn't even realized it.

When they'd been tossing around names, Luke kept coming back to one word that reminded him of what he felt for Sierra and Cole. With all of the crazy names that Trent and Xander came up with, Luke was still surprised that the moment he suggested it, the two men had looked at one another and instantly agreed.

Devotion

It sort of said it all.

As Luke and Cole led Sierra away from the crowd and toward the stairs, they had to endure hugs and pats on the back from various people, some probably the very ones whom Sierra had gotten advice from. Although he wasn't trying to disappear, Luke needed a few minutes of alone time with these two, and it would give the rest of the guests a chance to get back to normal. Whatever that meant.

When they reached the top of the stairs, Luke went straight to his office. Once the three of them were inside, he locked the door behind them and turned to face two of the people he cherished most in this world.

"I'm sorry for putting the two of you on the spot like that," Sierra began apologetically, but Luke quickly cut her off by stalking her across the room and pressing her into the wall, his mouth coming down on hers as gently as he could manage. It wasn't an easy feat.

Cole was right there with them, moving in close until the three of them shared a kiss hot enough to melt the polar ice caps and then boil the water afterwards. Before Luke had a chance to catch his breath, Sierra stunned him as she easily morphed into the aggressive one, seemingly fueled by her emotions. He didn't put up a fight when she pushed him down on the couch and straddled his hips. His cock immediately swelled at the feel of her heat against him, and he wasn't sure they'd get their clothes off fast enough.

"Naked," Sierra said between kisses, making Luke laugh. "I want you both right here. Right now."

"I can't wait that long," he told her, unwilling to wait until they were undressed. "And anyway, I want you to wear that just a little bit longer."

Turning to Cole, he locked his gaze with midnight blue eyes that seemed to be hiding the same emotion he was feeling. "I'm not wasting any more time."

Cole didn't move.

"Honey, I think he needs our help," Luke told Sierra when she stopped planting kisses along his jaw.

"I think so too," she said, eagerly reaching for Cole's arm and pulling him until he stumbled and fell onto the couch beside Luke. With hurried movements, Sierra moved off of him and over onto Cole's lap, straddling Cole the same way she had him.

When she had Cole thoroughly distracted, Luke stood from his seat, making quick work of removing his jacket and then unbuttoning his pants. As much as he wanted to take all night, he knew they'd be expected back down in the club soon so he would have to make this quick. There'd be plenty of time to take his time later, which he fully intended to do.

Sierra was already working to get Cole freed from his tuxedo pants as their mouths remained fused together. Luke used the time wisely, going over to his desk to retrieve the bottle of lube from his top drawer. When he returned, he noticed Sierra had managed to get Cole's pants down over his hips, and she was now riding his cock with her dress bunched up around her waist.

Lord have mercy, the woman didn't have on panties.

"Sonuvabitch!" Cole cried out when Luke leaned down, easing two fingers inside of Sierra's ass while fondling Cole's balls at the same time.

"Fuck that feels good," Cole groaned, his head falling back on the couch as he began pumping his hips, working his cock deeper inside of Sierra as she rode him hard.

Based on the urgency in Sierra's movements, Luke knew he had some catching up to do. Watching the two of them go at one another like wild animals right there in his office was certainly not hindering his progress either. This was the first time they'd taken advantage of this office, but he knew it obviously wouldn't be the last.

"Don't make me come," Cole begged, lifting his head and meeting Sierra's gaze, then looking past her at Luke. "I want him inside of you when I come."

Luke released Cole's balls, continuing to screw two fingers into Sierra's ass as Cole began fucking her with slow, measured strokes.

Getting himself situated took a minute because his legs were so damn long and he needed to get better traction. By the time he was sliding his cock inside of Sierra, Cole had managed to angle his body so that the three of them could almost fit on the couch together. With one leg on the floor, one knee on the couch, Luke began thrusting inside of Sierra while Cole picked up a rhythm of his own beneath her.

Luke's emotions were a tangled mess inside of his chest, and he couldn't seem to get close enough to either of them right then. Tonight, the two of them had made every single dream he'd ever had come true. There might have been a couple of doubts that disrupted his normal course from time to time, but Luke had given himself to them, heart and soul, a long time ago. To know that they had shared the same insecurity was bittersweet.

Between the love he felt for them, and the lust that he constantly battled, Luke wasn't sure he'd ever get enough. It didn't matter to him whether this was hard and fast, or slow and easy. Luke felt them right there with him. Three hearts, three souls, connected in ways he never even imagined.

"I'm going to come," Sierra whispered. "Make me come, both of you. And I want you coming with me."

Sierra's demand was fierce, and Luke aimed to please. Locking his gaze with Cole's he began thrusting inside of her, rocking Sierra back and forth on Cole's cock until the three of them were moaning in unison, their bodies covered in a fine sheen of sweat as they fought to reach that place that only the three of them could go.

"Fuck," Luke growled, leaning in closer to Sierra's ear, staring down at Cole's midnight blue eyes and willing him to see everything that was in his heart right then.

"I love you," the three of them said at exactly the same time, followed by Sierra's piercing cry as her orgasm took her, her body gripping Luke so hard, his orgasm leveled him at the same time Cole let go.

Chapter Thirty Three

From the outside looking in, Cole wasn't sure anyone would think his life was really any different now than just a few short months ago. As he sat quietly in Luke's office, Sierra's warmth settled against him as they tried to get their ragged breathing under control, he knew that it was.

Not only had they moved to a house that now reflected the three of them as a whole, but they were the proud parents of a beautiful little girl. They'd taken a risk and practically started over with a new club, and on top of that, they'd managed to open themselves up to one another.

It was the last part that Cole considered the most significant. Although he couldn't count on both hands the number of times they'd come together just like they had minutes before, never had it felt quite like this. Their love was real, there was no doubt about that. He'd known that from the beginning and always suspected it would be Luke who would have the hardest time expressing himself. Turned out that Cole was the one holding back.

Not anymore.

They'd made some promises to one another in recent weeks, and tonight they'd managed to seal their fate. Cole knew that they would definitely follow through because that was what the three of them had been searching for. They needed something concrete to tie them to each other. Glancing down at his ring finger, he smiled at the platinum band that adorned it.

For some, it might not be necessary, and many people might think that he and Luke were just loose cannons who needed constant reassurance and maybe that was true. For Cole, it was everything for him to know that he held the hearts of the three people he cherished most in the world.

Sierra and Luke completed him in ways he never anticipated. A traditional marriage might not be in their cards, but they were paving their own way, creating their own destiny, and living their lives in a way that would make them happy. Sometimes, there were bumps along the way to get to where you wanted to go, but Cole knew that, in the end, the journey was always going to be worth it. Especially when he had what he'd always been looking for right there beside him.

On top of that, they had the most precious gift that could ever be given to them. Hannah Gabriella McCoy-Ackerley. With Hannah, he felt there was a bond that could never be broken, and he knew as she grew up, she'd have the best of everything they could give her, but most importantly, she'd have their love and support. In all honesty, Cole wanted her to feel the same about Luke as she would about him because in his eyes, they were both her father and she was a very lucky little girl.

"So, I was thinking," Sierra said with a smile as she looked up at him, causing Luke to shift more to the side.

"What's that?" Cole asked.

"When are we going to start working on having another baby?" Sierra winked at Cole and then glanced over her shoulder at Luke.

As though he knew they were expecting him to answer the question, Luke leaned forward, kissing Sierra on the mouth gently. "Just as soon as you say the word. But this time, I think I'm going to let Cole have the honors of suiting up."

Sierra's smile widened, and Cole saw the tears that instantly filled her eyes. She tried to hide them by leaning over and kissing Luke and then him quickly before attempting to stand up.

"Well, honey. You heard him. This time you get to wear the condom," Sierra informed Cole as she maneuvered to her feet, before heading toward the bathroom. Before she disappeared inside, she stopped abruptly, glancing over her shoulder. "Since you're waiting for me to say the word, consider this your warning. I won't be refilling my birth control."

Cole smiled as he sat up, trying to right his clothes. With a quick look over at Luke, he noticed the gleam in his lover's eyes. "You ok?"

"I was just thinking."

"About?" Cole asked.

"Whether we actually bought a big enough house."

Chapter Thirty Four

Meanwhile, downstairs at Devotion…

"Please tell me we're going to be able to sneak away from these people for a little while," Sam whispered to Logan as they stood overlooking the club scene playing out in front of them.

She was almost a little surprised to see so much going on in one place, but it appeared that Luke and Sierra and Cole managed to release the flurry of inhibitions during their impromptu ceremony, and these people were quickly making up for lost time.

There was nakedness all around. It was vastly different from what Sam was used to from Club Destiny, although she did remember what she'd observed at the fetish club during the one time Logan agreed to take her. Not since the night that the Walker brothers were given a tour had she been allowed back. However, with Devotion, Sam knew Logan wasn't going to be able to control her attendance, and she fully intended for the two of them to visit on a much more frequent basis.

Logan shifted, pressing up against her back and Sam smiled as his erection ground sensually into her ass. So he was just as affected by the public indecency on full display around them as she was.

"What did you have in mind?" he whispered against her ear, sliding her hair back over her shoulder.

"Mmmm, I was thinking a tour of the upstairs would be a good start."

Sam had already received a tour of the entire club; however, that was before the doors had opened and before the excitement had built to a crescendo all around her. This was what she envisioned a sex club looking like. Between the sensual thump of the bass pumping throughout the open space, and the libidinous grind of partly or fully naked bodies in various places throughout the main floor, Sam knew this was going to be a place people would be begging to get into.

When Logan took her hand, sliding his large warm fingers through hers, her tummy did a little happy dance. As he led her across the room, he didn't seem to be in a rush, giving her plenty of time to absorb the scenes playing out around them.

The large glass rooms were all occupied, and there was a cluster of people gathered around, watching the various shows, most of them involving some form of BDSM at the moment. She knew from listening to Sierra that they had planned these scenes in advance tonight. Impressive, and her hat was off to Mistress Serena and her wild and kinky ways.

In an alcove beside the stairs, there was a man and a woman, both semi-dressed as though they couldn't wait to be naked before they devoured one another. The beautiful brunette was pressed into the wall, one of her legs lifted high – she was certainly flexible – as the man drove his cock deep inside of her. The music drowned out most of their moans of ecstasy, but the look of pure unadulterated bliss on the woman's face said what words or noises couldn't. She was clearly enjoying herself.

Sam focused on walking up the stairs as Logan fell into step behind her, his hand grazing the back of her thigh and slowly easing up beneath the short skirt that flared out from her hips. If he wasn't careful, he was going to give the other patrons quite a visual if he continued because the black lace thong she was wearing wasn't designed to hide much of anything.

Unlike the fetish club, there were some rooms that were made of glass, others that had solid doors. It was clear that the occupants within the glass rooms welcomed voyeurs; however, those with the closed doors had lights built in above them that would signify whether they welcomed company or not. The choice was either red or green. Sam noticed there were only a couple that currently were red. Of course, that piqued her interest even more than those with the green lights on.

Logan made his way in front of her once more, pulling her along as he moved to open the first door on the right. She was a little nervous about opening the door to a private room and seeing what was going on, but again, her curiosity got the best of her, and she wanted to kiss Logan square on the mouth for giving her the opportunity.

Once the door was open, Logan took a step back, allowing her to step in front of him. There against the far wall was a St. Andrew's cross, equipped with a sinfully attractive woman shackled and blindfolded. There was a woman on her knees between her legs, lapping at her, although, from this angle, Sam couldn't see much. There was a man on each side of them, attending to the restrained woman's naked breasts with their mouths.

Nice.

Logan pulled the door closed quietly and led her to the next room, which was three doors down. Logan once again took a step back as he allowed her to view inside the room.

This one contained a gigantic bed centered in the middle of the room and the current occupants were making good use of it. Two men with one woman sandwiched between them, both fucking her diligently as she moaned out her pleasure.

A sharp tingle shot right through Sam's clit as she watched them. It had been too long since she and Logan had ventured into that type of play. Ever since Tag fell in love with McKenna, they'd opted to refrain. Watching the woman being pleasured within an inch of her life made Sam suddenly wish they had another person who could join them.

It was actually a catch twenty two because Sam wasn't interested in a part time lover, nor were they looking for an addition to their relationship. Since Logan was only interested in watching another man pleasure her, they were limited in that regard as well. Sam had to accept that they didn't have many options since they chose not to be promiscuous in their activities.

Logan took her hand once again and led her back into the narrow hallway. Rather than take her to another room, he surprised her when he turned her to the wrought iron railing that encircled the second floor, offering an unobstructed view of the main floor below.

"Put your hands on the rail," he ordered and Sam immediately did as he instructed.

Logan pressed himself up against her, his cock thick and hard as he ground into her ass and she suddenly wished they didn't have their formal clothing between them because she was overly anxious to feel him inside of her.

"Did you like watching the woman being fucked by two men at one time?" Logan breathed against her ear, his words barely heard over the din of the music from above.

Rather than speak, she nodded, tilting her head at an angle so he could put his mouth on her neck, the one spot she was almost positive he could kiss and give her an orgasm. He didn't disappoint, latching his mouth onto her, nipping her with his teeth before chasing the sting with his tongue. A ripple of heat slid between her thighs and Sam was worried he might just make her come right then and there. Not that she minded.

"Have I told you how much I want to watch another man lick your pussy? I've been dreaming about it. I want to watch as you writhe against his mouth, letting him fuck you with his tongue."

Sam shuddered, her entire body heating from Logan's words.

"Spread your legs," Logan instructed and Sam immediately widened her stance.

The warmth of his hand slid over her thigh, then higher until he was sliding his finger into the elastic edge of her panties. She wanted to buck her hips against him so he'd move closer to where she needed him, but Sam knew not to rush Logan. He liked to take his time, and when he found that she was overexcited, he loved to draw it out even more.

"You're so fucking wet, baby," he groaned, his finger sliding between the swollen folds of her sex, briefly grazing her clit and making her body tense as the sensation ripped through her. She was lit up from the inside out, and she didn't have to tell Logan that it wasn't going to take much to send her flying. He knew her enough to expect it.

"Look down there," Logan said, his head barely angling to the right, signaling which direction he was referring to. Sam glanced around, noticing the few people standing below them, one couple dancing until her eyes landed on what she knew he was referring to.

A trio, one that she had met earlier, occupied the far corner. Two men sitting on a couch, their cocks visible as they stroked themselves while the fully naked woman kneeling before them alternated between pleasuring them both with her mouth. Another bolt of lust shook her at the same time Logan pierced her with one finger.

Her knees buckled, but her husband was quick to hold her up as he began fucking her deep, keeping a slow, steady rhythm that was driving her mad.

"I'm not going to let you come yet," he told her, and Sam fought the urge to scream.

"Why?"

"Because I have a surprise for you."

The starch in Sam's legs instantly returned, and she wanted to push him back, insisting that he give her the surprise now because she couldn't wait anymore. He must have sensed it too because his muscular body hardened and he braced himself so that she couldn't move out from between him and the railing. He thrust a second finger into her, and Sam bit her lip to keep from crying out as a couple walked past them.

Oh, God.

Xander. And the intensely sexy woman who had accompanied him tonight. Sam had yet to meet her, but she was hoping to. The woman was by far one of the most gorgeous women she'd ever seen and the air of confidence that surrounded her intrigued Sam even more.

Logan ground his cock against her ass and used his thumb to tease her clit as he continued to finger fuck her at the same time the woman with Xander turned and made eye contact. There was a gleam of heat in her pretty gray eyes and another shiver passed through her. Not that Sam had ever been attracted to another woman, but there was something about this one that drew her, excited her. Even made her curious about things she'd never thought about before.

Sam tore her gaze away, pretending to be staring down at the main floor activity once again, but she couldn't get the image of Xander's date out of her head.

A few minutes passed as she tried to get control of herself while still trying to outlast Logan's wicked fingers as he teased her relentlessly.

"Are you ready for your surprise?" Logan asked.

As if he even needed to ask the question. "Yes."

Logan removed his fingers from between her legs and then turned her to face him. She watched as he slowly cleaned his fingers with his tongue and Sam couldn't resist pulling his mouth to hers for a kiss, tasting herself on his mouth. She was never going to get enough of this man.

Probably to keep from taking her right there against the wall, Logan broke the kiss and then put his hand at the small of Sam's back as he continued down the hallway, offering her more glimpses into a couple of rooms along the way.

When they reached the last room with a green light above the door, Sam was suddenly saddened that her little tour was about to be over. On the other hand, she knew there were a few unoccupied rooms, and she couldn't wait to get to one so that Logan could give her the surprise he was offering.

Instead of simply opening the door, Logan knocked. Confusion rippled through her for a second as she tried to figure out why he didn't just open the door the way he had with the other rooms.

The door slowly opened, and there stood Xander, shirtless with his tuxedo pants unbuttoned, his rippled abs and clearly defined "V" drawing Sam's eyes. He gave a gentle nod, inviting them into the room, and Sam's entire body nearly froze right there on the spot as she tried to figure out just what was about to happen.

As she followed Logan into the room, she noticed the flogger in Xander's hand and an unfamiliar heat penetrated her core. Apparently she was turned on by the idea of the sex toy, but Sam had absolutely no idea why. Nor did she have any idea what they were doing in this room with Xander and his date.

Before she could turn to Logan and ask, the door closed behind them, and she looked up – way up – into the incredibly handsome face of Xander Boone, and it dawned on her just what they were about to venture into.

Sam had only one question...

Did he intend to use the flogger on her or was he reserving that for his date?

Epilogue

"Did you sign the contract yet?" Cole asked Luke when he passed through the kitchen a few days after their soft opening at the club.

They'd managed to slow down significantly since that day, enjoying some time together without the hassle of work, still riding a high from that night. And the days and nights that followed. As far as Luke was concerned, they seemed to be in the honeymoon stage. He certainly wasn't complaining.

"No," Luke answered gruffly, biting the inside of his cheek to keep from smiling. "I've read them, but I have one concern."

Cole stopped abruptly, but then again, Luke had practically predicted his response. If he knew Cole, he knew the man was thinking this was Luke's typical reaction.

"Something wrong?"

Luke knew Sierra and Cole had gone through a lot of trouble to get the contracts drawn up. Not only had he been surprised with the idea that they could have a legally binding relationship, quite frankly, he'd been a little stunned by the amount of work that went into them. At this point, they were working to have the two separate contracts merged into one, but there was one point that Luke wanted addressed before they sent it off.

"Yes," he told Cole truthfully. It wasn't anything bad, although the grim look on his lover's face told him that he was expecting the worst.

The contracts were fairly simple, outlining the details of assets acquired before and during the relationship, acknowledgement of children within the relationship, and various other legal stuff mainly related to possessions. There weren't any firm stipulations or any odd requests from Sierra or Cole, which Luke didn't find surprising at all. They weren't demanding people. The basic intention of the contract was to acknowledge their relationship legally which in turn would help to soothe some of the insecurities that even Luke knew needed soothing.

Sierra walked into the room a moment later, and she stopped right in between him and Cole. "Something wrong?"

"Maybe," Cole said with a glum expression.

Apparently he was waiting for the other shoe to drop. Luke wasn't going to tell him that they couldn't have been more secure in that moment than ever before. He'd find out soon enough.

"What is it?" Sierra asked as she turned to face Luke. Obviously she knew whom the source was, which seemed rather amusing, and Luke had to cover up a chuckle with a cough.

"There's something missing from this contract, and I'm not interested in signing it until it gets corrected." Luke put his pen down on the table and leaned back in his chair, his stern expression filling in the blanks for them.

Sierra nodded, appearing concerned as she moved closer to him to glance down at the papers spread out on the table in front of him.

"I can have the lawyer address it," she said without even knowing what he was referring to.

Luke gripped her hips and pulled her down onto his lap suddenly, and her startled squeal made him laugh. He managed a serious expression once again as he watched her face.

"We've made the decision that all children within this relationship would bear both of our last names," Luke began, feeling both Sierra's and Cole's gazes focused intently on him. "That doesn't solve the issue of Sierra's last name though."

Sierra glanced up at him at the same time Cole lowered himself into the chair across the table. They both seemed incredibly interested in where this was going.

"I want Sierra to share the same last name as the children. I want her to take *our* last names," he explained to them both before turning to address Sierra directly, cupping her face gently. "Baby, I want you to have my last name."

When her chin started to tremble and the sudden sheen of moisture filled her eyes, he pulled her flush against his body, wrapping his arms completely around her. "Is that too much to ask?"

"No," she sobbed against his chest. "It's more than I could ever ask for."

Luke swallowed the lump of emotion that had become a fairly frequent visitor in recent weeks. He wanted more than anything for Sierra to have their last names. This seemed like the only option as far as he was concerned.

A few seconds later, Sierra pulled away, wiping her eyes with the heels of her hands and then smiling back at him, a question already formed in her mind if her gently raised eyebrows were anything to go by.

"Now I have a question," Sierra stated.

Luke cocked an eyebrow, letting her know he was already expecting it. He loved that this woman was an open book. Although, he had to give her credit because she'd absolutely shocked both him and Cole at the club with her impromptu relationship ceremony.

"The two of you are wearing my rings, and I'm wearing yours. Will you be exchanging rings to signify your relationship?"

Luke stared at Sierra for a moment. Blazing blue eyes boring into his. He hadn't expected to have this conversation today, although it was one he'd given a significant amount of thought to.

Cole cleared his throat absently, but Luke didn't glance over at him.

"No," he replied to Sierra and out of the corner of his eye, he noticed the way Cole leaned back in his chair, apparently waiting for him to continue.

"No?" Sierra asked in all seriousness.

"We already have rings," he explained.

"So if not rings, how do you propose you do that?"

"How else?" he asked, seeing if she was going to guess.

"I have no clue, Luke," Sierra laughed, smacking him on the chest. "That's why I'm asking you."

"I was thinking more along the lines of tattoos."

Sierra glanced back at Cole as though waiting for him to approve, but Luke saw the smirk on his face. It was true, Cole's entire body was a blank canvas, but Luke was more than ready to get him inked. The thought of seeing him with a mark that reflected their love for one another while he was buried to the hilt inside of his powerful body had Luke's cock reacting eagerly.

"Do you have a design in mind?" Sierra asked.

Luke grinned at her and then over at Cole. "I do."

"When?" Cole asked.

"As soon as you're ready," Luke growled as the image continued to form in his mind. He wasn't interested in wasting any more time.

"Wait, before you run off and do that, I want to see what you're talking about," Sierra exclaimed, standing. She reacted as though Luke was going to drag Cole out of the house at any minute, which, honestly, didn't sound like a bad idea.

Luke stood, realizing that the evidence of his arousal was now front and center. Pretending that he wasn't aching to take this conversation in an entirely different direction, Luke headed toward his office while the two of them followed close behind.

Picking up the image he printed a couple of days ago when the idea began to fester in his brain, Luke turned to face them. Holding it out in front of him, Sierra easily swiped it out of his hands, a huge grin on her face.

"So where do you plan to get it?"

"Across our backs," he explained, realizing he was getting more and more worked up. Luke's erection began to throb as he once again envisioned the ink across Cole's back, staring back at him.

"Is it going to be the same on both of you?" Sierra asked, not waiting for an answer before turning to Cole. "Take your shirt off, I want him to show me where he wants this to go."

Cole tilted one eyebrow at Luke suggestively and lifted his t-shirt, pulling it over his head and setting it on the edge of the desk before turning around so that his back was facing them.

Luke moved forward at the same time Sierra did, his hands vibrating slightly from the sight of Cole's beautiful body. He knew exactly where the image was going to go. Sierra handed him the paper before placing her hands on Cole's naked back.

Cole hissed out a breath.

"Sorry. Are my hands cold?" she asked Cole, seemingly oblivious to the fact that she was instigating something that they weren't going to be able to control.

"No," Cole growled.

Sierra began tracing the outline of the image that Luke was holding across Cole's back. The subtle shift of Cole's body and the way his hands fisted at his sides caught Luke's attention. He was feeling it too.

"I want the yin yang symbol to be the base. We'll both have that. However, the dragon will be on him," Luke said, moving in closer, placing his palms against Cole's back, outlining the area he was thinking. "I'll have the tiger on me." Luke moved his hands showing how the tiger would be positioned differently.

Sierra glanced up at Luke, then back to Cole's bare skin. "Basically, if you were to overlay it then you'd see the whole picture, right?"

"Right."

Luke didn't take his hands off of Cole.

"Why on your backs?" Sierra asked, taking a step back. "Take your shirt off, I want to see."

Luke quickly shed his shirt, not answering Sierra's questions as he gave in to the inevitable. Regardless whether the woman realized what she was doing, they were all three about to get naked. Right there in his office.

Quickly returning to Cole, Luke pressed his chest against his back, leaning in close to his ear. "I'm going to be inside you in just a few minutes, I promise you that." He kept his voice low, the words only meant for Cole's ears.

"I'm banking on it," Cole replied just as softly.

It was Luke's turn to hiss when Sierra's hands made contact with his back, her fingers tracing the outline of what the tattoo would look like. When he thought he couldn't take anymore, Sierra placed her lips against his skin and his body hardened even more.

Apparently she was feeling the heat churning in the otherwise still air. Or maybe she had this planned all along.

"Your turn," Cole said, reaching behind Luke and grabbing Sierra's shirt, pulling her until she was stumbling back in front of him. "Little minx."

Luke slid his arms around Cole's waist, reaching for the button on his jeans as he ground his erection into Cole's firm ass. He flipped the button, then eased the zipper down before sliding his palm down Cole's washboard stomach until he was able to wrap his hand around Cole's iron hard cock.

Sierra laughed, pretending she didn't have a clue what Cole was talking about and Luke watched the interaction as he stood behind Cole, stroking him roughly.

"Strip," Cole ordered Sierra and a flash of desire sparkled in her ice blue eyes.

Without further hesitation, Sierra quickly slipped off her t-shirt and then her jeans.

"All of it," Cole ground out as he began thrusting his hips, forcing Luke to stroke him harder.

Sierra teased them as she removed her bra and panties, turning around to give them a breathtaking view of her magnificent ass.

"On the desk," Cole demanded.

The way Cole had taken the reins made Luke that much hotter. He liked this side of him, although he still looked forward to those times when Cole would submit to him.

Like right now.

"Take your jeans off," Luke growled in Cole's ear as Sierra moved into place.

Once she was sitting on the edge of the large oak desk that stood proudly in the middle of the room, Luke shed his jeans almost as quickly as Cole did.

"Fuck, baby, you're wet," Cole groaned as he moved in place between her legs, his fingers sliding through her glistening pink folds.

Luke alternated between watching Cole slide his fingers inside of Sierra and trying to find the bottle of lube that he kept in a safe place in his office. One never knew when it would be needed.

Once he had what he needed, Luke alongside Cole between Sierra's spread thighs. "We need to taste you," Luke said as he lifted one of her legs, opening her wide and giving him room to stand beside Cole.

His eyes met Cole's and they both zeroed in on her with their mouths until she was writhing and moaning against the desk, letting them both know in exceptionally vivid detail how good it felt when they both licked her pussy at the same time. Luke was a hairsbreadth away from coming right then and there by the time she allowed her orgasm to take her.

"Get down and turn around. God, baby, I need to be inside of you," Cole instructed, helping Sierra to climb down from her perch on the desk. Once her feet were on the ground, he retrieved the condom he'd apparently snuck in, sheathing himself in a rush.

Before Luke could even get in position, Cole was burying himself deep inside of Sierra, groans of ecstasy echoing in the room. Realizing the urgency, Luke lubed his cock before moving in behind Cole.

"Bend over," he instructed, forcing Cole's hips to still and making Sierra groan with disappointment. Apparently their little hellcat was enjoying herself.

Once Cole was in place, his body covering Sierra's as she leaned over the desk, Luke slid two fingers inside Cole's ass, doing his best to prepare him rather than just slamming home like he wanted.

"Fuck me, Luke," Cole begged, his hips shifting slightly so that he was grinding his length inside of Sierra's tight, warm body.

Luke moved into place, aligning his cock and pushing inside of Cole in one slow thrust. "Fuck."

It took a few moments to get situated so that he could fuck Cole at the same time Cole was fucking Sierra, but they managed. Luke leaned forward, his eyes trained on the spot on Cole's back where the tattoo would soon be and his cock swelled even more.

"I'm gonna love fucking you and seeing the ink right here," he told Cole, sliding his tongue over his warm, salty skin, holding his shoulders as he began thrusting faster. "I'm going to see it every time I'm inside of you while I'm reminding you exactly who you belong to. Damn, you're so fucking tight."

Luke began slamming into him, the image so vivid in his mind. With each punishing thrust, Sierra moaned as Cole's cock drove deeper into her pussy.

"I'm going to come again," Sierra moaned. "Please, fuck me harder."

Luke stood, gripping Cole's hips and ramming his cock deeper, over and over until Sierra was screaming her release.

"I'm gonna come," Luke groaned. "I can't wait."

Leaning over Cole once again, Luke pressed his lips against his warm, slick skin. He drove deep once, twice, and on the third time, he latched his teeth onto Cole's skin, both of them coming, Cole's groan echoing through the room.

Yes, Luke was definitely going to enjoy seeing Cole marked. And to think, this little afternoon rendezvous happened just from thinking about it.

Luke briefly wondered whether he should warn Cole about what was to come when he was inked and his body beckoned Luke even more than it did now.

Nah, what would be the fun in that?

Dear Reader,

First, I'd like to say thank you for reading Devotion. I hope you enjoyed the continuation of my most beloved threesome.

I have to say, you're love for them has been heartwarming. Luke, Sierra and Cole have been by far the most talked about of any of my characters. Between you and me, when I finished Temptation and hit the publish button, I was scared half out of my mind. I wasn't sure how readers would react to their story, but I had to stay true to them and give them the happily ever after that they sought, although it might not be seen as a traditional relationship. Although I love them and I believe they wouldn't have had their happily ever after without all three of them together, I was still petrified.

I will never be able to express my love for each of my fans and your continued support. You have made this journey worthwhile in every sense. I thank you from the bottom of my heart.

Much ♥,

~Nic~

Acknowledgements

I'm not sure I'll ever be able to personally thank all of the extraordinary people who have walked into my life and enhanced it more than I would have ever expected, but I'll certainly try.

My husband: You, above all else, are what keeps me going every single day. You've changed your entire life to accommodate my dream, and I am forever grateful that we get to take this journey together. I love you.

Nicole-Nation: Thank you for being there for me each and every day. Your continued support and humbling praise are more than I could've ever hoped for. I love each of you incredible ladies and look forward to meeting you one day face to face.

Bloggers: I wouldn't have made it this far without you. Not only have I enjoyed working with you, but your friendship means more than you'll ever know. There are so many, and I'm sure I'll miss some, but I want to give a big THANKS to Shh Mom's Reading, Sinfully Sexy, Swoon Worthy Books, Erotica Book Club, S&M's Book Obsession, The SubClub Books, Rock Stars of Romance, Sugar and Spice Book Reviews, Three Chicks and Their Books, Book Bitches Blog, We Love Kink, The Book Enthusiast, Mary Elizabeth's Crazy Book Obsession, Seductive Romance Reviews, Sarah's Book Blog, Reality Bites! Let's Get Lost!, Alpha's, Authors & Books Oh My!, My Fictional Boyfriend and Book Whores Page, BookSlapped, The Romance Cover, The After Dark Divas Book Club.

Want to see the tattoo that Luke and Cole are getting? Well, you'll want to sign up for Nic's newsletter on her website.

Website: www.nicedwardsauthor.com

Nicole would love to hear from you:

Twitter: https://twitter.com/NicoleEAuthor

Facebook: https://www.facebook.com/Author.Nicole.Edwards

Additional Books by Nicole Edwards

The Club Destiny Series:

Conviction

Temptation

Addicted

Seduction

Infatuation

Captivated

Devotion

The Alluring Indulgence Series:

Kaleb

Zane

Coming in 2013 –Travis

Continue reading for an excerpt from:

Travis
Alluring Indulgence, #3

Expected release July 30th, 2013

Chapter One

♀♂

Pictures certainly hadn't done the house justice, and Kylie couldn't help but smile as she stepped onto the wide, rickety wood steps of the old farmhouse. According to the tax records, the house had been built in the late 1800's. It was apparent that sometime in the last two centuries, someone had done some significant work to the exterior. It needed more work, definitely, but at least it was workable. She'd been hoping since the day she met Gage Matthews, and he went into detail about this little project of his, that he wasn't pulling her leg.

Granted, for the last two months, she'd spent more and more time with him, getting to know him not only as a client, but something else. What that was, she still had no idea. The fact that he was a cop hadn't helped in the getting to know him department, though. He tended to do that whole evasive answer thing that really got on her nerves. It was a good thing he hadn't been lying about this house though. At least she would get something out of the last sixty days she'd spent getting to know him.

"What do you think?" Gage asked from behind her.

Kylie turned to see him standing two steps lower than she was, yet he was still taller than her. "It's beautiful. On the outside anyway." Grinning, she felt like a kid at a carnival, excited about what came next.

"I assure you it only gets better."

Kylie didn't doubt it for one second.

Sidestepping her, Gage moved to the front door, and Kylie followed with a rush of adrenaline burning like jet fuel through her veins. Admittedly, she'd had her doubts about whether this house actually existed. For the last couple of months, she'd had a myriad of encounters with this sexy cowboy, but until now, he hadn't offered to show her this house he'd been so interested in hiring her to restore.

Now that they were here, the tiny town of Coyote Ridge, which was nothing more than a small blip on the Texas map, was growing on her. They'd stopped at a small convenience store as soon as they reached town to get sodas and Kylie had been amused when she talked to the cute little old man that ran the store. From the sound of it, the elderly gentleman knew Gage fairly well, which told her a lot about the small town. Although she had worked to pry some information out of Gage, he was the equivalent of a closed book for the most part, giving her remarkably few details about his home town. Or his life in general. He was born and raised here, that much she knew.

When he surprised her that morning by showing up on her doorstep once again, Kylie had been giddy with anticipation ever since he told her where he was taking her. The hour drive from her house in Killeen gave her plenty of time to think, and even more time to get worked up over the possibilities. It clearly didn't take much to impress her, and the opportunity to restore a house, seemingly untouched since the late 1800s, was like waking up on Christmas morning to find out the biggest present under the tree actually belonged to her.

She'd done a little research prior to their little road trip, actually begging him on a couple of occasions to take her to see the house. He had always had an excuse, but he somehow managed to take her mind off of it by spending more and more time together.

"How many acres does it sit on?" she asked when he opened the sun faded front door, swinging it inward, gesturing for her to precede him.

"Almost fifteen."

She wondered if he was planning to do anything with the land but she didn't ask. Thinking was the last thing she wanted to do when she got her first glimpse of the interior. As usual, as soon as she stepped inside, she felt as though she were in a time warp, imagining the life that passed through these walls for the last two hundred some odd years.

Just like she expected, there were walls everywhere. The term open concept hadn't played a role in the construction of this house back then. The small parlor entry was spacious but enclosed by a set of French doors that led to another smaller room where the wrap around staircase stood proudly on one side. The wood was well maintained, and with just a little buffing and a fresh coat of polyurethane, it would sparkle like the sun. To her right, there were two sets of double doors, both leading into an oversized living space that was probably two actual rooms back in the day.

Without slowing, Kylie made her way around, through the dining room, then through the small, fairly cluttered kitchen. She was excited to see a set of servant stairs, and probably even squealed a little as she followed the narrow, rather steep steps up to the second floor.

"This is amazing," she muttered, talking to herself.

Glancing into each of the three rooms and one bathroom as she passed, she noticed they were all decent sized. The landing that looked back over the main staircase was large enough to put a small settee or maybe even an antique desk.

God, she wanted this job. She'd been doing this – restoring historic homes – for the last eight years, but never had she taken on a project quite this large.

"Glad you like it," Gage's deep, thundering voice filled the interior of the tiny bedroom she was standing in. "You still interested?"

"Are you kidding?" She was grinning ear to ear as she stared at the cracked plaster and the hideous floor. She wondered whether there were hardwood floors beneath the dingy, olive green shaggy wall to wall carpet.

"Perfect."

Kylie stopped and took a second to stare back at the man filling the doorway. She could've sworn the room seemed larger before he walked in. As she stared at the sexy, dark haired cowboy, she still found it strange how he'd blown a mountain-size hole in her life in just a matter of weeks with his unexpected arrival at her house looking for her specifically. But yet here she was about to take on a project that would take her away from her home for a good number of weeks if not months.

Just that morning, Gage had talked to her about a timeline and getting things rolling. According to him, he was putting his house on the market and looking to move into his grandmother's old house in just a few months if she could be finished with the work in time. She didn't make him any promises because he hadn't even allowed her to see what she was getting herself into until now.

Although she didn't normally take such ambitious projects so far away from home, the longer she stood there, the more interested she became, and she couldn't help but wonder whether the attractive cowboy cop played more into her excitement than the house did.

The situation she found herself in was quite unusual, at least by her previous history. Although Gage seemed genuinely interested in hiring her to do the work, he also seemed interested in her on other levels. She knew she wasn't imagining it either because, over the course of the last two months, they'd actually gone on several official dates. Originally when he'd asked, she'd been taken aback, unsure whether it was a nifty idea to mix business with pleasure, but the longer she was in Gage's company, the more she found that she genuinely liked him.

Granted, she had little experience with dating mostly by her own choice. She chose to keep herself so wrapped up in work that she didn't have time to entertain the idea of a relationship. Not that what she and Gage had could be considered a relationship, but she knew for a fact that it was more than friendship. Or she hoped so. After all, the couple of times he'd kissed her sure didn't feel like just friends to her.

"You ok?"

Caught a little off guard, but more than grateful for the distraction, Kylie turned away, then back.

He really was one of the most attractive men she had ever seen. Dark hair, dark eyes, and a body that tempted her to sin like the devil. "Fine, why?"

The smile he shot her direction made her tummy dance with a sweet tingle that she'd been oblivious to for longer than she cared to admit. Or maybe she just hadn't had that tingle in a solid decade or so.

"You've really never heard of Coyote Ridge?" he asked, his attention directed to the chipped plaster that clearly needed some attention.

The way he asked the question made her feel as though she should've heard about the tiny little town that this man obviously called home. "Nope," she said casually, trying to stay focused on determining how much work the space needed.

That wasn't the first time he'd asked that question, and Kylie had to wonder whether it bothered him that she hadn't or if it was just another one of his random inquiries. He'd certainly asked more than his fair share over the last two months since she met him. Kylie attributed that to him being a cop. He was just naturally nosey, or so he'd told her.

Taking the opportunity to continue with her tour, Kylie ventured through the small bathroom that connected to another smaller bedroom. It could be considered a closet almost, she thought. As she took notes of the flooring and windows, jotting down the things that would need to be restored, fixed, or even replaced, Kylie's thoughts drifted back to Gage.

Ever since the first night he took her out to dinner, Kylie had been thinking some rather heated thoughts about the man. They'd shared quite a few intimate meals together, and some much more casual dates, most of them spent getting to know one another. Well, more like him asking her questions and dodging those she asked him, but she found it fascinating that he was interested in getting to know her.

In fact, Kylie couldn't help but think that a long time had passed since she'd actually dated a man who wasn't all about jumping into bed with her within the first ten minutes. Since she never obliged them, she figured this was actually quite nice. Well, with the exception that her hormones were beginning to overflow, and she wasn't sure how much more she could store up before the lid blew off due to the pressure. If Gage kept this up, she was going to have to buy stock in Duracell or Energizer just so she could function on a daily basis.

She still wasn't sure why they hadn't moved to the next phase of what felt like a potential relationship, but to this day, they had somehow managed to sidestep sex. How, she wasn't sure. That was one thing this relationship, or whatever it could be called, was lacking. The making out portion was testing the limits of her smoke detectors, but they still had never taken that next step. The chemistry was off the charts, but they both seemed to shy away at the last minute. It wasn't unusual for her, but for some reason, she sensed that Gage wasn't used to backing off quite so intensely, yet he somehow managed every time.

However, there were plenty of times when she wondered whether Gage Matthews might actually be getting too close for comfort. She found she genuinely liked him. They laughed, talked, and yes, he knocked her socks off with his kisses, but as far as going any further, she risked the possibility of getting too attached.

Kylie Marie Prescott did not roll that way.

Not after Travis Walker ruined her for all time.

Damn it.

As a rule, Kylie did her best not to think about Travis. Even all these years later, her body reacted in strange ways to those lingering memories that hadn't yet faded around the edges. Considering how he walked out on her after they'd been married only three weeks, it would make more sense if she wanted to slap him, not jump him, but damn it if she didn't want to just…

Ok, inappropriate. *Tune back into reality, girl.*

Some days were more difficult than others, but she figured that was because they were still married. A technicality, she told herself. It was just a piece of paper. Not that she considered it a marriage by any means. After he had walked out ten years earlier, she'd never once looked back. Ok, maybe just a little, but she tried her best not to. If only she had the desire to find him, she'd seek a divorce. She just knew it was better if she didn't. At least not right now. There was no way she could handle seeing him again. Not after what he had done to her. Ripping her heart right out of her chest and walking away with it still beating in his hands had been the worst thing anyone had ever done to her.

Ok, you're cut off now, woman. No more thinking. Her internal monologue with herself was enough to set her straight.

Ten minutes later, Kylie was doing her best to push the stray thoughts out of her mind and concentrate on the pen and paper in her hand.

"Let me know when you're done. I'd like to take you to meet some folks."

Kylie turned to look at Gage, who had obviously been following her through the house. Dropping her hands to her side, she exhaled and smiled. She was suddenly eager to get some fresh air. Whether it was the close proximity of this handsome man or thoughts of the one from her past, she wasn't sure, but the room was suddenly getting a little warm. "I'm good for now. As long as you promise I'll get to come back soon."

"Honey, you've got the job if you want it," Gage said, grinning.

"You don't even know my price," she informed him.

"Irrelevant."

Kylie had to wonder whether he'd done this before or if he just had money to burn. Either way, this project wasn't going to be cheap, but at least she could do the work in stages. However, she was going to have to try and find some crews that were local to help her. The ones she normally worked with weren't likely to venture this far out.

After Gage locked up the house and helped her into his truck, Kylie allowed her mind to relax as he drove. The familiar song on the radio made her want to tap her foot on the floor, but she refrained. It was rare that she was in a good mood after such pressing thoughts from her past, but for some reason, just being in Gage's company helped. That and the prospect of the new job made her smile, and for once, she just wanted to enjoy what life threw her way. It was high time she stop trying to hide behind those events that had changed her life irreparably. Time to move forward.

Still smiling, Kylie pulled herself back to the moment as Gage turned off onto a long dirt driveway. In the distance, she saw a lovely old farmhouse come into view, the fresh paint and new roof gleamed radiantly in the bright Texas sunshine. This one looked significantly different than the one they'd just left. This one was sporting a recent facelift.

She wasn't sure where they were, but she began to wonder whether Gage wanted to show her what ideas he might have. Refraining from asking questions, she paid attention to the details, noticing the men in front of the house. Two were carrying furniture, two more were talking on one end of the beautiful wrap around porch.

Did this place only breed hot, sexy cowboys?

When Gage pulled the truck to a stop, Kylie unbuckled her seatbelt and climbed out of the truck. She continued to eye the beautiful house, her eye for detail noting the few things they'd done to stick with the houses former glory, although there were quite a few enhancements they'd made to modernize it as well. Either way, she was impressed. Wouldn't have been her choice, but then again, it wasn't her house.

Gage surprised her when he walked around to her side of the Tahoe, taking her hand in his. That tingle that had been stirring in her belly erupted into a volcanic explosion of activity, and she wondered if her palms were going to start sweating. God, she hoped not. At least not while he was holding her hand.

Hoping she made a good impression on these people, whoever they were, Kylie pasted on a smile and fell into step beside Gage.